PEARLS IN ASHES

ALICE VL

Pearls in Ashes

Alice VL

Pearls in Ashes

Alice VL

Pearls in Ashes

DEDICATION

My friends, Donna & Bruce

It's always hard landing in a new country, on the other side of the world, and away from the only home I've ever known.

It can be mighty lonely at times, but gratitude is in abundance for the close friendships formed by friends who have stuck around, and remain staunchly in our lives.

I value you. I cherish you. I am thankful for God for placing you in our lives. Thank you for making our lives so much easier. It's because of you that we have not yet surrendered to drowning waves that seem to appear as thunderous storms out of nowhere.

Much love,

Alice

Alice VL

6

Pearls in Ashes

Alice VL

When Gabriel was assigned to Kenya with a team from Doctors Without Borders, Skyler never thought that their new beginning would end so abruptly after Gabriel went missing in war torn Kenya.

Angered by his family's betrayal, Skyler left the home she shared with him shortly after his memorial service, and moved away to a new city, hoping to never see them again. She slowly began picking up the shattered pieces of her heart when she unexpectedly met and fell in love with the kind-hearted and charming, Gavin Taylor.

Just when Skyler thought the years that had gone by had finally brought her the closure she so desperately sought, the news that Gabriel was found alive, left her reeling and devastated all at the same time. Can Skyler return to the town and the family she had left behind so many years before?

Will her love for Gavin shield her from the turmoil she is flung into by Gabriel's unexpected return? Are Skyler and Gabriel destined to become perfect strangers, while sharing a secret of the past Skyler can no longer hide from the world?

Alice VL

Pearls in Ashes

Alice VL

CONTENTS

Pearls in Ashes

CHAPTER ONE

Her eyes trailed down, overcome by sheer sorrow as she stared at the picture-perfect daughter she had given birth to only moments earlier. She was wholly consumed and entirely overawed with love for the tiny person she held protectively in her arms, but at the same time, her heart was shattering by the intense agony and desolation that was callously and gradually consuming her. She repeatedly counted her tiny fingers and her even smaller toes, and could barely imagine any living person as tiny as the bundle nestled safely in her arms. She smiled adoringly when she noticed her rosy cheeks and fiery red lips.

She had become grotesquely aware of an unexpected and overwhelming urge to offer up her life for the child sleeping without a care in the world, in her arms. Skyler Maxwell was overwhelming distressed by the fact that her daughter would in no way at all, be introduced to, or flourish in a world that would offer her a father, and he in turn, would never be acquainted with his daughter or ever know that he had even fathered a perfect little girl. He would never appreciate that he had begotten a flawless, beautiful daughter, and he would in no way at all, ever hold her in his arms.

Skyler was crushingly distraught to consider a reality where their daughter would turn out to be Gabriel Galicia's one great miss. She felt into her soul all that she could someday present her child with, would never matter. All that she would sacrifice for her in a heartbeat, would mean nothing much at all since she would still never be able to provide her with the only thing that her heart would come to yearn for some day, her father.

While gazing wretchedly at her daughter as warm tears had begun to roll down her cheeks, Skyler gently kissed her baby girl on her tiny forehead. "Hope ..." She whispered softly when she realized for the first time, that the little person lying so contently in her arms, had given her an endless amount of unforeseen courage. She had given her something new to live for when she was sure that she had nothing left to look forward to. There was nothing good in the stars for her that she could predict for her future, and there was nothing left to live for until she held her daughter in her arms for the very first time. She was convinced that Hope Maxwell was sent to her directly from God's arms and into hers, bringing along a kind bravery she had never known before, for her to face all her tomorrows from that day forward. Hope. It was what her daughter had given her over the last few months, and without her, Skyler was convinced that she would never have endured or survived losing Gabriel. She did not want to carry on without the only man she had ever loved, until the very moment she held his daughter in her aching arms.

Skyler gently placed her baby into the crib beside her, before she sluggishly climbed back into the bed where she laid staring lifelessly at the ceiling, unable to control the inexhaustible tears that perpetually and relentlessly, gushed from her eyes, and onto her cheeks. She sobbed irrepressibly at the sheer notion that she and Hope were compelled to face their lives alone, without Gabriel and without her family. She wept over the severe seclusion that consumed her, with every thought and each memory of Gabriel. She wept in undeniable sorrow when she considered a reality where she would never see him again. She longed for him, she longed for his comforting voice and she yearned to have his protective arms immerse her, and shield her from all that was threatening to destroy her. She ached for a life she had once shared with him, and she was terrified of raising his little girl without him. "I want you back ..." She cried out in desperation as she shut her eyes firmly, fiercely attempting to lock out the entire world around her. "I just want you back, Gabe. Ccome back to me, come home to our little girl ..."

Skyler's mind wandered back to the day she had first met

Gabriel Galicia, oldest son of Carlos and Sarah Galicia. Her parents, along with their three daughters, Skyler, Donna and Tallulah had only recently relocated to a quaint little fishing village in Logan's Bay on the West Coast. Skyler's father, Dave Maxwell and her mother, Tabitha, were both equally successful journalists in Willowton, but after many years of jet-setting and spending too many nights away from home, they both decided to settle down and semi-retire on the West Coast.

They reached a mutual decision that Dave would continue to write for various television networks while Tabitha's only role and desire was to become a round-the-clock housewife and mother. She was incessantly pestered by an inner struggle that provided much turmoil for her, each time she walked out the door of her home, and into her job. She was continuously harassed by the fact that her daughters were growing up far too swiftly, without her or Dave participating actively in their girls' normal, day-to-day lives. Tabitha was desperately afraid of her one great miss, as she often referred to the events that both she and Dave were missing out on. She was overcome by a scorching desire to become increasingly involved in their daughter's lives as they grew older. Donna had only recently turned four years old, while Skyler was slightly over a year younger and Tallulah, the youngest, was barely six months old by the time they had packed up and moved to the West Coast.

Years of saving diligently had enabled the pair to buy a beautiful beach front property for their family where their girls had acres of white sand and beaches to play on. It was a picture-perfect location with magnificent ocean and mountain views where Dave could finally begin the novel he had dreamed of writing for almost his entire life. Tabitha on the other hand, was only too pleased to settle down in Logan's Bay, and excitedly embraced her role of housewife and fulltime mother.

The Maxwell family had unexpectedly, but rather swiftly befriended their neighbors, Sarah and Carlos Galicia. Although Carlos was from Spanish descent, Sarah was born from a Scottish clan who had fled Scotland many years before she was born. Along with her parents, Sarah settled on the West Coast where she had met and fallen in love with Carlos. Tabitha was unceasingly astonished by their union, but could in no way at all, deny the love they shared for one another. Sarah and Carlos were doting parents to two sons, Gabriel who was seven at the time, and Christopher who was barely a year younger.

Gabriel had indisputably inherited his father's dark, masculine looks while Christopher on the other hand, took after his mother, sporting her fair hair and pale blue eyes. Gabriel was tall and sturdy, with a promise of curls between his almost raven hair, and eyes almost as dark. His eyelashes were endless, and his rosy red cheeks and lips were almost flawlessly perfect.

Carlos owned a fleet of fishing vessels along the coast, while Sarah too, favored her role as a housewife and round-the-clock mother. Tabitha and Sarah became best friends almost instantly, and the two families often spent weekends out on one of Carlos' many yachts.

The children played together and connected extremely well with one another. The Galicia boys took the Maxwell girls under their wing, and appointed themselves as older brothers by defending them whenever the situation called for it, and ultimately took care of them. Gabriel was keenly sensitive to Skyler's extreme introversion and vulnerability. He noticed how she habitually withdrew from a crowd when she thought no-one was watching. She would quietly, but invisibly slip away, and make her way down to the beach undetected. Gabriel would often follow closely behind her, and he would regularly join her in silence as she sat quietly, gazing out over the ocean. "Skye, what goes on in your mind when you sit here all by yourself?" He once asked her, greatly perceptive to her silence. "Nothing Gabe, I just think of life …" She would whisper bashfully, afraid to reveal the stories that were living in her head. "I see you often write in your diary, what's that about?" "It's not a diary, Gabriel, it's a journal, and if you must know, I am going to be a wonderful writer someday and live a wonderful life."

Gabriel placed his arms around her, and gazed out over the ocean with her, "Yes, you are, Skye, you are something wonderful, and I'll be right there to take care of you." "You will?" Skyler grimaced when she turned to face Gabriel, "I am going to cure sick children, Skye, and you, you are going to tell the world your wonderful stories." She smiled timidly before she gently kissed Gabriel on his cheek.

Skyler had grown predominantly close to Gabriel, and spent almost every waking moment with him. First as little children playing together on the beach, and then as they grew older, as teenagers who adored what every other teenager did, music and the movies. Skyler was entire dissimilar to Gabriel. Her hair flowed endlessly down her back, and was almost as fair as her mother's. Her eyes were a piercingly, arctic blue. Skyler was typically reserved and painfully vigilant, while Gabriel was extraordinarily flamboyant and sociable. He was entirely ignorant of the fact that his dark hair and equally dark eyes had made him stand out in a crowd. He was remarkably good looking, while Skyler repeatedly felt lesser compared to his manly beauty.

His intensity, coupled with his exceptional good looks had all the girls to flock to him and later, women gathered around him, hoping to attract the eye of Gabriel Galicia, who had barely seemed to notice the attention that had tirelessly encircled him. Skyler in contrast, closely resembled her father and dreamed of becoming a secluded, but lucrative writer someday. The world seemed far too busy and piercingly noisy for her. She dreamed of the day she could lock herself away in a cocoon of silence, and spend her days writing about all the characters that were living in her head, fighting to be liberated from her mind. She was desperate to give them a home, and she was anxious to give life to them, and become the crusader of their hearts. Skyler would consistently remain behind the safety of closed doors, during which she would jot down her stories in a notebook her grandmother had once given her. She would stumble on characters that she would incessantly fantasize about, and she would lay awake into the early hours of the morning, planning an unspoiled life and a fairytale ending for them.

Directly in divergence to her dreams, was Gabriel, who endlessly and with great enthusiasm, dreamed of becoming an astounding pediatrician someday. He adored children. They would herd around him, even though they had never met him before. Skyler on the other hand, favored her escape from reality and instead, flung herself into a world that she could invent for herself, and crawl into it whenever the world around her became too thunderous. She would often take time out from her homework, and write all about her fictitious characters in her ever-expanding imagination.

Gabriel loved the disorderliness and unruliness of children, and from a very young age, he was aware of an overwhelming need to nurture and protect them, to comfort them when an incident called for his guidance. It came as no surprise to Carlos and Sarah when Gabriel announced that he would be working in the children's ward of the Pedicare Hospital in Logan's Bay, during school breaks.

By the time Skyler was about to turn fourteen, Gabriel had only recently turned seventeen, and had just begun his second last year of high school. Skyler had reluctantly commenced with her very first year of senior school, and was surprisingly intimidated by Gabriel's seniority from the moment she set foot on her high school's premises. She felt entirely out of place amongst Gabriel and his peers, and she hated the fact that she was forced to once again, begin at the very bottom.

From a distance, Skyler watched closely as teenage girls gathered around him. She developed a discouraging self-doubt by his popularity almost at once. She found it despicable that girls would brazenly hurl themselves at him. She was sure that she could in no way at all, contend with any of the more matured girls, and she secretly wished that she was only a few years older.

Gabriel played outstanding rugby, and when he was chosen to captain the school's rugby team, his popularity increased ten-fold. Skyler was a loner, and would regularly find a corner during breaks at school to sit quietly, and shut off from the world around her. She would escape into the world that made sense to her, and write down the stories that were invading her mind.

Gabriel took it upon himself to act as an older brother to Skyler, but before the year had ended, she had become cautiously sensitive to untaught and unanticipated emotions for him, feelings that she knew were in no way that of a brother and a sister. It scared her that her heart would hammer so ferociously, and that her stomach would turn each time she would run into him in the school halls, or simply pass him by on the sports field. She became tongue-tied when she was around him, and she became acutely aware of the blood that would rush to her face each time Gabriel would glance in her direction. Skyler had never felt emotions such as those for any boy before, and she could in no way at all, understand why he had such a staggering effect on her. She would deliberately sidestep running into him at school, and in the afternoons, she would hide from him behind the safety of her bedroom door.

Skyler was horrified when she discovered that her stories had turned into fictions where Gabriel had evolved into her main character and love interest. By no means, was she able to expel him from her mind or from the stories that were living inside of her essence that had been consuming her every thought. When she ultimately accepted Gabriel as her storybook hero, she began looking immensely forward to escaping to her magical, storytelling world where she was free to live out her dreams with him, even if it was only in her mind. She would find any excuse to be left alone simply to flee into her fairytale world, and find Gabriel anxiously waiting for her. She ran into her happy-ever-after as fast as she could while she wholly embraced the life she had created for her and for Gabriel. She would hold his hands and touch his face, and he in turn, would smile adoringly back at her. She would kiss him on the lips, and he would subsequently, hold her firmly against him. It was a world Skyler had become addicted to, and could barely or willingly come back from.

She was no longer comfortable in the real world, and when Tabitha would demand her return to reality, she became irritated with her mother for intruding in a life she was familiar in. Gabriel too, had become zealously aware of an abrupt and surprising transformation in his own impressions of her. It tremendously frightened and unnerved him each time he felt a flutter in his stomach, or an awkward, untaught thump in his heart. At first, he would interrogate himself over the brusque and unexpected emotions that had manifested inside of him whenever he was around her, but after a while, he began looking at her in a way his heart had begun to nudge him to. He was frantic to spend more free time with her, and would intentionally bump into her as often as he could, even though he realized that she was deliberately avoiding him, and hiding from him as much as she could. He constantly dreamed up excuses to be with her, and he regularly declined invitations to hang out with his team members in the hopes that he could be alone with her. Gabriel would calculatingly make a point of finding Skyler on the school grounds, and would constantly run into her, even though he would never admit that he had intentionally, sought her out.

He would watch her on the sports field where she would sit with her notebook on the pavilion while the other girls would participate in netball or tennis. Gabriel was startled to realize how intimidated he would be whenever she engaged in fleeting conversation with another boy. He was at once overwhelmed by the feelings that he too, had never known before, and became subtler and gentler when he was around her.

Both the Maxwell and Galicia families secretly encouraged a union between Donna and Christopher, but instead, it was Skyler and Gabriel who found their way into each other's hearts from a very young age. Although Dave and Tabitha were clearly sensitive to Skyler's feelings for Gabriel, they in no way sought to sabotage their relationship, instead, they placed their confidence entirely in the two teenagers. Both Dave and Tabitha were evidently pleased that Skyler had found her first love in Gabriel. They thought of Gabriel and Christopher as the sons they would never have, and were pleased by their young romance and untainted love.

Skyler angrily swabbed at the warm tears that were flowing unreservedly from her eyes. She frantically swallowed past a restricting, overwhelming lump in her throat, where she lay motionlessly on her hospital bed. She glanced over at Hope often, and was thankful that her daughter would never know of the tears she had shed for her father. Tears she had surrendered to that were relentlessly overpowering her at that very moment.

She thought back to the day that Gabriel finally declared his love for her. Skyler was about to complete Grade 12, her final year of high school while Gabriel was nearing the end of his fourth year in medical school. Even though he was away from home attending university in Kennedy during the week, he made a concerted effort to return to Logan's Bay each weekend. He eagerly and effortlessly made the hour's drive to be with her, even though it was to spend only two days with her each weekend. Skyler would watch the time on her wrist watch as she sat on the seat at a bay window in her bedroom, and scrutinize the driveway next door for Gabriel's car to pull up. Her heart would flutter excitedly when he would finally park his car and climb out.

Skyler would stare at him and smile gleefully, while Gabriel would instantly glance up at her bedroom window. Each time he would spot her shadow in the window, Gabriel would smile and wave, aware of the quivering in his own heart.

On one particular Friday evening, shortly before Skyler's eighteenth birthday, she hurriedly made her way downstairs and ran into his waiting arms just as he had climbed out of his car. "Gabe! You're late!" She squealed with excitement before she flung her arms around him. "I know, I know. Traffic!" He placed his arms around her, and pressed her firmly against him. "So, listen …" He gently retreated until his eyes met hers. "We, some friends of mine have invited me to a get-together on the beach later. Do you want to join us?" "Oh? Me?" "Yes, you, Skye …"

Gabriel smiled when he realized that Skyler was entirely oblivious of her explicit presence in his life. "I, I don't know any of them?" "Well, let's see, you know Ana? She'll be there. Donna and Christopher will be there, and so will I. You know plent." He gently took her hands into his, "Skye, meet me there at ten, okay?" She smiled animatedly when she realized that Gabriel was eager to have her join him. "Okay ..."

A half an hour before Skyler was to meet Gabriel and his friends, she gently, but nervously knocked on Donna's bedroom door. "Donna?" "Hey Skye, what's up?" Donna had only just put her lipstick on, and was ready to head out to the beach. "Gabriel's invited me to the beach, I just, I don't know what to wear?" Donna embraced Skyler, and smiled adoringly at her, "I can fix that for you, that's what big sisters are for." She turned to her closet, and instantly handed Skyler a white pair of crocheted shorts and a matching top. "Just throw on a sweater over you, it's nippy outside." "Should I tie back my hair?" Skyler pointed to her hair, desperate to look older for Gabriel. "You have such beautiful hair, Skye, leave it hanging loosely." "Thank you, Donna ..." "You're welcome, sissy. I love you, and see you there?" "Sure, love you back, Donna." She hurriedly turned to leave, and sprinted back to her bedroom.

When Skyler apprehensively made her way down the

path that led to the beach, she was aware of the echoing of voices not too far from her. When she gazed out into the direction of the voices, she saw a burning fire, surrounded by the shadows of people engaged in chatter. Skyler approached slowly, aware of a frostiness in the air as the wind began blowing gently. When she approached the group, she was relieved to find Donna seated on a bedspread in the sand, with a handful of her friends. "Guys, this is my sissy, Skyler. Skyler, these are the girls and of course, you know Ana?" "Hey! Yes, hi Ana. Nice to see you again." Skyler smiled nervously before her eyes trailed over to the group around the fire, desperate to find Gabriel. When Skyler waved at him, he smiled affectionately at her. She quickly found an empty spot on the blanket, and did her best to avoid frequently glancing over at Gabriel.

"So, Skye, Donna was just saying that she only wants to be a mom when she's done with her course this year, what do you want to be someday?" Ana was eager to discover Skyler's future dreams and goals. "Really Donna, you just want to be a mum?" Skyler was surprised to hear of her sister's lack of ambition. "Yep, a wife and a mum!" She giggled when she grabbed onto Skyler's arm. "Wow!" "And you, sissy? What will you be doing next year?" "I want to write someday, so, I guess, I'll be enrolling in a literature course." "Really, Skye? Like, what do you want to write? Novels and such?" Ana was shocked to discover Skyler's love for writing. "That's all I've ever wanted to do. Novels, hopefully, and poems, and anything really ..." She smiled as she spread her arms out to indicate the entirety of her writing dreams, "And you, Ana?"

Ana turned to Gabriel who was staring at what seemed to be at the girls on the blanket, "I want to marry Gabriel Galicia." She whispered as she gazed over at Gabriel. Skyler gasped for air, and lowered her head at once. Donna glared incredulously at Skyler, before she turned to Gabriel. At that very moment, Donna realized that Gabriel was unintentionally, unable to take his eyes off Skyler. She reached out, and took Skyler's hands into hers, "Well I think Mrs. Gabriel Galicia will be someone pretty amazing." "I know, right?" Ana gushed when she giggled, and turned back to Donna.

When Christopher made his way over to the girls, he shyly caught a hurried glimpse at Donna, "Skyler, can I introduce you to the guys? Ivan is dying to meet you?" Skyler became anxious at once, and slowly rose to her feet, desperate not to come across as, or seem bad-mannered. "Sure ..." She followed Christopher to the bonfire, where Gabriel was standing with a beer in his hand.

"Ivan, this is Skyler, Donna's sister. Skye, this is Ivan, Joshua and Evan." "Hey …" She lifted her hand slowly, and smiled bashfully. Gabriel walked over to her, and placed his arm around her shoulder, "Don't get any ideas, guys, this one is taken." Skyler smiled anxiously, and hurriedly made her way back to the girls on the blanket. "Donna, I'm going home. It's cold and getting late. Enjoy your evening, and I'll see you tomorrow." She waved before she swiftly turned away from them and hurriedly made her way back to the path that would lead her home.

Gabriel's heart dropped when he noticed that Skyler was about to leave. He shoved his beer into Christopher's hand, and hurriedly followed Skyler, frantic to reach her. When she made her way through the parked cars, Gabriel finally caught up with her. He grabbed her by her arm, and turned her around to face him. Skyler was at once frightened by his sudden presence which seemed out of nowhere. She was entirely intimidated by the distinctive expression in his eyes. "Gabe?" "Skye …" He swept her into his arms, and shoved her against a car before he pressed himself firmly against her. He hungrily kissed her when she flung her arms around him, and held his head closer to hers. He kissed her feverishly before his hands began to trail downwards, and scrutinize every inch of her body. Skyler held him tighter, aware of the unidentified, never-before-felt sensations that were launching her body into the unknown. Her body had come alive, and intentionally began to pulsate for his. He abruptly liberated her, and stood gawking at her. He was acutely aware of an intense craving for her, that had entirely caught him off-guard, and stunned him. "Gabe?" She frowned while gasping for breath. "Skye …" "Don't talk, Gabe, don't say anything, let's go too far." She whispered breathlessly when she pulled him closer to her once again. Gabriel Galicia surrendered to the irresistible hunger for her, one that had unreservedly conquered him. He grabbed her and lifted her against him. With every thrust and every breath, she held on to him. She had never-before caressed the intimacy she had just touched with Gabriel. She had never-before known her body to react in the way that Gabriel had unwittingly encouraged her to respond to him. There was nothing in the world that could substitute or vanquish, all that she had felt at that very moment.

When he finally freed her body from his powerful grip, Gabriel placed his arms around her waist, and devotedly kissed her. She held him firmly against him, and kissed him back with equal enthusiasm. "Skye …" He whispered hoarsely as his lips continued to touch hers. "Don't say anything." She murmured croakily before she looked into his eyes. She straightened her clothes, and turned away from him. As she made her way up the path, she stopped and turned back to find Gabriel staring at her. "I love you, Skye!" He shouted out before she smiled back at him, "I love you back, Gabriel!"

Skyler's eighteenth birthday had finally arrived. Her parents had thrown her an elaborate coming of age birthday party, but, without wanting to impose on the youngsters, Sarah planned an evening off on Carlos' yacht for the adults. She had spent the entire day anxiously awaiting Gabriel's arrival, but when she finally realized that he was not attending her party, she half-heartedly and dejectedly joined her birthday guests. Her mood had turned somber by the penetrating disappointment and assumption that he had perhaps, forgotten her birthday. Her party was held on a warm Friday evening, and everything was so impeccably prepared and set up as the celebrations finally began. She was enormously disenchanted to discover that Gabriel would possibly not return to Logan's Bay until the following morning, and utterly disappointed that he hadn't called her earlier. She was entirely disillusioned that he had not called to make alternative arrangements for her birthday, which left her convinced that he had forgotten her.

Skyler could barely dismiss the insecurities that had been overwhelming her since Gabriel's departure from Logan's Bay, to continue his studies in Kennedy. She was desperately afraid of losing him, and she convinced herself that she could in no way at all, compete with any of the women who were attending University with him. She was after all, merely a young girl, still at school. Skyler was certain that after a while, he would forget her, and be captivated by someone more his own age, and more in his own league. Gabriel had frequently laughed it off as absurd when she revealed her fears to him, but she still couldn't rid herself of the inevitability that she would ultimately lose him. It was an enormous adjustment for Gabriel when he initially moved to Kennedy to commence with, and devote his time to his medical studies. He was deathly afraid that Skyler would meet a boy her own age, and fall in love with him. He regularly questioned Sarah about her whereabouts, and was relieved when she told Gabriel how Skyler would retreat into her own little world, lacking the need to be around people her age.

When Skyler finally joined her party guests, her parents along with Gabriel's parents at once surrounded her, anxious for her to blow out the eighteen candles on her impressive three-tier birthday cake. She beamed when she excitedly counted the candles which signaled the reality that she had finally grown up, and entered the world of maturity. Skyler firmly shut her eyes, and wished with all her heart for Gabriel to be there, with her at that very moment. That was all she wanted, the only wish she

Pearls in Ashes

had ever wanted to come true was for Gabriel to walk through the door, and take her into his arms while professing his undying love to her. When she opened her eyes, she tittered almost inaudibly when she was reminded of the fairytale that was living rent-free in her head. She had barely blown out her candles when she felt a gentle tug at her arm. Skyler turned around and was at once startled, yet ecstatic to find Gabriel standing behind her. "Happy birthday, Skye ..." He quickly kissed her on her cheek. "Gabriel!" She shouted out enthusiastically when her heart began to hammer ferociously. She impulsively threw her arms around him, and squeezed him with all her might, "I thought you forgot ..." She began telling him how afraid she was that he had forgotten her before Gabriel interrupted her, "What? How can I forget my own girlfriend's birthday?" He smiled as he took her hands into his. "Come, I have something for you." He held her hands steadily in his, as he led her outdoors. He directed her to the driveway, and what Skyler saw, left her wonderfully speechless. She was sure that her eyes were delightfully deceiving her when she noticed the brand-new car embellishing a bright red ribbon around it. "Happy birthday, Skye." Gabriel turned to her before he placed a set of keys in her hands.

Skyler was left speechless and elated by Gabriel's generosity, and when the extravagance of his gift had fully sunk in, she jumped up and down as exhilaration had made its way through her entire body. She devotedly embraced Gabriel once again before she teasingly planted kisses all over his face. He laughed out loud as he gently pushed her away from him, before he caressed her cheek and gazed admiringly into her eyes. He smiled when he once again noticed the ocean in her wintry blue eyes. Gabriel gasped for breath when he was again, overawed by her incredible beauty. "I love you, Skye. I've loved you from the very beginning." He kissed her gently while absorbing everything about her. Her lips were soft, but pleading for him as his passion grew for her. He pressed her body firmly against his, and it felt as though his heart was about to hammer out of his chest. Skyler gently pulled away from him, her hands still clasped around his neck. She gazed into his dark eyes, and noticed again how unbelievably beautiful a man he was. "Gabriel Galicia, I love you so much. I miss you. I miss you when you're not here. I hate it when you're over there, and I'm here."

She was at once aware of an agonizing thud in her heart when she realized that that moment could someday, become a mere memory. They were instantly distracted when they heard applause from behind them, and was at once startled to find the entire Maxwell and Galicia families standing around them. Although Donna had owned her own car, she was overjoyed and excited that Skyler now too, had her own. "You are sooo lucky! May you have many safe miles with her, Sissy!" She excitedly embraced her older sister. "Now I don't have to drive you around anymore!" She giggled before she winked at Skyler. It was not long before Tallulah joined them, and placed her arms around her sisters, "I'm so envious, Skye!" She giggled playfully. "Come on guys! Let's leave Skye and Gabriel to take a drive in her new car." Tabitha had noticed the sudden discomfiture in Skyler's eyes.

"Would you rather fancy a walk on the beach, Skyler Maxwell? The first as an adult?" Gabriel took Skyler by the hand, and lovingly squeezed it. "I would love to, Gabriel Galicia." They silently made their way down the path between their homes as they walked hand in hand to the shore. Both Gabriel and Skyler revered at the beauty of the ocean that had served as a tranquil backdrop while they were growing up. As soon as they began their stroll on the beach, they were relieved to find that the beach was abandoned, and that they were finally alone. Still clutching his hand, Skyler reflected on the moments that she and Gabriel had spent as children, joyfully filling their days on the exact same spot they were walking on. They had spent hours flirting with the waves that had crashed ruthlessly on the shore, screeching with laughter until Sarah or Tabitha would call them back home long after the sun had set.

They adored meeting up before sunrise, and they would habitually sit in silence as they waited in anticipation for the sun to set. Sunsets were vital to Skyler. She loved the idea of the universe showing her the end of another day. It was as though it was swearing to her that it was bringing her closer to spending the rest of her life with Gabriel. Just as much as she adored the setting of the sun, so did she immensely look forward to the sunrise which in turn, promised her a new day and a new adventure with him. Gabriel persistently studied her as she gazed out over the ocean with each sunset. He was awe-struck by her beauty as the sun would cast the last of its light on her face. She would close her eyes, and embrace all that was left of the warmth of the sun, that wholly engulfed and liberated her, all at the same time.

After sauntering in silence for just a moment longer, Gabriel stopped and turned to face Skyler. He placed his hands on her shoulders and lifted her chin until her eyes met his. Skyler became anxious when she saw the expression in his eyes. She could by no means quite place the untaught countenance on his face, and it scared her to realize that she had never seen such concern in his eyes before. "Skye, I am so anxious for you to finish school this year. I can't wait to bring you home with me to

Kennedy. I miss you so much when I'm not with you, and sometimes, sometimes I just feel as though you might never get there. I love you, Skye, and I don't want us to lose this, us." Skyler placed her arms around his neck, and held him firmly against her. She smiled sadly when she listened to his fears, but at the same time, she was elated by the fact that he had felt as insecure about her as she had about him.

Gabriel had been waiting for her from the moment he had left Logan's Bay, and was willing to wait for her until she could finally join him. He was desperate to believe that she would wait for him too. He sat down on the exact spot they had sat on, so many nights before and gently pulled her down beside him. "I was thinking, you have been writing for as long as I can remember. You have been dreaming of becoming a writer all your life. You should follow your dreams, Skye. You should do that. I spoke to the Dean of the university, and he told me about great English literature courses that you could take next year." Skyler beamed, and felt excitement well up inside of her. "I mean, I haven't really decided what to study yet. What if I am no good as a writer?" Skyler was utterly insecure and slightly self-conscious by her less than perfect writing skills. She in no way at all, ever imagined her stories good enough for the rest of the world. She had never shared her writings with anyone, and was rather reserved when it came to permitting the world a glimpse into her stories. "You will be a great writer, Skye. I'll care for sick children, and you can write all day long, if you want." Skyler chuckled as she listened to Gabriel plan their lives. "I'll be starting my internship next year. It will be perfect. We can get a place closer to The Tygerberg Children's Hospital where I will be doing my internship. I've looked at a few places that I think you'll really like." He took her hand and placed it on her knee. "You mean, we should live together? I'll be a student, Gabe." "Yeah, I know, but I mean, my father wants to invest a portion of our inheritance, and what better way than property? A place we can call our own? It makes no sense that you live on your own while I live on my own." Gabriel became edgy when he heard the reluctance in Skyler's voice. "I'm not sure my parents' will approve? I mean, my dad, you know?"

She hesitated when she considered her father's possible reaction to their intended living arrangements. "I'm pretty sure your dad will rather have you live with me than in a hostel? I know I can talk him into it, but, that's only if you want to?" Skyler was thrilled at the sheer prospect of a future with Gabriel, but became disheartened at once when she realized that she would have to wait another four months before she could join him. "Of course, I want to, Gabe! Then, we can stay up all day and all night if we want to!" Gabriel swept her into his arms, and kissed her gently before he laid her down on the beach. Skyler smile timidly as she gazed into his eyes, acutely aware of his captivating dark eyes that were incessantly penetrating her soul. "I love you, Skye. I've always, always loved you, let's run away." He pressed himself firmly against her as he delicately kissed her at first, before he could no longer fight against a fervent force that had entirely begun to overwhelm him. His hands made their way down her entire body as he slowly began to unbutton her blouse. "I love you too, Gabriel. I love you, let's go too far." She whispered hoarsely as her body began to tremble while she unintentionally began aching for him. She felt an unfamiliar shudder inside of her as fear began overpowering her. She could not at all wholly comprehend or identify what she was feeling, and she was in no way at all, prepared for how her body was beginning to react to his. It was different somehow, and it scared her to navigate the untaught emotions that were engulfing her. "Gabriel ..." She moaned hoarsely as her body instinctively and almost unconsciously, moved closer to his, searching for the warmth of his skin on hers. "Let's go too far ..." He let out a faint whimper before he kissed her again, overcome by an urgent need for her. He did not plan to make love to her, and he had no intention of soaking up her body that night, but almost as though he had no control over his own emotions, Gabriel made love to Skyler in the sand with only the sounds of the waves crashing down on the beach, while the stars shone brightly down on them.

Gabriel turned and held her in silence, unsure of what to say to her. Skyler was once again conscious of a confining lump that had shown up unsolicited in her throat, while her tears began to unexpectedly, shimmer in her eyes. "What's the matter, Skye? Did I, is something wrong?" He sat upright, afraid that he may have unintentionally hurt her. She pulled him closer, and gently touched his face, "Nothing's wrong. I just, I love you. I don't want to lose you, Gabe. I don't want you to forget me." "I love you, Skye. You will never lose me, do you understand, never ever?" Skyler smiled when she pulled his face closer to hers, and gently kissed him.

When the year had finally come to an end, Skyler was excited to begin her new life with Gabriel in Kennedy. Dave and Tabitha had ultimately agreed to allow Skyler to move in with Gabriel. Although Gabriel had continued his weekend visits to Logan's Bay, she could barely shake the feeling that they were living past one another. He was spending his days in class while his evenings in the hospital were wearing him out. He was profoundly affected by the children that were ill, and he felt personally responsible when he could not save a terminal child. He spoke incessantly to Skyler of how desperate he was to work harder, and offer up more of his time and effort to the children that needed him.

Gabriel became uncharacteristically silent after an enormously discouraging day at the hospital. By the time had had finally reached Logan's Bay, he was noticeably aloof and distant. Skyler noticed the utter misery in his eyes, and for a moment, she was sure he had aged ten years. "Gabe? Why do you look so sad? What's the matter?" Skyler was horrified to detect how entirely removed he was from her. Gabriel wretchedly shook his head before his eyes found hers, "It was just one of those days …" He lowered his head and grimaced, entirely overwhelmed and distressed. "What happened, Gabe? You're scaring me …" Gabriel looked away and shook his head before his eyes trailed back to hers, "We lost a little girl today. She was beautiful. She had the most beautiful, biggest brown eyes I have ever seen. She looked so healthy. She was only 26 months old. She was diagnosed with DIPG which turns out to be an untreatable form of brain cancer in children." Skyler felt an instinctive shudder in her heart when she saw the tears make their way into Gabriel's eyes. She took his hands into hers, and gently squeezed them, "I'm so sorry, Gabe. You can't save them all, Gabriel. Cancer is ugly, and it asks no age, you know that? There just are no rules." He inconsolably nodded in agreement, before he lowered his head in torment, "The thing is, Skye, we can do more. There's a lot more we can do. Too little funding goes into childhood cancer. Scientists get only 4% funding for research for cancer in children, we must do better. We can save more children with better equipment and better research." He was at once frustrated as he hurriedly explained the hitches that he, as a doctor, faces daily. "We are the ones that have to tell a mother that her child won't survive. We must tell them that there is nothing we can do for them, except make them comfortable as they hold their babies in their arms and watch them die." He paused to take in a deep breath, "Have you seen the pleading in a mother's eyes when you tell her that her child will inevitably die? Have you ever asked a mother to give up on her child? That there was nothing, *nothing* left to do? Nothing left to try? No medicine, no trials, just nothing? And, when the child finally dies after suffering so severely, the grief and despair on the face of that mother is excruciating. It's unbearable, Skye. I hate that. I hate cancer. Fuck cancer!" Gabriel lifted his hands to his face and began sobbing violently. Skyler took him in her arms, and held him protectively against her. "You care, Gabe, that's enough for now." She whispered sadly as he wept in utter anguish.

Each time he would leave to return to Kennedy, Skyler was plagued by a ghastly fear that she may never see him again.

She was indisputably bothered about the toll his work would take on him, and she wondered how he would survive his internship in the pediatric unit, watching terminal children inexorably die. She studied diligently for her finals. She worked harder than any other year, and by the time the year was over, she had enrolled for an English literacy course in Kennedy. Tabitha and Dave fervently supported their daughter, and placed complete conviction in Gabriel by allowing Skyler to leave for Kennedy with him. Donna and Christopher had been in Stafford attending Juliette College for almost a year by then, leaving the Maxwell's saddened that their daughters were growing up too fast. Still, Tallulah was at home for another two years, but at the same time, they knew all too well how swiftly time had passed by for their older two daughters. It often amazed the Maxwell and Galicia parents that Donna and Christopher had always simply remained friends, but they accepted the fact that the two of them adored and cared for one another almost as brother and sister.

Gabriel took a well-deserved break from his studies and from Kennedy during the Christmas holidays at the end of what he often referred to as an emotionally exhausting year, to spend much-need quality time with his parents and with Skyler. He was scheduled to begin his fulltime internship in January, which would mean that his regular weekend trips to Logan's Bay would soon become a thing of the past. The two families spent Christmas and New Year's together as they did each year before. Skyler was anxious and eager to return to Kennedy with him, and begin the life she had dreamed of with Gabriel, for almost as long as she could remember. On the fourth day before they were to leave for Kennedy, Gabriel asked Skyler to take a traditional stroll on the beach late one evening. Skyler could barely refute the fear that she had unexpectedly noticed in his eyes. She had no reason at all to think that anything had happened to influence or change their plans, and there was nothing that occurred to indicate that anything had gone wrong, yet, she was convinced that Gabriel was tormented by something balancing profoundly on his mind. She was overcome with instant dread as apprehension fearfully tugged at her heart. She had never seen Gabriel display such an enormous amount of restlessness on his face, and she instinctively sensed that something between them had changed.

"Skye, you know that I am about to start my fulltime internship at The Tygerberg Children's Hospital in January?" He nervously took her hands in his as he studied her interrogative eyes. As he stood staring at her, he was frenetic to identify the feelings that began to confound him, before he could respond to the questions Skyler would inevitably seek from him, following the announcement he was about to make. "Yes?" He could barely ignore the anxiety that had crept up into her eyes when he caught the uncertainty and dread in her voice. Gabriel made an enormous effort to remain composed, desperate to avoid the quiver that was threatening to expose his own fears. "A selected few of us have been assigned to begin and complete our internship in Kenya on a fulltime basis. I am on the list, and we leave on the fourth. I have no say in this, Skye, I have to report for duty with the others the first week in January." Skyler glared at Gabriel in confusion and downright devastation as she began to understand that Gabriel was forced to leave Kennedy, and complete his internship away from her, and in a whole different country. "No Gabe, you can't go! Not now, just not now!" Skyler was intensely dedicated to defeat and rebelled against what he referred to as his duty, before she bellowed out in anguish. Gabriel could barely look her in the eye as his own tears began brimming in his eyes. He bowed his head and hurriedly swabbed at a lost tear that had rolled carelessly down his cheek. "Gabriel? They can't force you to go, can they?" She was silently begging him to say no before he abruptly and exasperatingly interrupted her, "They can, and they did. There is nothing I can do, I must go. The Tygerberg Children's Hospital is a massive and substantial partner of the Doctors Without Borders project, Skye. It's my duty as a doctor to go, and it is my duty to my country to go and do what I can to help. It is too late to apply for my internship at another hospital now. Besides Skye, what message would I be sending as a doctor?" Skyler lowered her head before she began sobbing. Three years were far too long to be without him. For the next three years, and in less than a week, she would hardly see Gabriel. She would have to rely on weekend passes or mid-year breaks for him to come home, and it scared her to consider a reality wherein those breaks may not be enough for them to survive a separation as great as this one. Her mind became chaotic when she grasped that she alone, would be building their life together, without him. She had never lived away from her parents, and now, she would have to live in a strange town, and if that wasn't enough, entirely on her own. She at once considered the uprisings and unrest in Kenya. She had only recently seen a news report exposing the warfare that was consuming the African continent.

"But, Gabe? It's not safe?" She terrifyingly grabbed at his arm, when she implored him to consider the consequences of his intended trip. "Gabe! Look at me! It's not safe over there!" She yelled out in hopelessness when he remained silent. Gabriel knew that there was nothing he could say to repudiate what she had already known. "You don't have to do this, you can quit. You can take a year off and apply at another hospital next year? I don't want you to go, Gabriel! I don't want to see you once or twice a year for the next three years! I don't want you to go! You don't have to go!" Skyler was overcome with desperation as her mind began racing incessantly. "Skye! Take a year off? That just doesn't make any sense at all! Stop! I must go. I am going! All I ever wanted was to be a doctor, and if this is how I become one, then so be it. I want to make a difference, and I want to do better for the children in our war-torn African countries. They have no medical care and they barely have food to eat or clean water to drink. There is no care whatsoever for children with cancer over there. I need to do this. I don't want to leave you. I don't want to go away to Kenya and leave you to figure things out without me, but, I just, I just have to go. I have to do this, Skye. You have to let me do this. I swear, Skye, I'll come home every chance I get."

Gabriel was certain that he could essentially see the physical shattering of Skyler's heart. He was convinced that there was nothing in the world that could crush him anymore, than the expression of utter devastation on her face at that very moment. He had only days before considered giving up all he had worked for, but becoming a doctor was all that he had dreamed of, and had shaped him into the man he wanted to become. By the look in his eyes, Skyler knew that nothing she could say to him would change his mind or alter his heart. There was nothing in the world that could make him stay, even the consequential fact that her entire world had come crashing down on her. Gabe was overwhelmed and extremely sensitive to the suffering of children in war-torn and disadvantaged areas. He was overcome by enormous guilt for the lack of suitable medical care that he knew he could provide impoverished children. Gabe was duty-bound to fulfill his obligation as a doctor, no matter where it would take him. "Go then, Gabe, just go, but you better come back to me. Always, just come back to me. Please just come back to me, Gabe." She wept uncontrollably in his chest as he contemptuously held her firmly against him. "I'll always come back to you, Skye, just wait for me. Please don't hold this against me and please, please don't punish me for this someday." He hurriedly swabbed at the brutal tears that began drowning out his eyes, and roll eagerly down his cheeks. "I'll wait for you forever, Gabe, we have time and I'm not going anywhere. Three years is nothing, just come back to me."

She retreated slightly from him and took his hand into hers before she let out a faint, forced smile, even though her face was drenched in her own tears. Gabriel gently wiped them away before they turned to head back home in silence, both crushed by their penetrating sorrow and the excruciating agony in their hearts.

When they reached the front door of her parents' home, Gabriel turned to Skyler, "I still want you to go to Kennedy and do all that you planned to do, Skye. I want you to live in our home, and I want you to go to your classes. I want you to write. I don't want anything that we've planned, to change. But more than anything, I want you to find your feet as though I'm there, and wait for me. I'll come home as soon as I can and every chance I get, I promise." Skyler burst into tears before she hopelessly collapsed into his arms once again. She was dreadfully afraid that if she let him go, she would never see him again. "Do your parents know?" "Yes ..."

CHAPTER TWO

The entire Maxwell and Galicia clans accompanied Gabriel and Skyler to the airport where they said their goodbyes to Gabriel in January, moments before he boarded the plane from Kennedy International Airport to Kenya. Skyler remained close to him, and when he finally said goodbye to their families, she alone, accompanied him to his departure terminal. She clutched his hand firmly into hers, and the closer they were to saying goodbye, the tighter she gripped it. "I don't want you to go, Gabe, I changed my mind. I don't, don't want you to go. I will do anything, just stay. Please, just stay?" She desperately held onto his hand with both her hands, unaware of how forcefully she was squeezing them. Gabriel gently freed his hands and took his passport and plane ticket from his pocket, before his eyes found hers, "I know, Skye, I am so close to backing out." He whispered softly when his lower lip began to quiver, before Skyler clasped his hands into hers once more. "Then do it, Gabe, turn around and come home with me! We'll figure it out." Gabriel reluctantly freed his hands from her powerful grip and took her face into his hands, "Skye, I love you. God only knows how I'm going to miss you. I can't back out, those kids, they need people like us, Skye. I swear, I'll write as often as I can. This is for us, Skye, for our future. Look after yourself for me, and call my mom if you need anything, okay? Wait for me and don't forget me. I'll be home before you know it." He gently kissed her before he turned away from her. Skyler watched him leave, and was certain that her heart would not survive the devastation and destruction it felt as it began to smash into a million pieces. As Gabriel walked away from her, a floodgate of tears opened inside of her, and she sobbed for the man she was convinced, she would never see again. Gabriel turned back one more time and waved miserably before he disappeared into the crowd.

When Skyler finally moved into their home in Kennedy, she was delighted and overjoyed by the impressive sea views that welcomed her. She was immediately charmed by the sight that greeted her through almost all the windows in the house he had so carefully chosen for them. She was ecstatic by the fact that she could watch the sunrise and set over the ocean, on any day she wanted to. She began attending classes almost immediately, and she grew increasingly impatient for Gabriel's letters to arrive. His letters were on time, yet short and to the point. He told her about the poor conditions the children were being raised in. He spoke of how diseased-stricken the village he was assigned to was. He wrote her about the scorching heat that had become almost unbearable for him at times. He explained the lack of clean water, and how the children were severely suffering from malnutrition. He told Skyler how often he dreamed of her, and that he could barely wait for the day they would be reunited again. He missed her, and longed for the day he would return to her. Skyler wasted no time in replying to his letters as they arrived. She swiftly wrote of her classes, and how she missed having him watch the sunsets with her. She reminded him of her never-ending love for him, and she continuously begged him to take care of himself, and come home to her, unharmed.

She had deliberately padlocked herself off to the world, and surrendered to the safety of her cocoon. She had barely gone to see her parents in Logan's Bay anymore, and spent virtually all her free time writing. She longed for Gabriel and she missed him terribly, and by the time his letters had ended, she was exhausted and defeated by a debilitating fear and extreme anxiety that something terrible had happened to him. It was unlike him to discontinue his letters to her. They were on schedule, each week. Skyler was unreservedly consumed and wholly beleaguered by concern for his well-being from the moment she realized his letters had stopped reaching her. Gabriel's crew had little to no access to mobile communications, and when Skyler discovered that there was no way at all to successfully make contact with him, her fear devoured and crippled her entirely. She contacted the headquarters of Doctors Without Borders often, but they were unable to reassure her of Gabriel's safety, while they unceasingly investigated, and searched for his group. Skyler stopped attending classes, and spent her days in a total daze. The nightmares were never very far from her as she laid awake at night, and fervently pleaded with God to bring him safely back to her.

She would routinely make her way to the postbox, and wait edgily for the Postman to arrive. He had grown so accustomed to Skye's repetitiveness, that he hoped that soon, he could deliver what it was that she was so anxiously waiting for. Skye called Gabriel's parents often, but they too, were unsuccessful in locating him, or heard anything at all from him. She sustained her letters to him, and prayed that he was, at the very least, reading them. The hours turned into days, and finally, the days turned into weeks and still, she received no word from Gabriel, or his team. She refused to turn on the television, she had learnt to despise its place in the living room out of fear for the news it might bring her.

Not quite a month after she had received his last letter, Skyler reluctantly called Sarah once again. "Mrs. Galicia, have you heard anything at all from Gabriel? Anything?" Skyler was keenly aware of the panic that was apparent in her voice. "No Skye, nothing. Have you?" Skyler could at once detect the anxiety and equal concern in Sarah's voice. They were both frantic with worry, and for days after their phone call, they desperately tried get in touch with the Kenyan authorities. It was of no use as they were constantly reverted to Doctors Without Borders, which left Skyler feeling destitute and helpless, as she grew increasingly apprehensive with each passing day. For around two weeks after Skyler's phone call to Sarah, she had continued her decline in attending class. It was enormously complex for her to find balance again, and return to her typical day to day routine while she received no word from Gabriel. She was engulfed by thoughts of horror that were beginning to entirely devour her as she considered all that could have happened to Gabriel. She persistently called Doctors Without Borders and without fail, she would beg them to go in search of Gabriel in a frenetic attempt to locate him or his group.

Late one night as she desperately tried to trace and map out Gabriel's journey, the ringing of her phone caught her off-guard and alarmed her almost at once. Skyler instinctively reached for her mobile phone, and swiftly glanced at the alarm clock on her night stand, "Hello?" She began trembling when she held the phone to her ear. "Skye?" Skyler was at once familiar with Sarah's unsteady voice, and she instantly sensed that something was drastically wrong, "Mrs. Galicia, what?" Panic had begun to demolish her almost immediately when Sarah's silence unnerved Skyler at once. She instinctively knew that something had happened to Gabriel. "Mrs. Galicia! Please tell me!" Her hands were trembling violently as she tightened her grip on the phone, afraid that she would drop it when she heard Sarah sobbing hysterically on the other side. Skyler could barely breathe when her heart began to hammer irrepressibly. She felt the blood drain from her face as she desperately implored God for Gabriel's safety. "Oh God, Mrs. Galicia, don't do this to me!" She yelled through the phone. "It's Gabriel, they can't, they can't find him. There was an explosion just outside their camp, that's all they can tell me, they don't know anything more than that." "No! No!" Skyler yelled out hysterically, instantly debilitated by an incapacitating grief. "Don't, just don't! Don't say that! Gabriel is fine! Gabriel is coming home! It's been weeks! Why are they only telling us now? No, Mrs. Galicia, do you hear me? No!"

She dropped the phone and fell to her knees while excruciatingly releasing the tears from her eyes as she clutched her aching stomach that was at once overwhelmed by intense biliousness. She rocked herself back and forth, and cried out for

Gabriel to come home to her. She shouted out in prayer and begged God to discharge the torture and anguish that had entirely submerged her shattered heart. She appointed God as the Crusader of her heart, and begged him to mend the broken pieces of her. She pleaded with Him to find Gabriel, and bring the only man she had ever loved, back to her. She sat in the dark while she negotiated with God, her life for that of Gabriel's. She spoke delicately when she told God that she could not face life without him, and that she could barely breathe when she thought of him. She undertook to be better and do better for God. She reminded God of how much she loved Gabriel, and she told Him that her heart could no longer endure the devastation of Gabriel's loss. She begged Him to take her, and bring Gabriel back. She pleaded with Him to look into her heart, and pay attention to the crushed pieces bouncing around inside her. She said a prayer to God, to make her braver than she was.

As the silence began to overwhelm her, she no longer tried to wipe the tears from her face, and she no longer wanted to talk to God. She was encircled by a disconcerting silence as she listened to the clock tick in the living room, one second at a time. It comforted her to hear the echoing of life through the darkness that had suddenly and repellently surrounded her. She lay curled up on the floor, listening to the sounds of the darkness. She was numbed by the anguish she had felt only moments before while her tears continued to relentlessly dribble from her eyes. She thought of Gabriel and the dark eyes that had once imprisoned her. She closed her eyes, desperate to conjure up his protective arms around her. From where she was lifelessly laying, she studied the memory of the image of Gabriel saying goodbye to her at the airport, one that was vindictively burnt in her mind. She smiled sadly when she could faultlessly imagine him looking at her. At that very moment, Skyler decided to return to the world she had once created, the world she knew he'd be waiting in for her. She squeezed her eyes tighter, and instantly entered the universe that bore no pain, hurt or anger. When she found Gabriel there, Skyler knew at once that theirs was one story she could never tell the world of, a story her broken heart had abruptly compelled her to live in. "I thought you were gone, Gabe? They told me, they said that you were gone?" "I'm never gone from you, Skye, never." "I was so afraid, Gabe, I was so afraid that, that I would not find you here …" She burst into tears when Gabriel seized her into his arms, "You'll always find me here, Skye, just close your eyes. But right now, you have to go back, Skye. You can't stay here, you must go back …"

It felt as though hours had passed by before Skyler was yanked back to reality by a deliberate and urgent knock on her front door. She leaped from the floor, and sprinted to her front door as fast as she could. She was sure it was Gabriel, who would dry away her crushing tears, and tell her that it was all a huge misunderstanding. "Gabriel!" She snatched open the door, but was instantly disappointed to find her parents standing with Tallulah on her doorstep. "No ..." She wailed out in excruciating pain as she collapsed in her father's arms, howling violently into his chest. He held her close as Tabitha and Tallulah made their way inside, both desperate to hide their own sorrow from Skyler. "Honey, let's go inside." Dave Maxwell placed his arm around her when he noticed that her legs were growing weak underneath her. They slowly made their way into the dining room where Tabitha and Tallulah were seated, both crying inconsolably. Skyler clung to her father, and desperately prayed that he would tell her they had found Gabriel, alive. "I'm so sorry, Skye ..." Tabitha rose to her feet and placed her arms around Skyler. They sat late into the night in a deafening silence before Tabitha realized that Skyler would by no means at all, get any sleep, anytime soon. As the sun greeted them, Tabitha frantically called a doctor who had worked with Gabriel. She hurriedly explained Skyler's situation to him, and asked him to prescribe something to help Skyler sleep. Dave wasted no time in collecting the sedatives and handed it to Skyler who willingly swallowed the pills. She wanted to sleep. She was desperate to escape the anguish and hurt that was mercilessly crippling her. She wanted to shut herself off from her parents and the rest of the world, until Gabriel found his way back home. She no longer wanted to breathe while awake and be conscious of his absence. She wanted to sleep so she could find him in her darkness. She curled up on her bed, and drifted off almost at once.

Skyler was unyielding in her decision to remain in Kennedy while her parents returned to Logan's Bay a couple of days later. She had resolved to patiently wait for proof of his death before she would simply accept that he was gone. She categorically decided to continue as normal with her classes as though nothing had happened, and wait unwearyingly for him to return to her. With less than a week before her semester was to end, Skyler noted that her entire body had been continuously aching and that she felt overwhelmingly strained and run-down. She had been working longer hours on her projects lately, while at the same time, she was studying for her tests that were around the corner. When she took a break from her studies, she was writing, and hardly ever indulged in a good night's sleep, ever since the phone call from Sarah. She found it immensely trying to sleep at night, which left her tremendously exhausted in the mornings. She no longer woke up to watch the sun rise, and as the sun was about to set, she would draw the curtains in a desperate attempt to miss the once-loved vision. She called Dr. Alden to schedule an appointment for that same afternoon hoping that he would prescribe vitamins and possibly, something to help her sleep at night. After confirming her appointment for later, Skyler ran out to the postbox, hoping to find a letter from Gabriel. When she opened the post box, she once again found it empty. Each time she closed it, she was reminded of her dreadful sadness and increasing anger towards the postman, and towards Gabriel.

"Ms. Maxwell?" The desk nurse smiled when Skyler got up. "Come with me." She followed her to Dr. Alden's consulting rooms, and sat in the first empty seat, patiently waiting for him to show up. "Skyler Maxwell?" Dr. Alden was a tall, masculine man with dark hair and a grizzled beard. She was pleased by his friendly demeanor when he held his hand out to introduce himself. She smiled before she gently shook his hand. "What seems to be the problem?" "I don't really know, doctor? I mean, I haven't been sleeping. Each time I try and eat something, I become nauseous. I've been studying late at night, and my boyfriend is missing. I haven't really slept since." Dr. Alden frowned as he listened to her talk, aware of a shudder in her voice, "Your boyfriend is missing?" She lowered her head and began fidgeting, "He's, he's a doctor who was sent to Kenya with a team from Doctors Without Borders. They, they can't find him. It's been a while ..." She explained briefly as she desperately tried to swallow back her tears. "I'm sorry to hear that. I'd like to run a few tests just to rule out any concerns, then I'd like to give you something to help you sleep at night, and eat better. Okay?" Skyler nodded without looking up. After running a few minor tests to rule out anything serious, Dr. Alden was satisfied that he had diagnosed Skyler's problem. "How old are you, Skyler?" He stared at the sheet of paper he was holding in his hands while waiting for her response. "Nineteen, why?" She was anxious almost at once. He made his way to an empty seat next to her, and took her hands into his, "What I'm about to tell you might come as a tremendous shock. Given your circumstances ..." He paused, unsure of how to carry on. "What are you trying to say, Dr. Alden? What's wrong with me?" "You are going to have a baby, Skyler." He smiled sadly when he correctly predicted how unasked for, or intimidating the diagnosis came to be. Skyler could hardly believe what she had heard him tell her. She was stunned to discover that she was going to have Gabriel's child. "I'm pregnant?" She was shocked and bewildered by the very notion. "Yes, very much so. Yyou are, give or take, 8 weeks along." Skyler was numbed with shock, vaguely hearing him schedule a follow-up consultation before he handed her a prescription to improve her appetite. "Unfortunately, I can't give you anything to help you sleep, but I'd like to monitor you closely for the next few weeks." He smiled when she nodded and got up to leave.

When Skyler returned home from the doctor's office, she instinctively called Donna. "Hey, Skye, how are you holding up?" Donna had been avoiding Skyler since they were all informed of Gabriel's yet-unverified death. She could in no way yet, bear to hear Skyler's broken voice each time they spoke on the phone. "Donna ..." Skyler was hesitant to tell her sister that she was going to have a baby. "What, Skye? What's going on? Did something happen?" Donna could hear the nerve-wrecking trembling in Skyler's voice. "Please Donna, I want to tell you, but you can't tell anyone. Not yet." "Tell anyone what, Skye?" "I, I'm going to have a baby ..." She whispered, afraid that the walls that were closing in on her, may betray her. Donna gasped in shock, desperate to digest what Skyler had told her only moments ago. "Are you sure?" "I've just come from the doctor. I am 8 weeks, give or take, pregnant." "Have you told mom and dad?" "No, I will, but I just need a few days to process all of this. You can't say anything, Donna." Skyler was at once terrified that Donna would be unable, or unwilling to keep her secret. "I won't do that, Skye. I think it's comforting to know that Gabriel left a little part of him behind for all of us." Donna's voice had begun to quiver when she considered all that Gabriel's leaving had cost Skyler, and how terrific the price was that she was paying for loving him. "I just, I don't want to upset Gabriel's parents right now. Everything is still too raw, you know? There's just no point in reminding everyone that Gabriel isn't here, that, that he might be gone ..." She had spent another hour on the phone with Donna, before she was able to ultimately convince her not to utter a word to Christopher. Donna valued Skyler's decision to withhold the news from their families, even though she in no way at all, agreed with her methods. "I'm the one stuck in this madness, Donna, let me do it my way, please?"

Skyler conscientiously continued writing her stories as she successfully completed her literature course. She flung herself into her chronicles, and created a world wherein she could find, and stay with Gabriel. Each night as she closed her eyes, she was swept away into her fairytale where she would once again see him. As though on schedule, he would wait for her, and take her into his arms while she desperately held onto him. She had existed flawlessly in a life that no-one knew about, one where she could see his eyes and feel his lips on hers once more. She would sit beside him as she spent hours captivated and enchanted by the world she had created for only the two of them. It was a universe she escaped to when her longing for him became too much to bear.

She felt no pain or wretchedness. Her shattered heart became whole again the moment she stepped into her world with Gabriel. When she awoke in the mornings, she could still feel his eyes on her, and she could hardly wait for nightfall, so that she could find him even only one more time.

She had stopped visiting her parents in Logan's Bay in a vehement effort to avoid the Galicia family at all cost. Skyler was comforted by the fact that Donna had kept her promise, but she frequently reminded her of how frantic she was for her sister to keep her secret. Their child was due in August, and by June, Skyler had slowly succeeded in picking up some of the shattered pieces as she instinctively and involuntarily, moved on with her life. She was determined to never surrender to a reality that Gabriel would never return to her.

Alice VL

"It doesn't even look like you have just given birth. Nice to see you again, Skye." Dr. Alden greeted her when he entered her hospital ward. "How are you feeling?" "I'm fine …" She lied when she bowed her head, desperate to hide the fact that she was no longer convinced that she would be able to cope with raising Hope without Gabriel. "Is there any news of her father, yet?" He was at once saddened by the prospect of her having to raise her daughter entirely on her own. "No, nothing yet …" He squeezed her shoulder as he made his way over to her new-born daughter. "She is so adorable. You're going to get through this, Skye, I promise you." Skyler had openly discussed her fears and apprehension during her scheduled visits and check-ups with him, and by the time Hope was born, he was well acquainted with her less than favorable circumstances. "When can I go home?" "Well, if everything checks out, you can go home tomorrow." He smiled before he quickly made notes of the day's updates in her file. "Thank you, doctor Alden." She was anxious to go home and begin her new life with her brand-new daughter.

At Sarah's nagging persistence, Skyler was forced to sell the beach house she had once shared with Gabriel. It was entirely against her will and she was sure, against Gabriel's. Sarah was strong-minded and determined that Skyler move on with her life, convinced that she was pointlessly clinging to the hope that

Gabriel would return to her. She stubbornly nudged Skyler to claim back her independence, and finally accept that Gabriel was gone. As Hope's birth loomed, the Maxwell and Galicia family ultimately accepted that Gabriel would never come back from Kenya. They were firm in the belief that he had died in the explosion. Skyler fought them tooth and nail when she distraughtly tried to convince them to wait for him for just a while longer, but much to her evident hopelessness, they went ahead and held a formal memorial service for him that she refused to be a part of, or even attend. Skyler was overcome with antagonism and resentment. She scolded them for their lack of faith in Gabriel, and then she vowed never to speak to any of them again. She made a solemn oath to Donna that neither of their families would ever see or know Gabriel's child, the child he left behind for all to remember him by.

Donna unstintingly understood how profoundly tormented Skyler was, and reluctantly supported her in her decision to keep secret the fact that Gabriel's child was about to be born, out of fear that Skyler might disappear as Gabriel had. Skyler assured Donna that she would call her often, and as soon as she had settled into a new town and a new home, she would inform her of her whereabouts. Skyler was anxious to take Hope away from the city she shared with Gabriel, and leave for Point's

Reach as soon as she was discharged. She had found a home on the beach which she bought from the proceeds of the sale of her and Gabriel's home. A few months before Hope was born, she published her first novel which would allow the two of them to live off comfortably for a few months, and until she started her second book.

CHAPTER THREE

When Skyler unlocked the front door to her new home, she gazed down at Hope before she opened the door to their new life for the very first time. "Welcome home, baby ..." She softly whispered before she gently kissed her daughter on her forehead. As she stood gazing at the little girl in her arms, she was once again reminded of how strongly Hope resembled her father. She was sad that Gabriel would never get to know and love the little girl that had changed her life so radically. As she casually strolled through their new home, Skyler made a promise to her daughter that she would evolve into the very best mother and father she could be for her daughter. She swore to the little girl sleeping in her arms that she would offer her the sanctuary, stability and love she knew Hope would need someday. She instinctively picked out Hope's bedroom, and smiled when she noticed the beautiful views and perfect sunlight that would greet her as she awoke each day.

She sat down on the carpet in front of the burning fire place in the empty living room, thrilled that she had so effortlessly lit the fire. She reached for the photo album she had so immensely cherished and clung to. She laid Hope down in her cradle, and when she was sound asleep, Skyler cautiously paged through the album. Each time she would see Gabriel's face, she gasped for breath by the careless hammering of her heart. She stared at a picture of him, overwhelmed by an incapacitating sadness that penetrated the very core of her, and silently wished that he was there, with her and their daughter.

After all the months that had passed since he boarded his flight to Kenya, Skyler deeply longed for him, and his absence in their lives grew profoundly with each passing day. She could not escape the anguish that would overcome her when she least expected it. The album was all she had left to remind her of the memories they had once made together, in a life they had chosen to include one another. When she glanced at Hope sleeping in her crib, she was acutely grateful to Gabriel, for having left something of himself behind for her. It was all she had to get her through the rest of her life without him. When her mind drifted back to her parents, she quickly grabbed her mobile phone from Hope's diaper bag, and hurriedly dialed Donna's number. It had barely rung once when Donna anxiously answered the call, "Skye?" "Hey Donna, how are you?" Skyler smiled when she heard her sister's familiar voice. "Fine, where are you?" "I'm on the east coast, Donna, just please don't tell anyone. Please?"

Donna interrupted her almost at once, "I know, Skye, I won't break my promise!" She was instantly agitated with her sister. "Well, we just got here, and it's nice ..." "We?" Skyler giggled when she detected the disbelief in Donna's voice, "Yes, my daughter, Hope and I. She is healthy, beautiful and has all her fingers and toes! She has hair just like Gabriel's, and sleeps all the time!" "Oh Skye, that makes me sad! You had a little girl? Who does she look like? Please sissy, please send me a pic!" Donna was overcome with wretchedness when she considered a life for Skye and her daughter, without Gabriel. She was saddened by how cautious and distrusting of their family Skyler had become. Donna was tempted on more occasion than one to betray her sister, and expose all Skyler's carefully laid out plans to her parents, and then, tell them about the granddaughter they would never know. But, Donna could hardly betray Skyler. She was desperately afraid that if she told anyone, they would never see Skyler again. "She looks just like Gabriel, Donna, just like him. I'll send you a pic after our talk, okay?" Skyler tearfully began whispering as she gazed longingly at Hope. "I wish he was here. I wish he could see her." "I'm so sorry, Skye, I wish he was there too. Is there anything I can do for you?" "We're fine, Donna, we will be. Just please, I trust you, sissy." "Listen, Skye, have you thought more about telling Gabriel's parents, and mom and dad yet? I feel bad for them. What if that's all that they'll ever have of Gabriel?"

Donna was desperate for Skyler to introduce Hope to their parents. She was terrified of the fact that Skyler was entirely alone after she had placed great distance between them, and determined to raise her daughter on her own. "They have a right, Skye, this isn't right. I don't know how you are going to keep this up and hide her forever. Don't you ever want to see us again? It's cruel, Skye. We are your family, and we are Hope's family now. How can you hate us so much?" "No, Donna! We talked about this! I don't hate any of you! I am angry! I don't want Hope to know so much anger right now. I don't want them to ever forget what they've done. I don't hate you, Donna, and I do want to see you again, just let me figure this out. I just need time …" "Skye, please, Mom and dad are so worried. They have no idea where you are?" "Donna, if you ever want to hear from me again, then you will never say a word, okay? I will go so far that none of you will ever find me, I swear it. Tell mom and dad that I called and that I'm fine. Tell them I just want to be alone for a while, and that, that I will reach out to them when I'm ready. Just tell them that, okay? They don't need to know more and if they ask, you just say you don't know anything more than that." Skyler was desperate to keep her distance for just a while longer. "Okay, Skye, fine! I hate this, and I hate lying to dad. Dad will do anything for you, you know that?" Donna unenthusiastically and despondently agreed to Skyler's terms. "How are mom and dad doing?"

Skyler longed for her parents when she realized how desperately she needed her mother's guidance in raising Hope. "They're fine, they just can't understand what got into you. I told them to give you some time, but you know how they are? Dad's very upset about you leaving and all, and asks me all the time if I know where you are. He is looking for you sis …" "I'll get a postcard off to them tomorrow morning, Donna, I promise." "Skye, I just don't understand why you don't want mom and dad to know? It's hard raising a child as a new and now single mother. Mom and dad love you, and they will love Hope too. They've done nothing but support you and side with you." Donna was frantic to try one more time to convince Skyler of her madness before Skyler rudely interrupted her, "I don't want mommy telling Gabriel's parents yet. I can't tell them, and then ask them to keep it a secret from the Galicia's. I don't want Sarah to think she's got Gabe back. I don't want her to ever feel that it was okay to bury him. They gave up on him! And then, Sarah asked me to move on with my life without Gabriel. As though, almost as though he was never here. I can't do that, Donna. I hate her for asking me to do that! Gabe wanted me to live in that house, and she forced me to move out." Donna was silenced by Skyler's outburst, and felt sudden dread and immense anguish tug at her heart,

"Then, where is he Skyler? If we've all just given up on him, where is he? Why hasn't he come home? Why hasn't he called? Maybe you should accept that Gabriel is gone …" Donna was distraught when she considered a reality for Skyler that did not include Gabriel. "No! And don't you ever say that to me again! It was too soon …" "No Skye, it will always have been too soon for you. Tthere will never have been a right time for you to accept that Gabriel is gone and never coming back, Skye, he isn't coming home." "No Donna, not you too? I have to go …" Skyler hung up before Donna could respond to her sister's incensed and embittered words.

Unnerved by her argument with Donna, Skyler glanced over at Hope who was still sound asleep. Skyler got up from the carpet and soundlessly made her way to the kitchen. She swiftly glanced at her wristwatch, and realized that the furniture removal company would be arriving at any moment. She quickly made her way from room to room to decide which of her furniture should be placed where, and as soon as she had made her way back to Hope, she was alerted to the removal van pull into her driveway. She gently took Hope into her arms, and made her way out to meet the driver that was hauling all she had ever owned, all that was left of her life with Gabriel and the home they had once shared. "Ms. Maxwell?" He smiled unenthusiastically when he held what Skyler realized, was an inventory form in his hands. "Yes, you must be Derrick?" He nodded when she looked up at him. "Pleased to meet you." He held a hand out as introduction before he gently shook hers. "Well, if your guys can just unload everything into the house, I can take it from there. I don't expect you to move anything around. It's been a long drive and I'd rather you all get home to your families before night fall." She smiled when she glanced around and noticed half a dozen of his workers. "Are you sure we can't move everything into place for you?" "No thank you. I'll be fine." Skyler hurriedly made her way over to a palm tree out by the pool, and sat down on the grass with Hope still calmly sleeping in her arms. She looked back at the men who began unloading her possessions one by one, before they carefully carried them into her new home. She gazed down at Hope's angelic sleeping face, and smiled sadly before she gently kissed her on her cheek. "I love you so much, Hopie, it's just you and me now. We are going to be fine, just the two of us." She whispered almost indistinctly, as she rocked her baby girl back and forth.

By the time Skyler had unpacked a dozen or more boxes

after she had fed and bathed Hope, she realized that it was long after midnight. She was incapacitated by exhaustion when she was suddenly reminded of the fact that Hope would awake every couple of hours for a feeding. Skyler became anxious and decided at once to get some sleep, and continue unpacking in the morning. She had not as much as brushed her teeth or changed her clothes when she climbed into bed, and laid Hope down beside her. She closed her eyes and instinctively, her mind wandered back to Gabriel once again, "Gabe, come find me …" She whispered in exhaustion as every muscle in her body began to ache. Her feet were throbbing unsympathetically as fatigue entirely overpowered her. Skyler turned on her side, and fell asleep almost at once.

Skyler woke up shortly before 7am the following morning. When she opened her eyes, she was keenly sensitive to how hefty they felt. She turned to Hope who was still fast asleep beside her, "You would be sleeping, wouldn't you, Hopie? You had me up every two hours …" Skyler smiled at her daughter who looked like an angel right out of God's arms. She was reluctant to admit that she was compelled to employ a nanny, if she wanted to get started on her next book. Skyler sluggishly strolled into the kitchen and mindlessly, switched on the kettle while dialing the number of an employment agency she had researched before making her trip to Point's Reach. After confirming several interviews with suitable nannies for noon that same day, Skyler poured herself a cup of coffee, and made her way back to Hope who was still sound asleep.

Satisfied that she was dry and comfortable, Skyler took her packet of cigarettes from her sling bag, and grabbed the baby monitor with the other hand. Turning back to check on Hope, she hurriedly made her way out to the pool. She had no sooner lit her cigarette when her mind involuntarily drifted back to Gabriel. Skyler cringed when she considered how angry he would be if he knew that she had concealed Hope from his parents. She carelessly admitted her failure to consider their emotional states and once again, she justified her decision simply by admitting that she could in no way ever, exonerate the Galicia's for so readily, giving up on him.

By early evening, Skyler had unpacked what was the last of her possessions before she placed Hope down for the night. Other than writing her novels, Skyler was convinced and eerily comforted by the fact that her life would be filled to the brim with raising Hope, and escaping into the world her stories would create for her.

She had employed a nanny that came highly

recommended earlier on in the day, and she was confident that Maria Diego would be wholly competent to take care of Hope. Maria was a Mexican woman in her early fifties who had lost her husband to cancer almost a year ago. She had bounced around between her children who had begun raising families of their own. Maria was desperate for some sort of independence from her children when she eagerly applied for Skyler's nanny position. Skyler liked her; there was something motherly and comforting about her she could not quite place. She was anxious for Maria to assume duties the very next day, and eagerly handed her the keys to the granny pod that was scarcely furnished. Skyler made it clear that Maria's only duty to her was the well-being and care of Hope, and that she would be required to relieve Skyler only during the day.

Skyler was determined to begin writing on her next novel, but she was desperate to balance her time so that she could be present for Hope. It frightened her to identify how unchartered her territory had become, but she was frantically determined to make sure that Hope grew up attentive of her mother's presence.

Skyler and Hope's transition to Point's Reach turned out to be far less complicated than Skyler initially considered it would be. They were enamored by their new home, and uncannily captivated by their new town. Skyler adored the views of the ocean that was present from almost every room in their new home. She loved the idea of watching the sunrises and sunsets once more, this time with Hope in her arms.

Skyler regularly sent postcards to her parents, and was diligent in placing regular, weekly phone calls to Donna. Donna never again brought up the issue regarding Hope and her parents again, but Skyler knew that it demanded an enormous amount of restraint on her behalf to guard her secret after Skyler had silenced her shortly after Hope's birth. Donna loathed the fact that she was betraying her parents, yet, she knew that Skyler would never absolve her for deceiving her if she were to utter a word of Hope to her parents. She knew the risk was too great, and she knew that she would lose Skyler, and Hope in the process.

By the time Christmas showed up, Skyler was stunned to realize that Gabriel had been gone for almost a year. She was nearing the end of her second novel while waiting patiently for Hope to start crawling. Maria was as wonderful and as competent with Hope as Skyler hoped her to be, leaving Skyler feeling calmer and relaxed around her. Skyler relied wholeheartedly on Maria, and it allowed Skyler the free time she needed to run errands anytime she needed to.

Skyler glanced at her wristwatch. It was just after 10pm on Christmas Eve when she reluctantly, but longingly decided to call her parents. "Hello?" Skyler felt a thud in her heart when she recognized Tallulah's gentle voice. "Hey Lu, how are you?" "Skye!" Tallulah squealed with delight when she heard Skyler's familiar voice. When Tabitha heard Tallulah call out Skyler's name, she hurriedly picked up an extension from the kitchen, "Skyler?" Skyler was moments away from bursting into tears when she heard her mother's voice. "Hello, mommy ..." "Honey, where are you?" Skyler could barely ignore the concern and despair in her mother's voice, "Mommy, I just called to let you all know that I am fine, really, I am. It's Christmas, you know? I miss you guys, and I just wanted to wish you all a Merry Christmas." Skyler's voice began trembling when her tears began shimmering in her eyes. "Thank you, Honey, we miss you. Where are you?" "Mommy, please don't ask me that, I don't want to have to lie to you. I just miss you, and I miss dad, and Donna and Tallulah. I miss you." Skyler hurriedly swabbed at the tears that were rolling down her cheeks. She swallowed back on the lump in her throat that had transformed her voice into a hoarse whisper. "Listen honey, the Galicia's miss you terribly and are very worried about you. They ask about you all the time. After your fallout with Sarah, they felt very badly and they want to reach out to you?" Tabitha was desperate for Skyler to pardon Gabriel's parents for the unintentional agony they had caused her. "It's done, mom! She can't go back and change anything. She can't fix what she has done. I'd like to call you more often, but if this is all you want to talk about, if all you want to talk about is the Galicia family ..." Skyler had become irritated before Tabitha interrupted her. "No, no, not at all. I just want to know that you are safe. We'd like to hear from you more, Skye?" Tabitha was terrified that Skyler would abruptly end the call. "So, baby, I read your book! Oh, my gosh, I couldn't believe that you wrote it. To be honest, I read it twice. It was beautifully written. It was just beautiful. I am so proud of you, Skye, it was such a beautiful story ... you did wonderfully!" "You did? You actually read my book? You actually know about my book?" Skyler was overawed by Tabitha's unexpected revelation. "I most certainly do know about your book. And yes, I did, and so did your father, and so did Tallulah. We loved it. Dad is so excited for the next one!"

They spent almost an hour on the phone discussing her next book, and all the comings and goings of her family before Skyler finally hung up to turn in for the night. She knew that in Logan's Bay, the Christmas celebrations were only just about to begin. She missed their traditions. She thought about how Tabitha insisted that Santa Claus show up each year, even though her daughters had grown up, and no longer believed in his magic.

Each year without fail at midnight, Santa Claus would come around the corner, bearing an armful of gifts for both the Maxwell and the Galicia family. Each time Skyler would spot him, her stomach would turn, and excitement would overwhelm her. At that very moment, she became a little girl again and would enthusiastically clasp her father's hands in hers. Skyler was sad to miss out on Christmas with her family. All she wanted to do was fall asleep, and awake on Christmas morning, to hold her daughter in her arms.

She hastily checked up on Hope before she changed into her pajamas, and climbed into bed. Skyler was emotionally depleted, but pleased to have heard her mother's voice. She had almost forgotten how comforting it was to speak to her mother. She turned off her bed lamp, and laid staring at the ceiling while listening to the waves crash onto the shore. Skyler's mind drifted back to Gabriel as it always did when she was alone in the darkness and deathly silence of the night. Those were the very moments that she found Gabriel again. Skyler would wait for the blackness to bring him to her, and for a while, when the whole world was asleep, she would find him in her dreams and go too far away from reality. She would submerge herself into an alternate reality, ready to fly away with him, knowing that the storms were never far off. She lived in a world where she thought her life as a shining star, even though her fears were closer than she would have like them to be. Before she would drift off to sleep, she always seemed so much braver than she ever was. Those were the secrets that she could never tell, her shadows of darkness between Heaven and hell, fantasy and reality. They were wounds that could not heal without a world in which Gabriel existed in. When her nightmares became real, she was forced to add up the cost of her frequent escapes to him. She was never sorry, and never once regretted finding him in their secret world. Skyler ached dreadfully for Gabriel. She had no idea of how to move on without him. Hope would continuously remind her of him, especially when it appeared as though her little girl worshipped her. She thought about her next novel and about the clues she would once again, leave for Gabriel. They were important for him to find if he ever was to return. Her first book was riddled with messages and signs for Gabriel, and her second book would be no different. If he was alive, Skyler knew that he would find her in her books.

On Christmas morning, Skyler handed her daughter the gifts she had bought for Christmas. Although Hope was all of four months old, Skyler smiled when she realized that she had no intimation of who Santa Claus was, and she had no sense of Christmas. She decided to take her out to the beach later that morning to enjoy a Christmas day picnic. There was no point in cooking a large meal just for her after Maria had left the day before to join her children for the holidays. When they reached the beach later that morning, there were barely a handful of people frolicking in the waters while others were stretched out in the sun. She was thankful for the small crowd, and immediately placed a blanket down on the sand before she sat Hope down. Hope adored the beach, and relished in playing in the sand and the water. After Skyler had taken her into the ocean for a while, she saw her daughter's eyes fight to remain focused. Skyler knew at once that Hope was exhausted. She swiftly dried her off, and laid her down on their blanket. Once Hope had devoured her bottle, she was sound asleep. Skyler sat quietly beside Hope as she gazed out over the ocean. She noticed the ships passing through the bay, and she wondered whether they were celebrating Christmas on the ship or whether they had families at home, waiting for them to return to them, just as she had been waiting for Gabriel to return to her and Hope.

"Hi there …" Skyler was at once unnerved and alarmed to hear an unexpected coarse, masculine voice. When she looked up, she noticed a tall, unfamiliar man standing over her. "Hello?" She was uneasy and muddled all at once. "My name is Gavin. Gavin Taylor …" He extended his hand in an attempt to offer her an introduction. Skyler cautiously shook his hand, unsure of who he was, or what he wanted from her. "Skyler …" She hesitantly introduced her, aware of the abruptness in her tone. "Can I help you with something?" She frowned before she got up to face him. "I saw you here with who I assume is your daughter, and I was just wondering why you two aren't out celebrating Christmas with your family?" "That's none of your business, besides, why are you here and not celebrating Christmas with your family?" She glowered, desperate to draw his attention away from her. "Well, maybe the fact that I don't have a family has got something to do with it, I can't be sure. What's your excuse?" Skyler was mortified by his forthcoming answer, and silently berated herself for her total lack of deportment, "I, I don't have family either …" She lied after lowering her head.

Gavin was partly lost for words when she responded, and when he realized that he had nothing left to say to her, he uncomfortably turned to leave. Skyler watched him walk away, and suddenly realized that she had failed to notice a similar heartache in his eyes earlier, "Wait!" She yelled out after him. Gavin stopped and turned almost at once. After staring at her for a moment, he made his way back towards her. "I was rude earlier. I am sorry. My daughter and I were about to have a Christmas picnic, and seeing that she's not really a fan of sandwiches yet … would you like to join us? I'd hate for all this food to go to waste." Skyler began blabbering and at once, she regretted inviting him to join them. "Thank you, I would love to." He smiled timidly when he accepted her invitation. They ate their sandwiches in silence and after smiling courteously at one another, Gavin turned to face her, "Do you live around here?" Skyler turned and pointed to her house, "I'm over there …" He pointed to his own house only two houses away from hers. "What do you do for a living?" He was curious to know more about her. "Write, I'm an author." She replied bashfully, unable to look him in the eye. She was severely uncomfortable all of a sudden when Skyler realized that she had never interacted with any man, other than with Gabriel. She eyed Gavin, and realized how unlike Gabriel he was, but how alluringly attractive he was in his own right. Gavin adorned sun-bleached blonde hair and piercing blue eyes. Skyler thought him to be at least a good ten inches taller than her, while his physique exposed him as a dedicated surfer. "What do you do for a living?" "Me? I'm a lawyer, criminal law." He replied simply before he gazed out over the ocean. "Where is your baby's father?" Skyler was caught entirely off-guard and wholly unprepared for his candor. She felt bare and exposed as he glared inquisitorially at her. "That's personal, but, if you must know, he's somewhere in Kenya. Lost I Kenya. They all believe he is … gone …" "Sorry, I shouldn't have snooped."

He was at once profoundly remorseful for his unrestrained curiosity. Skyler glanced over at him again, and instinctively began telling him about Gabriel that was missing and presumed dead. She told him about Hope, and how the Galicia and Maxwell families knew nothing of her existence. She expressed her distress of the fact that they so effortlessly surrendered to the news of his supposed death. She told him how infuriated and distressed she was that they had all given up on any hope for his survival and refused to search for him. She wanted Gavin to know how she adored Gabriel and how she incessantly prayed for his safe return. Gavin sat in silence while mulling over all she was spilling to him. "You, you have a family, Skyler, mine are dead, and I would give anything to see them just one more time. You shouldn't shut them out like this. Hope deserves to know her aunts, uncles and cousins someday. She needs to grow up knowing that her family extends beyond you. She deserves the pleasure of knowing her grandparents, and who her father was … is …" He was saddened to realize that her stubbornness and unwillingness to forgive her family, was what was withholding Hope from her grandparents. "I have never met that one special someone to spend my life with, but my parents passed away very recently. And Donna? You are so sure that she will never expose your secret?" "No, she won't, at least, I pray that she won't … yet." "Yet?" He was confused by her hesitancy, "When the right time comes, I'll tell them. Of course, I'll tell them, Gavin, just not yet. I can't deal with them yet, and I need to carve out a life for Hope and I first." She was adamant of how she had planned to deal with Hope in the future. "When will the right time be?" Skyler bowed her head when she realized that she couldn't answer him truthfully. She did not plan for a perfect time to introduce her daughter. She had remained indignant and dreadfully wounded by Sarah Galicia's actions. She wanted to punish her. With a demoralizing shudder, Skyler realized that she could never chastise Sarah over something she would never know about. "Do you think I made a mistake?" Fear had begun to penetrate the very core of her. "Yes, I think you did, and I think you still are."

Gavin was unyielding and without hesitation. For the first time since Hope was born, Skyler allowed herself to consider the fact that keeping Hope from their families was perhaps, an enormous error in judgement. "Well, it's too late to go back now." She shrugged off her guilt before Gavin interrupted her, "It's never too late, you know?" Skyler considered what he had said for just a moment, but she knew into her soul, that she did not have the courage to expose her lies to the world. Her thoughts were unexpectedly interrupted when Hope woke up. Gavin gently picked her up, and held her on his lap. Skyler was uncomfortable at first, but managed a smile when she discovered how proficient Gavin seemed with Hope on his lap. "Do you have kids?" She was curious to know more about him while he playfully spoke to Hope. "No, never been married. Never even crossed my mind." "Oh?" Skyler was authentically and unpredictably surprised.

They sat on the beach for the remainder of Christmas day while comfortably spilling facts of one another's lives to each other. They discussed the crooked roads their past had taken them on, and they admitted to their dreams and goals for the future. Skyler was relieved to discover how uncomplicated he was. She was intensely thankful that she had stumbled across a perfect stranger; one she could confide in, one who had called her out when she deserved to be questioned. Just as the sun was about to set, Skyler swiftly excused herself. "I must go, Hope has her bath before dark. It was really nice meeting you." Gavin helped her pack up the picnic basket, and gently shook the blanket they sat on. "Merry Christmas, Skyler, and good luck. If you need anything at all, you know where to find me." He quickly kissed Hope on her forehead, "I'd like to see you again, as friends, of course!" Skyler smiled and agreed almost at once.

Skyler called Donna later that evening just as she had put Hope to bed. Donna excitedly told her that Christopher had proposed to her, and that she was about to plan her wedding. "I didn't know you two were dating?" Skyler was flabbergasted and stunned by Donna's unanticipated revelation. "It kind of just happened, Skye ..." She paused to take in a deep breath, "I love him. I've always loved him, you must have known that?" "No, I had no idea? Oh, Donna, I am so very, very happy for you! I guess, I guess I've just been so absorbed in my own life that I didn't even ask what was going on in yours? I am so sorry, sissy." Skyler was pleased to hear the joy in Donna's voice. "There's more, Skye, I'm pregnant. I'm going to have a baby!" Skyler was speechless and could not help but wish that Gabriel was with her so that Donna could break the news to him, and tell him that he was about to become an uncle. "Skye?" Donna became anxious when Skyler's silence alarmed her. "I'm here, that is such awesome news! Mom and dad, what did they say?" "They're happy for us! Dad was a little upset at first, and you know how mom is, but after the initial shock, they've given us their blessing. Come home, please, Skye." Donna pleaded with Skyler to return home to Logan's Bay. Skyler struggled to find the words to tell her sister how desperately she wanted to go home, but that she did not have the courage to face any of them after all that she had done. "I can't, Donna, I can't ..." "Will you at least come home for the wedding?" "When is the wedding?" "Next weekend …" Donna bit on her lip. She instinctively knew that Skyler would not attend her wedding at such short notice. "It's too little notice, Donna?" "Yeah, yeah. Anyway, I'll send you some pictures of the wedding." Skyler smiled wretchedly when she realized how much she is missing out on, and how time was not being kind to her. She quickly asked about Tallulah before she ended her call to Donna.

Pearls in Ashes

CHAPTER FOUR

Hope's fourth birthday arrived almost out of the blue for Skyler. When she awoke that morning, she was stunned and horrified to realize how carelessly time had passed her by. She could barely acknowledge the fact that Gabriel had been gone almost five years, and it saddened her that she had finally accepted the reality in which he was never coming back to her. Somewhere along the way, Skyler had acceded to the veracity that he was gone. She was forced to face the reality that he had died while over in Kenya. Even though she had made a heroic effort to remain as normal as possible, she was constantly faced with waves of sorrow that threatened to drown her on more days than she would care to admit to.

Skyler and Gavin were making their way out to the pool with Hope's birthday cake when they stopped and chuckled at the sight of a dozen other four-year olds. Skyler glanced over at Hope, and was happy to discover how contented and well-adjusted she was. Skyler and Gavin began dating less than a year before, and although Skyler never quite recovered from losing Gabriel, she appreciated having Gavin around. He adored Hope, and spent the majority of his free time with her. Hope in turn, fell hopelessly in love with Gavin, and cheerfully referred to him as Daddy-Gav. Gavin was constantly nudging Skyler to get married so that he could legally adopt Hope, but she chose to keep their relationship as uncomplicated as it had been right from the very start. Secretly, Skyler did not favor the idea that Hope be adopted by another man. She was convinced that she would betray Gabriel and his legacy by passing her off as another man's child. She would never disclose her fears to Gavin, and convincingly told him that they were perfect as they were. She was afraid to unreservedly commit Hope and herself to him. Gavin knew that he would lose her if he pursued her contractually, and accepted that Skyler was in no way at all, ready for a marriage. He was only too happy to carry on with things as they were for the time being.

After impatiently blowing out her four burning candles, Gavin seized Hope into his arms as she threw hers devotedly around him. "I love you, Hopie …" He kissed her tenderly on her cheek. "I love you too, Daddy-Gav!" Gavin was the only father Hope had ever known. Skyler had often told her the story of Gabriel, her real daddy, but she was convinced that Hope didn't fully understand when she tried to teach Hope about death, Heaven and angels. Gavin was only too eager to take on the role of Hope's father, and stood in with pride each time he held his daughter in his arms. Skyler knew that they both loved each other dearly, and was often saddened by the fact that she could never love Gavin the way he deserved to be loved, the way she enduringly adored Gabriel. She had a distressing feeling that her soul belonged to him, but for now, she had given Gavin the pieces of her that was left.

The three spent much of their free time together, but Skyler had at no time permitted him to stay overnight at her house. She would often arrange for Maria to babysit Hope, before she stealthily made her way over to Gavin's house. The arrangement eventually suited them both, but Skyler was unyielding in her decision to be home before Hope awoke in the mornings. Skyler increasingly began calling her parents during the past few months, as she slowly began to accept the fact that Gabriel had died almost five years ago. Although Donna was living her very own dream as Mrs. Christopher Galicia, she never ceased to encourage Skyler to introduce Hope to the rest of the family. Donna became a mother to two boys in quick succession of one another. Skyler was pleased when Donna told her how their father had doted on both her boys. She would regularly be overcome by guilt for withholding Hope from them. She was horrified and shaken when she realized that it was no longer anger keeping her from telling them about Hope, but debilitating and crippling fear. She was frantically restless of their undeniable anger and criticism towards her, and she was desperately afraid of the possibility that they may reject her, were they to discover that Skyler had been deceiving them for all of Hope's life. She was overwhelmingly apprehensive of the repercussions that her actions would bring about, and she was desperately afraid of the sorrow her lies would inflict upon the Galicia family. For the first time in her life, Skyler was ashamed of who she had become, of what her anguish and heartache had turned her into.

Later that night, after Hope had finally fallen asleep, Skyler sluggishly made her way to her study. Hope had been over-active and unwilling to lie down for the night, leaving Skyler frustrated by the fact that she refused to settle down. Gavin returned to his home just as Hope finally agreed to take her bath and brush her teeth. When Skyler reached her desk, she slumped into her chair in utter exhaustion and total defeat. She was frantic to complete her fourth novel. She promised herself that she would publish a novel each year shortly after her daughter's birthday, and she pressured herself to adhere to her schedule. As she glared blankly at the screen in front of her, Skyler's eyes caught a framed picture of Hope on her desk. She smiled when she was again reminded of how beautiful her daughter was, and how striking her green eyes and raven black hair was. Smiling sadly, she was once again reminded of Gabriel, and how much Hope resembled him.

She had barely opened her file, when her phone rang unexpectedly, shattering the stillness of the night. "Hello?" "Skye?" Skyler was pleased to hear Donna's gentle voice. "Hey Donna, what's up? Twice in one day! Or was earlier just to wish Hope for her birthday, and now you realize you miss me, and want to speak to me too?" Skyler giggled softly, happy to hear her sister's voice. "Skye, please, be quiet and please listen to me. You can't interrupt me, okay?" She paused for only a moment, "I don't know how to tell you this? I just don't … it's … shit!" Skyler was alarmed by Donna's sudden and absolute frustration. "Donna, what's going on? Did something happen? Is mom and dad okay? Is it Tallulah?" Skyler became anxious when fear and dread began to submerge her entire body. She sat straight up in her chair, and waited impatiently for Donna to respond. "Donna, you're scaring me!" "Skyler, it's, it's him, Gabriel …" Donna burst into tears and wept wretchedly into the phone. "Gabriel? What about Gabriel? What do you mean, it's Gabriel? Did they find his body?" Skyler felt her throat restricting the air she was anxious to breath in when her heart began to hammer irrepressibly at the mere mention of his name. "Donna!" "They found him. They found Gabe, and, and … he's alive, Skye, and he's coming home!

Gabe is alive! You were right! You were right, Skye! All these years, you were right!"

Skyler became giddy almost at once. Her entire body began to shudder, and her heart raced wildly as she desperately tried to catch her breath. "Skye?" Donna remained silent, waiting for Skyler to respond. "Skyler!" "Gabriel's alive? Are you sure it's Gabriel?" The call she had dreamed of since the day he disappeared, had finally come through. "They found him somewhere in Europe. He was held hostage in Kenya and escaped. I think dad said he escaped about two years ago from a camp. He was beaten and tortured, and for a while, he couldn't even remember his name. Dad says he suffered from a temporary form of amnesia, but that he is okay. Still, somehow, he ended up somewhere in Europe …" Donna paused to wipe the tears that were rolling uninhibitedly down her cheeks, "He'll be home tonight, Skye. Sarah and Carlos left as soon as they got the call. They went to pick him up at the airport, and asked me to call you and tell you that Gabriel is coming home …" Skyler sat in silence, unable to take in all that Donna was saying. "They say he's okay, Skyler, are you there?" Donna was at once anxious when her sister's silence turned deafening, "Skyler?" "I'm here, Donna." She whispered hoarsely through the tears that had begun to drown out her face. "Christopher says he's been asking for you. He wanted Sarah and Carlos to take him home, but Christopher had to tell him you don't live there anymore. Home isn't there anymore. All he wanted was just to go home to you …" "Don't tell him anything. Don't say anything about anything, Donna. I'll come home for a few days. I'll be there as soon as I can, just don't say anything to him, Donna."

As though in a shocking haze, Skyler abruptly ended her conversation with Donna, and sat shuddering unrestrainedly when she replayed the phone call over and over in her mind. Gabriel was alive, just as she was sure he had been for the first few years after he went missing. Skyler's heart was racing against the clock, before her entire body erupted into a massive tremor when she finally conceded to the idea that Gabriel had returned to her. Skyler sat in a silent daze for what felt like forever. When she glanced at her wrist watch, she realized that it was just after 11 pm. She hurriedly called the airline, and hastily made a reservation for the next flight out to Kennedy. She swiftly made her way out to the granny pod, and prayed that Maria was still awake.

When she hesitantly knocked on her front door, Skyler was relieved to hear sounds from her television in the background. "Skye, are you alright? It looks as though you've seen a ghost?" Maria was entirely caught off-guard by Skyler's appearance at her doorstep in the middle of the night, incapacitated and overpowered by an ashen expression on her face. Her eyes were bloodshot and enflamed, while her tears continued to torrent unapologetically from her eyes. "I'm okay. I just, I just need to go away for a few days. Something personal has come up, but I don't want you to worry about it, okay Maria? I just, I can't take Hope with me so I need you to stay with her and take care of my little girl for a few days. My flight leaves in a few hours, please don't ask questions, Maria, just take care of my baby until I get back." "Of course, whatever you need." Maria placed her hand on Skyler's shoulder when she realized that Skyler had turned pallid.

"Please just carry on as normal with Hope for a few days." She turned around to make her way back home, before she hurriedly turned back to Maria, "Please tell Gavin that I had to leave for a few days and that I'll call him tomorrow evening, okay? Please, don't tell him what you saw tonight. Please Maria, I need you to do this for me?" Maria nodded her head before Skyler made her way back into her house, as though caught up in a foggy mist. She stood staring at Hope who was fast asleep in her bed before she gently kissed her on her forehead. All she wanted to do was climb into bed with her, and hold her in her arms until the sun came up. When she packed an overnight bag, her mind drifted back to the last time she saw Gabriel. He was about to board a plane, and disappear from her life for the next five years. She speculated about the torment he may have suffered, and she was curious to know whether he had become the pediatrician he had always dreamed of becoming. She remembered the plans they had made in the past, and she considered the life they had so carefully laid out. Skyler burst into tears again when she realized how her mendacities had finally caught up with her, and how they were coming back to haunt her. In less than twenty-four hours, she would be in the presence of both the Maxwell and Galicia families again for the first time in years, and she would finally see Gabriel again.

Pearls in Ashes

CHAPTER FIVE

Skyler glanced tensely around her as she cautiously stepped off the plane, at once alert of Donna's presence. She continued to glance around nervously, and was relieved to notice that Donna was accompanied only by two boys running circles around her. She smiled when she spotted Donna entirely flustered and overwhelmed. Skyler's smile expanded when she descended further down the stairs. Donna was desperate to calm her boys down. Skyler was overcome with immense guilt for forcing her to keep Hope a secret, one that had kept Hope from being a part of their family and a cousin to two little boys. Hope had missed out on knowing her grandparents, aunts, uncle and cousins. Skyler knew that she had made a senseless mistake, and indirectly blamed her broken heart as the reason for her utter stupidity all those years ago. At the same time, Skyler was convinced that she had missed her chance to raise Hope around the family that would grow to adore and protect her. At that very moment, Skyler realized that her faults were overwhelming her, and that she was Hope's worst enemy. She was at once overawed with remorse, but had no way of knowing how to try and reverse all the wrongs she had done, not only to their families, but to Gabriel. "Skyler!" She heard her sister frantically call out for her while mercilessly clutching her boys by their arms before she made her way towards Skyler. "Donna! Wow! You look just wonderful, and the boys are gorgeous! I've missed you, sissy."

Skyler bent down and kissed each boy on the cheek while chuckling inaudibly at Donna's flustered appearance. When the boys retreated bashfully from Skyler, it saddened her to realize that she might seem nothing more than a stranger to them. She stood gazing at them in silence, immensely saddened by the fact that she had missed out on their lives. She was at once flung into unsympathetic despondence when she grasped the fact that she would never have the memories of witnessing all their firsts, to someday return to. "This is Antonio," Donna smiled sketchily when she pointed to her eldest son, "And this is Gabriel …" Skyler's heart began to hammer when Donna introduced her youngest child, Gabriel Junior. Not only was he named after her Gabe, but he bore a striking resemblance to the man she had once loved, the man who had been responsible for turning her life outside down one time too many. "Gabe for short. Christopher wanted to name him after Gabriel. He just wanted to, urgh, Skye, you know what I'm trying to say?" Donna was overcome with an intense need to explain their decision to name their son after Gabriel, yet she had no idea of how to quite end her sentence. "I am so happy for you, Donna. You deserve all of this. Just you and Chris and the boys. I screwed up so badly ..." Skyler felt the tears roll down her cheek when she became desperate to swallow back on the growing lump in her throat.

She had disregarded her sisters, her parents, and her old life but more than anything, she longed for them. She had pined and ached for Gabriel, and she desperately missed her parents. She had been alone in her grief, yearning for her family, and she missed being shielded from harm. Skyler took her sister's hand into hers, and gently squeezed it, "You feel like home, sissy." "You are home now, Skye, where is Hope?" Donna turned around, frantic to find Hope. "I didn't bring her. She's back at home with Maria, her nanny and ... Gavin." Skyler was at once aware of the scowl on her sister's face when she stared questioningly at Skyler. "I've been seeing him for a while, Donna, we've been dating a little over a year." Skyler was at a loss as to how to accurately and honestly explain Gavin's presence in her life. She at once felt as though she had not only betrayed Gabriel or their families, but that she had bitterly deceived herself and Hope.

They made their way to the luggage collections hand in hand, but in silence. Skyler persistently dabbed at the tears that were slithering from her eyes when she once again realized how in-over-her-head she was. She had allowed herself to fall in love with Gavin, when she fiercely loved Gabriel with all the broken pieces of her shattered heart. Hope knew only one father, and Skyler knew how deeply Gavin had fallen in love with Gabriel's daughter. Skyler was terrified by all the inner turmoil that had engaged in a bitter warfare within her. She was angry at the cold-blooded deceits life had handed her, but undeniably, she was elated and thrilled that Gabriel had come home. She had begged and pleaded with God on so many nights to bring Gabriel back to them. She had beseeched Him and negotiated with Him to bring Hope's father back to her. Skyler thought back to the day they were given the news of Gabriel's disappearance, and she despondently recalled how she had offered her own life to God, in exchange for Gabriel's. She no longer knew where she belonged in the world. She failed to understand the universe's forbidding plotting against her. She had no idea of how her life would change, yet, she was once again trapped in the aftermath of the destruction that Gabriel's disappearance had left behind. She had no plans for tomorrow. Skyler was untaught as to how to move on from that moment forward. She was certain that she was brave enough to face him, but she never thought she would have to be so much braver than she was.

She hastily retrieved her luggage and followed Donna and her nephews to the car. They had barely driven out of Kennedy when the two tots were sound asleep. "Donna, how is he? Is he hurt? Did they hurt him?" Skyler was anxious to learn more about Gabriel, and what had happened to him. "He looks fine, Skye. I mean, on the outside you can't tell whether he's been hurt or anything like that, but he is quieter, you know? He doesn't say much, and he doesn't talk about what happened over there? He so badly wanted to come and pick you up today, but I had to insist that I come alone. I wasn't sure with Hope, you know? I can tell you this, sissy, he's been through hell. He doesn't understand why you left. When Sarah told him that we haven't seen you in years, he was so sad, Skye …" Donna paused to take in a deep breath, "He was frantic when he found out that you were gone. I mean, mom and dad couldn't tell him where you were, and when he found out that you had broken off all contact, he was devastated. It hurt him, Skye. He kept asking what happened, but we couldn't tell him because nobody really knew?" Donna became silent as she gulped down on her own tears. Skyler was at once aware of a piercing ache that had rushed through her heart, and she prayed desperately that Gabriel recover from the torture and pain he was involuntary forced to endure while over in Kenya.

During their drive back home, Donna was pleased to fill Skyler in on all the events she had missed out on. Donna told Skyler of how the Galicia and Maxwell families had come together after Gabriel's disappearance, and then again when Skyler had left without a trace. She spoke of her and Christopher's relationship that thrived on the grief they had both shared when they lost Gabriel, and then, Skyler. "When Gabriel left, Chris was shattered Skye, and then you left, and I was crushed, and it just almost destroyed us all. All of us. Nothing was the same again. None of us were ever the same again, and none of us really knew what to say anymore. It tore us all apart, and nobody knew much of anything anymore." Donna was once again dismayed by the events that had taken place not too long ago. "I'm sorry, Donna. I never quite thought this through. I thought I knew it all. I thought I could punish them, and it would make me feel better, you know? And it did, for a while. The thing is, I wasn't punishing them when they had no idea Hope even existed, and for that, I am truly sorry, sissy." "You should be, Skye. I mean, I get it. I know why you did it, but at the same time, I don't understand why you had to leave and hide Hope from us. Mom and dad miss you, Tallulah misses you and me, I miss you. Did you never miss us?" Donna wiped fiercely at a lost tear that had rolled down her cheek. "Donna? How can you ask me that? Of course, I did. I miss you guys every day. Don't you think I know what I've missed? Your wedding. Your boys. I would do anything to get a do-over. Anything, Donna. Your boys don't know me? I've missed birthdays, the first tooth, the first steps, the first words. I know what I lost, Donna. I know …" Skyler sobbed when she realized that she alone was to blame for all the hurt and anger that had entirely devastated and overwhelmed her family's life. "I, I know I was wrong. I just, I just didn't know how to move forward. I don't know what to do now, Donna?" Donna took Skyler's hand and gently squeezed it. "We'll figure it out, sissy. Gabriel is back, and you're home …" Skyler interrupted her before she could continue, "I'm not home, Donna, I can't come home. Not yet. Not now. I've fallen in love with Gavin. He is a good man and he is a good father to Hope." "But, Skye, he isn't Hope's father. You owe Gabe this! None of this was his fault. He didn't ask for this, and none of this is Hope's fault either." "I know, just give me time, Donna. Please, just let me do this one step at a time." "That's your problem, Skyler. You're always asking for time that never runs out. I just don't get why you were so angry with us all? What really happened, Skye?" "I thought, I just felt like everyone was wrong to move on so easily after Gabriel disappeared. I was angry that everyone just gave up on him. Nobody looked for him, and nobody waited for him. I was so mad at Gabriel, and I wanted to punish his parents and, and, even though I am still so mad at them, I know now that I was just lashing out at the world. I just wanted to punish everyone I loved. But Donna, now that it turns out I was right, I don't feel any better. I don't feel like my actions can be justified. I feel like a traitor. I wish I could go back, Donna. I wish I could change everything."

When they finally pulled up at the Maxwell house, Skyler began to intuitively tremble as her heart hammered fiercely in her chest. She quickly glanced around her, and noticed how nothing seemed to have changed, yet from the innermost core of her; she knew that nothing would ever be the same again. There was nothing she could say to excuse herself for all the anguish she had brought upon those she had loved the most, especially the one man she couldn't bear to lose. Without warning, anxiety and extreme fear crept up on her as she scanned over her parents' front porch. Skyler knew that she was hoping for much too much when she silently begged for a warm and innocuous welcome. Her heart began trouncing when she thought of Gabriel and the fact that he was some mere meters away from her. The reality of seeing him again entirely overwhelmed her when her heart began racing irrepressibly. She stood numbly and in silence, and questioned how she could face her parents after all she had done to them. She felt a hand fold into hers, and when she turned around, Donna squeezed her hand firmly. "Come on, sissy. They have been waiting a long time for you." Skyler smiled nervously before she turned back to the porch.

As they were about to walk into her childhood home, Dave, Tabitha and Tallulah rushed out to meet them. Donna let go of Skyler's hand, and hurriedly excused herself from the reunion. "I have to get the boys home, we'll all pop around later." She turned to Skyler and placed her arms securely around her, "It's going to be okay, sissy, see you later." Tabitha placed her arms firmly around Skyler's neck as soon as Donna let go and held her closely against her for what felt like forever, "You've changed, Skye. You are terribly skinny and drawn. Are you alright?" Tabitha gazed into her daughter's eyes, saddened by the pained expression on Skyler's face. "I'm good, mom, just the life of a writer!" She squeezed her mother's hand before she turned to Dave, "I've missed you, daddy ..." She collapsed into his arms, and clung desperately to him. Dave swallowed back on his own tears, and held Skyler protectively against him, "Oh, my girl, we've prayed so much for you to come home." Skyler hurriedly wiped the tears from her cheeks before she veered towards Tallulah, "Who's this girl, dad? You didn't say anything about trading mom in for a younger model?" She teased before she embraced her youngest sister. "You are beautiful, Lula, look at you!" Tallulah smiled bashfully.

Skyler's parents led her into the kitchen where she

cautiously glanced around her. She at once felt almost as a stranger to a warm and welcoming family, virtually as though she was merely a guest. Skyler gazed at her mother repressing the tears that were brimming in her eyes. "It is so wonderful to have you home again, Skye. For a while, I wasn't sure we'd ever see you again, angel, but you're here now." Dave took his daughter's hands in his, and held firmly onto them. "Daddy, I am so sorry for everything. I made a mistake, a terrible mistake ..." Skyler was desperate to explain why she had turned her back on them. She wanted so frenetically to tell him about Hope, but Dave hurriedly placed his index finger on her lips, "Not now, my child. Let us not get into any of that right now. You are here now, and for now, that's all that matters. If there is anything else to say, we'll discuss it later. Right now, we are a family and we need to put the past behind us for Gabriel." Skyler burst into tears when Dave held her possessively against him. Tabitha swiftly made her way towards them, and placed her arms around both Dave and Skyler. "We love you, and we are so glad that you're home. That my baby, is all that matters." Skyler buried her head in her mother's chest and wept inconsolably. "Mama, if you don't mind, I'd like to go and see Gabe. I can't, I just want to see him. Can I put my bags in my old room?" "Of course, honey. We'll meet you later at the Galicia's. Go, he's waiting for you." Tabitha placed a hurried kiss on her daughter's forehead before Skyler and Tabitha made her way into her bedroom. "Let me help you unpack while you go and see Gabriel."

Skyler hesitated nervously as she walked up the path which would lead her to the Galicia house. She was profusely aware of the hammering of her galloping heart, and that her legs were growing heavier with each step. Her heart was crushed when she believed she had lost Gabriel, and the mere notion of seeing him again after so many years, frightened her almost to death. She had only just begun moving forward with her life without him. Gradually, she had come to terms with the harsh reality that she would never see him again. For a moment, Skyler's thoughts drifted back to Gavin. She had grown enormously fond of Gavin, and could barely imagine how she would have survived the years without him. She missed the comfort she felt around him, and for a moment, she was desperate to have him at her side. She smiled when she thought of the shelter he had offered her, but she realized that she could never submit her heart wholly to him, as she did to Gabriel. The sheer thought of seeing Gabriel again after all the years that had passed made her stomach turn with excitement, yet, her heart was in agonizing conflict with the emotions clashing inside of her.

As she was about to knock on the front door of the Galicia home, Carlos appeared in front of her after abruptly opening the door. He smiled fondly at Skyler and longingly placed his arms around her, "Thank you for coming, Skye, we've missed you." Skyler was aware of the shudder in his voice when he spoke in the hefty Spanish accent she could so vividly remember. "Skyler?" Sarah hurriedly approached her, "Tabitha said you'd come. I wasn't so sure but, we're happy to have you." She swiftly turned away from Skyler, unable to look her in the eye. "Come, I take you to Gabriel …" Carlos took her by her hand, and led her into their backyard. From the porch, Skyler could see Gabriel standing on the beach, and was once again sensitive to the overpowering thudding of her heart. "Thank you, Mr. Galicia …" She stood motionlessly for a moment as she absorbed the reality that it was, in fact, Gabriel standing on the beach. She knew him well, and at once, recognized the man she had watched from a distance so often. Skyler was anxious to see him, but even more so, she was desperate for time alone with him. She had much to tell him, but more than anything, she wanted to learn about his time away from them. She instinctively wanted to run up to him and leap into his arms. She wanted to tell him that she knew he would come home to her. She just could not quite tell him about Hope yet, the daughter she had hidden from the world, the daughter that had kept him alive for her from the moment she was born. Carlos was instantly aware of the burning questions and equal agony in her eyes. He squeezed her hand and turned to leave, offering her much-needed time alone with Gabriel. Skyler urgently, yet deliberately made her way down to the beach while acutely aware of the same intense fear she had felt when she arrived home earlier. She was overcome with guilt, and had no inkling of how to keep Hope a secret any longer. She knew that Gabriel would in no way at all, ever absolve her for veiling Hope from the world, and their families. At that very moment, Skyler convinced herself to hold on to her secret, just a while longer.

She hesitantly walked down the path they had strolled hand-in-hand along so many times before. She glanced around her and smiled when she realized that not much had changed around them, yet everything had been altered for them. They were no longer the two teenagers who had recklessly fallen in love with one another. They were no longer enthusiastic about what the future would hold for them. Instead, they had become broken pieces holding onto what was left of them. Their lives were merely a reflection of all they had once dreamed of.

When Skyler reached Gabriel, she was agonizingly aware of her feelings for him, and that they had in no way been tainted, almost as though no time had passed them by. As though in a trembling daze, she moved closer to him, and gently touched him on his shoulder. He was at once startled and unnerved by her presence when he turned around to face her. Skyler gazed into his dark, familiar eyes, and at that very moment, she felt into the crux of her soul, that there was nothing to question. Simply by looking at him, her heart reminded her of her unforgotten and intense love for him. Time had failed to remove, or in any way at all, diminish the love she had once felt for him. While she stood studying his eyes, she knew once more that Gabriel Galicia was all that could mend her crushed heart. Her tears were shimmering cruelly in her eyes, as she took a moment to soak him up one more time. "Gabriel, it is you …" She whispered hoarsely when she saw the tears begin to glimmer in his own eyes. She instinctively flung her arms around him, and held distraughtly onto him, desperately afraid to let him go. She was terrified that he might leave her again or worse, that he might not be real. She held on tightly as she once again, absorbed the way she felt in his arms. She sensed him and recognized him deep into her soul as he held her protectively in his arms. He had folded his arms tightly around her, and firmly pressed her against him, just as he had done so many times before. Skyler was deeply thankful that he did not seem physically hurt. He appeared to be the Gabriel she had said goodbye to, only a little older and entirely overwhelmed. "I've missed you, Skye. I've missed you so much. God, I've missed you." Gabriel was choking back on his tears, but his voice remained forgiving and gentle. She gradually freed herself from him, and allowed herself to drown in the eyes that had captivated her each time she would gaze into them. There was something transformed in his eyes. Stained. The reflection in his eyes spoke of wretchedness, as though they had a thousand broken stories to tell her. She loved him still. It felt to her as though she had finally woken up from a bottomless sleep and that for the first time, she could breathe again. "I'm so glad you came home, Skyler. I've missed you so much." Skyler knew that he loved her still. She could feel it in his touch, and she could see it in his eyes, almost as though nothing had changed between them. "I can't believe you're here, Gabe? We, we all thought that ... I can't believe it's really you, and that you're here, home again?" Skyler began weeping irrepressibly when it finally sunk in that Gabriel had come home. He was real. He was standing in front of her as though he had never boarded that plane.

It was only a few months before that she had finally accepted that he was gone, yet, at that very moment, he was standing in front of her, just as she was standing in front of him. He was safe, and had come back from the dead. "Don't cry, Skye. I'm home and I am okay. I'll never leave you again, I swear." He placed his arms around her shoulders, and held frantically onto her. They stood in silence while clinging to one another for what felt like an eternity. They both realized that they had lived in an in between world that meant nothing without the other. Skyler held on with all her might, desperate not to lose what she was feeling at that very moment. She had grown so entirely accustomed to the agony that had uncompromisingly lingered inside of her, and for the first time, it felt as though Gabriel had wholly glued her back together. She felt him into her soul, and she never wanted to let go of him again.

Gabriel eagerly absorbed all that he could remember about Skyler, and he soaked up all that he had forgotten about her. He had forgotten how her skin smelled, or the way she would dreadfully cling to him. He had never forgotten her eyes, or her voice, or the way she felt in his arms. Nevertheless, Gabriel knew that there was something changed about Skyler. She no longer seemed as happy or as carefree as the young girl he had once left behind. She seemed angrier, and she looked sadder. Gabriel thought she had aged far beyond her actual years, and prayed that it was not the result of losing him so many years ago.

Skyler was at once jolted back to reality when she reflected on all that had happened during Gabriel's disappearance. Even though he had come back to her, her life was undeniably bound to end in tragedy yet again. She loved Gabriel in a way she had never loved anyone before, or after. Hope was proof of the love they had once shared, but for the very first time, Skyler felt as though all they once meant to each other had taken place in a universe she was no longer a part of. She could not tell him about their daughter, the child that saved her, the child she had hidden from the world. It was not the lie she feared as much as his brutal rejection that would inevitably follow. It was not anger that she expected from him, but the disgrace of her betrayal that had overwhelmed her.

They sat down on the beach in silence. Gabriel seemed to be lost in his own thoughts, while Skyler felt as though she was drowning in her treachery. At that very moment, she knew without a doubt that the bliss she had shared with him in a far-removed lifetime, had ended the day he boarded the plane to Kenya. "Were you able to complete your internship?" Skyler discreetly realized that she was still clutching his hand. "Yeah. I, I'm thinking about opening my own practice in Kennedy early next year." He stared at her and smiled forlornly before he lowered his head. Skyler's heart came alive when she saw him smile, and for a moment, it again felt to her as though no time had passed between them. He was familiar to her heart and she realized once more, how hollow she was without him. While gazing at him, she realized again how stunned she was that he had returned, and come home to them. Skyler bowed her head and drew circles of frustration in the sand when she realized that she couldn't do the same, and come home to him. "How have you been, Skye? Your dad says they haven't seen you in a while and that, that you live permanently on the east coast now?" Skyler could hear the confusion in his voice as his eyes desperately searched for an explanation from her. "I, yes, I don't really know where to start. I sold the place in Kennedy and just packed up and moved to Point's Reach four years ago today, actually. I wasn't really thinking, I just wanted to get away from everything and everyone, you know? I was all alone in that big city, and when you left, I just didn't want to stay there anymore. I've published a few books since then, and have sort of found my feet again." She whispered carefully before Gabriel interrupted her. "I know, I've got them all actually, mom got them. We need to take a minute and talk about them sometime …" He playfully winked and chuckled softly, knowing how mortified Skyler would be. She was uncomfortable at once when she evoked the clues for Gabriel in each of her books, that she hoped would reach him and guide him back to her, even if it was only in her mind. "Are you married, or, have you met someone?" He could barely face her and turned back to the ocean. Skyler lowered her head in dishonor, suddenly feeling as though she had unforgivably betrayed Gabriel. "I'm not married. I'll never marry, but I have been involved with someone for a while. We, we have a little girl together …" Skyler's heart began profusely hammering as she desperately and continuously cautioned herself against blurting out all the veracities that she had withheld from him and from their families for so long. By the look of utter surprise and synchronized sadness, Skyler at once regretted telling him about Gavin, and shamelessly lying to him about Hope. 'Why did I just do that?' She silently berated herself for irresponsibly announcing yet another lie. Gabriel was aware of the trouncing of his heart when he heard her tell him about the family she had created without him, and while he was away. He was astounded by the fact that neither Tabitha nor Sarah had mentioned Skyler's child before, but more than anything, he was shattered that she had moved on, without him. "Your mom didn't say anything? Nobody said anything about you having a child or a family? I didn't know, I'm sorry." Skyler was once again aware of the mystified chaos in his eyes. "They don't know about her, Gabriel. I haven't told them. Don't be sorry ..." She whispered sadly when she once again identified the total disarray she had found herself in.

Gabriel abruptly rose to his feet as anger and disgust made its way into his heart. "They don't know, Skye? What do you mean, they don't know about her? Are you kidding? You're hiding your life from your parents? You have a child that nobody knows of? Why would you do something like that?" Skyler sprung to her feet and stood directly in front of him, devastatingly sensitive to the shudder that had begun to consume her entire body. "I know what you're thinking, Gabe, and I know it was stupid. I was so, so stupid. We had, we had an argument shortly after you supposedly died, and I was so mad at them all. I was angry and hurt, and so incredibly stupid! And now, now so much time has passed, I just don't know how to tell them anymore. I made such imprudent mistakes when you left, Gabe. I just wanted to hurt them. I wanted them to feel my pain, but how could I have hurt them when they didn't even know about Hope? I was so stupid …" "Yes, Skye, you were reckless, and you still are! You haven't seen your parents in four years, probably more? Your child is growing up without grandparents, or aunts, or cousins? You see, Skye, I just don't get that? It's like, like I am standing in front of someone I don't know, a stranger. What could you have been so angry about that you would lie to everyone about your child? There I was, fighting for my life, trying to get home to you and our families! I would have given anything to come back to a child, and yet, you had just that. You have it all and still, you punish everyone around you. What happened to you, Skyler?" "You happened, Gabe, you happened! I just, I just wasn't thinking anymore. I was drowning in everything that was wrong, and I just, I just didn't know how to be normal again, you know?" "Skyler, no! Don't stand there and tell me how rough things were for you, don't do that! At the end of the day, that's what family is for. That's who we turn to and that's, that's where we get strength from. You, you just decided to shut everyone out! You deleted them all?" He yelled furiously at her and for a moment, he was entirely overwhelmed by an all-consuming repulsion for her.

Skyler felt her entire world shatter once again when she discovered in his eyes, his disgust for her. "It didn't take you too long though ..." He muttered softly, leaving Skyler to detect overwhelming resentment in his voice. There was nothing she could say to him, nothing came to mind that would alter the sudden disposition he had found himself in. She could not tell him about her repugnance for Sarah at the time, and when she thought about their argument once more, she realized at that very moment, how utterly trivial it was. Skyler grimaced as she tearfully glared at the sea sand under her feet, and remained guardedly silent. "So, a little girl, huh? How old is she?" He glared distantly at Skyler when she began fidgeting nervously. "Hope, her name is Hope." She looked up at him and whispered softly, knowing that Hope's age would make him suspicious of her greatest invention yet. "Hope, how old is she?" Gabriel asked with devastating wretchedness in his voice. "She's four years old, it was her birthday yesterday."

Gabriel gasped for air when he roughly calculated his leaving and Hope's birth. He convinced himself that Skyler had strayed from him, the very moment he had left for Kenya. His heart was crushed, and his lower lip began to quiver wildly. He remained silent and turned away from her, unable to face her any longer. He was consumed with fury for her, but determined to hide his bitterness. He made a valiant attempt to hide his heartache from her, but when he opened his mouth, the lump in his throat had hampered all that he had still wanted to say to her. "I'm so sorry, Gabriel. I know what it looks like, but ..." Skyler became silent when she realized that there was nothing else she could say to him. Her lies and betrayal had not only devastated his heart, but were crushing hers with each untruth she was so effortlessly and carelessly coming up with, almost as though she had spent the last four years rehearsing that very moment.

Gabriel turned to her once again. When his eyes met hers, he recognized the fact that she still felt like home to him, and even though he knew that it was he who had left her, he was desperate to hear that she waited for him. Instead, she was telling him how she had met someone else and had started a family with another man. He noticed the look of utter dejection in her eyes, while Skyler was acutely sensitive to the agony he was in. She could think of no way at all, to make Gabriel grasp the pain she had been feeling and living with since he had been gone. Gabriel glared at her, overpowered by a penetrating sadness, while anguish had begun invading his entire body and soul. "I, I suppose you did what any normal person would do, Skyler, and I can't blame you for that, not really. I can't stand here and be mad at you for trying to find your place in the world again, but what I don't understand is how things could turn out this way? I didn't really expect to hear that you placed your life on hold over here, for me, but I love you, I've loved you for most of my life. Doesn't that count for something? Was it really too much to ask of you to wait for me? You wasted no time at all. It's as though you were just waiting for me to set foot out the door!" Gabriel became increasingly enraged, but more than his overwhelming antagonism, he was incapacitated by his all-consuming desperation. "Your daughter is as old as the time I have been gone, give or take your pregnancy. I mean Skyler, really?" His voice was trembling while his despondency became increasingly apparent in his eyes.

Skyler stared at him, and knew that what he was saying made more sense to her in her life than she could ever deny. She knew Gabriel well, and she knew that his entire life was crumbling around him. She turned away from him when she realized that she could no longer bear to witness Gabriel in such extreme despair. Skyler was convinced that she could not rescue what little was left of them, and whether there was anything but ashes that could be saved. All that was left of their love and burning desire for one another was a heap of burnt-out ashes that had piled up between them, with one pearl she had managed to rescue, and hide from him. What they once had, and who they once were, had incinerated right in front of their eyes. There was nothing left to pick up. There was no starting point that would help them rise up again, and fight once more for a love they had once conquered. A love Skyler knew she could barely breathe without, a love Gabriel knew he would lay down his life for.

He gently, but firmly placed his hands on her shoulders. Skyler hesitantly gazed up at him, and noticed the tears that were sparkling in his eyes. "Gabriel, I'm so sorry. I know what you must think, but I don't know what else to say to you. I am sorry, I have so many regrets. I have so much remorse, and if I could change anything, if I could go back and do things differently, I would beg for that chance. You were gone, just gone. Everyone told me that you were dead, and that you weren't coming back. For a while, it felt as though my life had come to an abrupt end, and there were days that I was so sure I couldn't carry on without you. I, I began to write, and somehow, that just managed to drag me through each day. I created these worlds for us in my stories and they became worlds I wanted to escape into when, when I just missed you so much. I gave us a life in a universe that existed for only you and I, and for a while, that was all I needed. That was the only place I wanted to live in. It never changed the way I felt about you, and it never changed the love I had for you, but then Hope came along, you know?" She paused as she swabbed angrily at the relentless and cruel tears that were rolling down her cheeks. "I had to pull myself together, you know? For her, but for me too. I had to wake up from my dreams, and face the harsh reality that you were never coming home to me, and that I had this little girl who needed me. I had to be present for her, you know? But at night, Gabe, when the world became quiet, the noises in my head were deafening, I would meet you there. I would find you waiting for me, and I never, Gabe, I never, ever let go of that, but I made my choices with my daughter. I didn't plan on having her. She was definitely not what I intended for my life after you left but, she showed up and she saved my life." Skyler disintegrated into his chest and desperately held onto him, afraid that she may never feel Gabriel close to her again. Gabriel pressed her firmly against him while they sobbed mercifully in each other's arms.

He had reminisced about how perfectly she felt in his arms. He breathed her in one more time, and he held her closer to him. Skyler clung to him as though she wanted to climb into him, but she knew into her soul, that her betrayal to the only man she had ever loved was beyond brutal, it was inhumane. She was not only deceiving Gabriel, she was deceiving Hope and denying her of her father. Skyler felt like a fraud, and wondered for a moment whether she deserved Hope or the love that Gabriel had offered her. While in Gabriel's arms, she thought of Gavin, and reluctantly reminded herself that he was purely a consolation prize, a replacement and one she willingly accepted for herself and for Hope. He had walked into her life when she was convinced, and had reluctantly accepted, that she would be alone forever. He picked her up, and brought the sunrises and sunsets back into her life. She felt safe with Gavin. He had saved her, but she still, undeniably, loved Gabriel. "Skye, do you, do you love this guy, the father of your child?" Gabriel whispered in his trembling voice while still holding her in his arms. Skyler hesitated before she wretchedly gazed up at him. She wanted to shout out that she still loved him.

She wanted to tell Gabriel that her heart had chosen him a long time ago, but that Gavin had protected her endangering heart. She wanted to tell Gabriel that he was the only man she had been dreaming of and yearning for, for her entire life and that had never changed. She wanted him to know that because of Hope, she had kept him close to her heart, and had seen him in their daughter's eyes. Skyler was overcome by anguish when she realized that to tell Gabriel the truth, was a far greater risk than to lie to him. Hope had become her entire purpose of existence, and betraying her daughter was far too dangerous for Skyler. She loved Hope more than life itself, just as she loved Gabriel, but to risk losing them both, was an option not available to Skyler at that very moment. "I do, Gabriel, I love him. We're a family. Hope loves him. I didn't plan for any of this to happen. I didn't go looking for someone else to love, it just happened. You were gone, Gabe, they buried you ..." She didn't want to let go of him, yet, she could no longer hold onto the man who had come back to her. At that very moment, nothing else mattered to Skyler, than to preserve her daughter's untainted heart.

Gabriel felt almost as defeated as he had felt during his captivity in Kenya. He knew that he had lost Skyler forever, and he wondered whether coming home was not perhaps, his greatest fault yet. Gabriel stared at her while Skyler was once again aware of how wonderfully attractive he was, almost as though she was seeing him, and meeting him for the very first time. His eyes were sadder, but he was never more striking than at that very moment.

With fear gripping at her heart, she was excruciatingly aware of the fact that he would never be left with a scarcity of beautiful women by his side. She knew that he would ultimately let go of her, and move on with his life with another, just as she did. Soon, it would become a world where they would be strangers to one another, a simple memory of a life that once might have been. A life that would offer him no proof of the love they had once shared. Skyler had Hope to remind her of the only man she would ever truly love, the only man her heart would regularly look to find. It was a world she had chosen in anger and bitterness, but it was a life she could not escape from, unscathed. The truth of her betrayal, would wholly destroy Gabriel and their families, and it would eventually, destroy her too.

Gabriel remained static while overcome with emotion when he leaned forward and kissed her on the forehead. "I admire that, Skye, and I honestly don't blame you. I'm not going to lie, it hurts as hell, but I want you to be happy. All I want is for you to be happy, and to just once in a while, I want you to remember what we once had. I want to know that I didn't claw my way back for nothing. I will never forget our time together, and I will never forget you. I let you down, I know that, and I am sorry too. I did this. This is all my fault and that, I can never forget either." Gabriel paused to take in a deep breath, "I love you, Skyler, I still do. I fought my way back because I just love you so much. I would not have survived without you. I just, I just wanted you to know that. I don't want anything from you, just have life and be happy." He slowly moved away from her and took her hands into his. Skyler was saddened when she realized that he was letting her go.

She felt rejected and discarded. She was overcome with an intense throbbing that had unexpectedly, entered her heart. He was surrendering and giving up on her, and she was in no way at all, prepared for how excruciatingly painful it was. She turned away from him, and realized that the sun was about to set as the tide was slowly coming in. The slow advancing tide together with the sun that was about to hide from them, seemed so significant to Skyler at that very moment. It felt as though she was drowning in the tears that were fighting to reach her eyes. She swallowed with difficulty when that well-acquainted, curbing lump in her throat threatened to give way to her tears. She was angry at Gabriel. She wanted him to try harder, to fight for her, for them and for their love, but when she gazed up at him, she saw a broken man, unable to fight for her and unable to love her as fiercely as he once did.

"Gabriel …" Skyler wanted to blatantly accuse him of being weak. That he had come back defeated and frail. The Gabriel she had once fallen in love with would fight with all his might for her. She wanted him to know that he was giving up too easily on her, but she was afraid that her tears would overwhelm her as soon as she began to speak. She wanted to tell him that she loved him still, that she had always adored him, and that she forever will. She wanted to yell out to him that Hope was back home, waiting for him, waiting to meet her father. But, when she gazed further into his eyes, she realized that telling him the truth was something she could never do. Gabriel had come back, but not to her.

He had come back to a life he had lived, and to a family he had lost, but he had not come back to a woman he once loved, a woman who would lay down her life for him. She was powerless to control her tears, and could no longer bear the anguish that he brought to her. She abruptly turned away from him, and hurried down the path back to the house she was raised in. She had made a heart-wrenching decision to walk away from Gabriel, from the only life she had ever desired or ever known. While she swiftly made her way back up the path that led to her parents' home, Skyler was horrified to discover that she was stepping out of her dreams with Gabriel, and into a life of lies and betrayal, a life that would terrifyingly reject her if ever the truth was discovered.

Gabriel watched her walk away from him. He was

desperate to run after her, and stop her from leaving his life. He wanted to plead and beg with her to stay. He wanted to remind her that she had so aggressively loved him once, and he wanted to beseech her to find him again. Gabriel wanted to tell her that he would never leave her again, and that he would love Hope as his own if she would ask him to. He wanted a brand-new chance to love her again, but when he could no longer see her, he knew that they would be the two people that would miss each other their entire lives.

When Skyler rushed into her childhood home, she found her father seated on the porch while sipping his whiskey and smoking a rum and maple cigar. When he glanced at her, Skyler realized that her father had seen the tears that were still warm on her face. "Daddy ..." She collapsed hopelessly in his arms and sobbed brutally into his chest. Dave Maxwell was horrified to realize that he could almost see his daughter's devastated heart. He could barely recall when it was that he last saw her smile. "My angel, I don't want to tell you what to do, just give this whole mess some time. Things always seem to work itself out." He gently stroked his daughter's beautiful hair. "I was a fool dad, and an idiot. I messed up so badly, daddy." She glanced up at him, desperate for her father's comfort. He wiped away the hair that were shielding her eyes, he could barely ignore the anguish that were telling him a thousand stories through her desolated expression. "Skyler, nobody can blame you for this?" He began comforting her before she frantically interrupted him. "You don't understand, daddy, none of you know? Nnobody knows ..." She paused before she lowered her head in shame. "I, I have a little girl daddy, a daughter ..." She buried her head in his chest and wept as she did when she was only a little girl. Dave Maxwell gazed at his daughter in what appeared to be bewilderment and amazement, "Skye?" He lifted her head and glared at her. Skyler stared at her father, overcome with degradation, unable to stop the tears from rolling recklessly down her cheeks. "I'm so sorry, daddy." Dave stubbed out his cigar, and abruptly stood up while holding only his glass of whiskey in his hand. He gazed agitatedly over the ocean as he sipped silently on his drink before he turned back to face Skyler. "Why would you hide this from us, Skye? Why didn't you tell us?" Skyler was at once unnerved by how surprisingly calm he was, even though she was sure she could hear a hint of disenchantment in his voice.

As Skyler urgently swabbed at her tears, she was anxious to regain her composure. She no longer wanted to hide Hope from her family. It had become a substantial burden to carry, and it was exhausting. "She's just turned four years old, daddy. She is beautiful, and bright and just, she just makes the world a better place for me. She is so innocent, daddy, how can I expose her to any of this?" Skyler nervously began explaining while Dave continued glaring at her in what appeared to her as utter disbelief. "Daddy, it's just, there is so much more that you don't know. Things that nobody else knows, and its beginning to smother me, daddy. I am such a fraud. Can I talk to you, dad? I mean, just you and I, daddy?" Skyler sluggishly stood up, and moved hesitantly towards her father. He glowered at her in silence before he realized that she had much more to tell him, more than what she had already said. "Skye, you can tell me anything, you know that?" Skyler took her father by his hand, and led him out to the pool. They sat down on a carefully placed pool lounger before she turned back to her father. The tears had remained shallow in her eyes, and for the first time in years, Dave Maxwell realized that his daughter was suffering, and that she had been enduring a pain he could not begin to understand. "Skye?" He felt a sudden twinge of sadness and ambiguity well up inside of him when he studied the look on her face.

Skyler took her father's hand into her own, and when Dave looked into his daughter's eyes, he was sure she was somehow and possibly unwittingly, pleading with him to save her. "Dad, you have to promise me, you must swear to me ..." Dave squeezed her hand before he abruptly interrupted her,

"Skye, whatever you say to me here, today, will remain between us. Unless you ask me to, I will never breathe a word, not to anyone." Dave was desperate to gain his daughter's confidence once more. Skyler knew she could tell her father anything, and although she knew that she was risking both her sanity and reverence, she also knew without a doubt, that she was compelled to tell him the truth. Skyler could no longer live with the deception that she had created. She was overcome with remorse as she mercilessly berated herself for living her lie so effortlessly. "It's about Hope, daddy, my little girl. When Mr. and Mrs. Galicia wanted to bury, when they accepted so easily that Gabriel had died ... Oh daddy, I don't know how to say this!" She became silent as the apprehension began overwhelming her. Skyler lowered her head in disgrace when she realized just how awful her lies were, and what her father would think of her. "Just tell me, Skyler." Skyler swiftly dabbed at a lost tear from her cheek, and nervously gazed up at her father, "Hope is Gabriel's little girl, daddy, and I just told him that she was another man's child! I don't know why I did that?" Skyler failed to detect the factor of surprise in his eyes, and for a moment, she wondered whether he had not already known the truth. "Daddy?" Skyler was anxious at once. "Skye, I know. I mean, it could only be Gabriel's daughter." He wiped the tears from her cheeks when she began swallowing profusely through the foolish and confining lump in her throat. "Besides, I was lying too. I haven't been truthful either, but it ends right here, right now and today! Donna told me in confidence shortly after Antonio was born. Don't be mad at her, she swore me to secrecy. It was a terrible burden for your sister to bear, and then it became a horrific burden for me when I was faced with lying to your mother and our friends, over and over."

Through the narrowing in her throat, Skyler distraughtly whispered, "So, mommy doesn't know?" "No, she doesn't, but I would like her to know. We would like to meet our granddaughter, Skyler. Keeping her from us and your sisters is wrong. We are her family, even if everyone thinks she is another man's child. I can live with that for know." Skyler was mortified when she realized that Dave had known the truth all along. She turned away from him, unable to look him in the eye. "I know that, daddy. Obviously, you are right. Please, just don't tell mommy just yet, please, please daddy?" She squeezed her father's hands in downright uneasiness. "No, it's not my place to say anything, but you must tell her, Skye. This must end now. You must let go of your anger, for your sake and for your little girl's sake. For ours too, Skye, it's not fair towards any of us." He paused to take in a deep breath, "How long will you be staying for?" "A day or two. I can't stay longer, daddy."

Skyler got up, and lovingly embraced her father before she turned back to the house, and urgently made her way into the kitchen where Tabitha was preparing lunch. "Can I help you with something, mom?" Tabitha spun around, and smiled when she heard Skyler behind her, "You can make the salad, if you want?" Tabitha smiled tensely when she spotted Skyler's red and swollen eyes. Skyler grabbed a bunch of tomatoes, afraid that Tabitha would sense her distress and at once, began preparing the salad. She knew she had to tell her mother about Hope, she just had no way of knowing where to start, or how to tell her that she had been deceiving them for far too long. "Mommy?" She whispered softly as she anxiously began chopping the tomatoes. "Yes?" Tabitha made her way over to Skyler who was strained to focus her attention solely on chopping the tomatoes. "Nothing, it's, its nothing, mommy. I have to leave again tomorrow." She was desperately afraid to tell her mother about Hope, and silently begged for a more appropriate time to break the news of her deliberate deception. Tabitha placed her hand on Skyler's dejected shoulders, "So soon?" "Yes, I want to stay a little longer, but I can't, I just can't." "But why, Skye? You only just got here?" Tabitha was at once dissatisfied that Skyler would be leaving the following day. "We haven't seen you in so long?" "I, I just need to get back, but I'll come back soon and stay a little longer next time. I promise, mom, I'll come back real soon." Skyler struggled immensely to find the words to tell Tabitha about the little girl back in Point's Reach, the daughter waiting for her mother to come home to her. "Are you still angry at Sarah and Carlos?" Tabitha glowered when she scowled at Skyler. "No, no, mommy. That's in the past and forgotten. I don't want to go back to that. I don't want to be in that place again, I can't." Skyler lied, but she was determined to put an end to her resentment towards the Galicia family. "What about Gabriel?" Skyler lowered her head once again while hurriedly making the salad. Without turning to face her mother, her voice become soft and husky, "I'm seeing someone else, mom. I've met another man. We've been together for a while, and he is so good to me and ... he is such a good man, mom. I told Gabriel about him today, he knows about Gavin."

Skyler whispered miserably, desperate for Tabitha to understand that nothing much would change. Her mother circled around her. Skyler could sense her disappointment and immediate disapproval. With not much left to say to one another, Tabitha and Skyler continued with supper in silence. After an hour of awkward and inevitable silences at dinner, Skyler quickly excused herself, and made her way straight to her bedroom. She took a speedy shower, and was anxious to call Hope before she went to bed, "Hello, this is Hope speaking?" Skyler was ecstatic to hear her daughter's gentle, childlike voice on the other side of the phone. "Angel face!" Skyler felt as though the entire world had stood still, and realized once more how unfussy her life seemed when she heard her daughter's voice. "Mommy!" Skyler smiled broadly when she detected the excitement well up inside of her daughter. "Hello baby. How are you?" "Fine, but, mommy?" Hope became somber all of a sudden. "Yes, my girl?" "When are you coming home?" Hope's mood fell instantly when she became disheartened almost at once. "Tomorrow, my angel!" "Yeah! Daddy-Gav brought me a puppy today!" Hope yelled out in excitement as she feverishly told her mother all about the puppy Gavin had picked out for her. Skyler smiled at the thought, and was immensely grateful to him for distracting Hope. "That's wonderful. Listen honey, I can't speak too long, but I'll see you tomorrow. Be a good girl and remember that I love you." Skyler blew imaginary kisses into the phone before she hesitantly and despondently hung up on her call to Hope. She quickly dialed Gavin's number, hoping to update him on her plans.

"Hey!" Skyler was relieved to hear his reassuring voice on the other end of the phone. "Hey yourself! Where are you?" She could at once sense the concern in his voice. "Just, just a family crisis." Skyler was hesitant to explain Gabriel's return to him over the phone, "Are you okay, Skye?" "I will be when I get to see you and Hope again. Listen Gav, I don't want to talk about anything right now. I'll be home tomorrow; can we talk then?" "Yes, of course. Text me your flight details, and I'll pick you up the moment you land. Have a safe flight, okay?" Gavin was at once perturbed, but happy that she would be home in less than a day. "Okay, and thanks for the puppy. Hope was over the moon! See you tomorrow then?" "See you tomorrow. I love you, Skyler." He whispered almost inaudibly before Skyler brusquely ended the call.

She climbed into bed and restlessly lay thinking about Gabriel. She thought back to the life they had planned together, and became angry and resentful at all that had gone so wide of the mark for them. She was sad that he had been missing from her life for so long, and devastated that he would possibly never know that Hope was his daughter. She appealed desperately to God that Dave and Donna would keep her secret. She longed to tell him the truth about Hop. She was frantic to step back into the past, and pretend that his absence never happened. But, the more Skyler thought about it, the more she knew that too much time had passed, and too much had changed between them. She closed her eyes as she prepared to fall asleep while thinking of Gabriel. She secretly confessed to how wonderful it was to have him back again, and how enormously she loved him still. She longed to feel his arms around her, and she prayed that what they once had, would be enough to last her an entire lifetime. Before she ultimately drifted off to sleep, her mind floated back to Hope.

She became anxious when she considered Hope a grown woman some day. She wondered if Hope would ever absolve her for her deception, but most of all, she doubted that she would ever excuse herself for lying to those she loved the most.

Alice VL

CHAPTER SIX

Skyler awoke early the following morning, and was instantly startled to find Tallulah sitting at the foot of her bed. "Morning Skye!" Tallulah smiled when she detected her sister's confusion. "Hey, what's going on? What's the matter?" Skyler was barely awake, but entirely unnerved by Tallulah's presence. "Mommy wants to know if you'll be here for lunch? Donna is coming just after breakfast, and will stay for lunch. She told mom that she'd take you to the airport afterwards ..." Skyler thought about it for a moment, and although she was in a hurry to get back to Hope, she was keen to spend just a little while longer with her parents. Skyler was certain that they all had questions about her life since they last saw her, but Donna swore to her that they would not discuss any of it until Skyler was ready. She was eager to see Gabriel one more time before she returned to Point's Reach, and to her new life. "Sure, Tallulah, I can always leave after lunch. My flight out isn't till early evening." She smiled forlornly when she detected the uncertainties in Tallulah's eyes. When Tallulah left her bedroom, Skyler hurriedly changed into an old pair of jeans and a sweater.

She quikly brushed her teeth and combed her hair before she swiftly made her way into the kitchen where Tabitha was busy preparing breakfast. "Good Morning, Skye, did you sleep well?" Tabitha smiled as soon as Skyler appeared in the doorway. "Thanks for asking, mom, I did. I've missed this place and it smells good in here!" Once again, Skyler realized how she had missed her family, but more than that, how she craved her mother's sumptuous breakfasts. "The Galicia's, along with Gabriel will be joining us for breakfast, would you mind laying the table out on the porch?" Skyler froze at the mere mention of Gabriel's name. "Sure." She was hesitant to face and deal with Sarah and Carlos just yet, but she was enthusiastic to see Gabriel again.

In less than fifteen minutes later, the Galicia clan had made their appearance at the breakfast table. Other than being consumed by an enormous amount of overwhelming culpability, Skyler was deeply discomfited when she saw them again. Carlos hesitantly approached her and placed his arms firmly, yet lovingly around her, "It's so good to see you again, you're such a sight for sore eyes." He smiled broadly before Skyler lowered her head, and turned to Sarah, "Hello Mrs. Galicia, thank you for coming." Skyler was at once reminded of the unfortunate events that once led to her selling their home in Kennedy, and was unintentionally consumed with anger for Sarah once again. "Skyler ..." The ambiance and distinct aloofness between them was evident for all to see when they each took their seats at the breakfast table on the porch. Skyler knew that there was an enormous amount of lingering tension between them, but she was eager to refrain from dealing with, or confronting any past issues with Sarah just yet. She would be back in Point's Reach by evening, and had no desire to leave with one more haunting argument between them.

"Gabriel, good morning ..." Skyler smiled when she greeted him, happy to see him again. "Morning Skye, did you sleep well?" She smiled bashfully when she was reminded of the acquainted thrashing of her heart when he spoke, "Thank you for asking. I did. You?" He nodded his head, and gazed into Skyler's eyes for just a moment longer than was needed. She was once again saddened to detect the utter dejection and hopelessness in his eyes. They all sat in silence on the porch where Gabriel had taken an empty seat beside Skyler. They had barely begun indulging in breakfast when Gabriel stood up, and in one motion, raised his glass of juice out in front of him, "Shall we make a toast?" He smiled before he hurriedly glanced around him. Skyler lifted her glass, and held it out in front of her. "I'd like to make a toast to you, Gabriel, for coming back to us, and I would like to thank God for bringing you home safely." Dave quickly blurted out the first toast, and smiled sorrowfully as he held his glass out to Gabriel. "Thank you, sir. Thank you for having me back. It's really wonderful to be home and back with all of you." Gabriel swung around to face Skyler, "I, in turn, would like to toast Skyler. I wish her and her daughter, yes, the daughter she doesn't want all of you to know about, and of course, the father of her child, that you all probably do know about either, all of God's richest blessings in the world. May they have a long, and happy life together." He sipped slowly on his juice, unable to ignore the fact that Skyler was stunned and shaken by the sudden and unexpected disclosure that she was desperate to keep a secret. "Gabriel? What's the matter with you?" She glared up at him, horrified by his deliberate maliciousness.

Skyler could feel the eyes of the entire breakfast table on her while Gabriel sat smiling arrogantly. Yet, the longer Skyler watched him, the more she empathized with him when she realized that his actions and retaliation was a direct, undoubted result of his shattered heart and conquered spirit. She knew without a doubt, that Gabriel Galicia was a broken man, crushed by her departure and conflicted by all that he had been through not too long ago. Skyler understood for the first time that he was appallingly immersed in resentment for her, and that it was likely that he probably would never exonerate her for leaving.

Dave hurriedly took a speechless, pallid Tabitha by her hand, and quietly led her indoors, while Sarah and Carlos remained composed before Sarah uninterruptedly glared at Skyler. "I didn't know that you were seeing anyone, let alone that you have a child?" Sarah was upset and in utter disbelief. "You would know more about me if you didn't force me to sell Gabriel's home …" Skyler was lost for words and could barely find a way to explain herself, but when she glanced over at Gabriel, she realized that she was just as enraged as he was. "Please excuse me, I want to see my mom."

Skyler was anxious to find her mother and expound Hope to her. She was desperate that Tabitha allow her an opportunity to explicate, and hear her side of the story. She wanted to tell her mother how dreadfully she felt she had to run, even though, she never really knew why, even though, it no longer made any sense to her. She wanted Tabitha Maxwell to understand that she was crushed, angry and overwhelmed, but that she never once considered the aftermath, or the pain that would be inflicted upon her, because of the thoughtlessness of her egoistic actions. She found a devastated Tabitha seated limply in the sun room. She was staring out straight ahead of her, her eyes not quite focused on the ocean in front of her. Skyler carefully approached her mother, and hauntingly noticed that her eyes were filled with crushing tears. "Mommy?" Skyler apprehensively placed her hand on Tabitha's shoulders. "Your father has just told me. He's just told me the whole shebang about Hope, about Gabriel and about your lies! How? How could you not tell me?" Tabitha inadvertently yelled at Skyler when her voice began to tremble huskily, "How could you keep something so profound and so insanely important, a secret from us for so long? What about Gabriel? What about his parents? Hope's grandparents? What about us? That's why you would never say where you are? That's why we never saw you again? And I just thought, I just thought you were punishing the world when really, you were just punishing all of us!" Tabitha continued to bellow out in anguish as her tears began to roll unreservedly down her cheeks. Skyler deflected away from her, unable to face her mother, overcome and instantly degraded by emotions of indignity and culpability, "I thought he was dead, mom, so did you and so did they!" "And that makes it alright? That gave you the right to lie to us all? You come here, and you continue to lie about the fact that you have a child? How could you do this to the Galicia family, Skyler? How could you do this to your father and I ... your sisters? How could you so blatantly lie to us? And now, now I find out that Gabriel thinks Hope is another man's child? It's just one lie after another? What is one more lie, after all? What happened to you? I didn't raise you this way?" Tabitha became hysterical, as Skyler became quiet and withdrawn. Dave leaned in to Tabitha, and placed his arms devotedly around her. She was sobbing unrestrainedly before she pessimistically, buried her head in his chest.

"Please don't say anything. Mom. I am begging you, please don't tell Gabriel the truth. Not now, not now, mommy. I know you think I'm a horrible person. I know you don't understand …" Skyler pleaded with her mother before Dave irately interrupted her. "We won't tell him anything, Skye, for now, but you are going to have to fix this! This is your doing, your mess, you must do the right thing now, for all of us. But, most of all, you will fix this for Hope and for Gabriel, do you understand? We are not going to let things carry on like this, not even a day longer." Skyler nodded in horror and reluctantly acknowledged that it was unfair of her to assume that her parents would keep the one secret that could ultimately destroy her. "Alright, daddy, but I have to tell Hope first. I want to go home and talk to Hope before I speak to Gabriel. She is just as innocent as Gabriel is in all this. She won't understand unless I go home and talk things over with her. She is fragile and so sensitive to the world, I have to handle her so carefully …" Dave glanced over at Tabitha who nodded wretchedly. "I'll come back in a few days, mom, I promise. Please, just give me a chance to prepare my daughter for the news. She thinks he's with the angels …" She moved closer to Tabitha who shot her one final glare before she gave her the cold shoulder. "I'm so sorry, mommy. I was so scared you'd tell them ..." Skyler was desperate to defend her behavior, and tried her utmost to offer a reasonable explanation.

By Tabitha's sudden aloofness, Skyler knew that her mother was acutely distressed by her for hiding the truth from them all and denying Hope her grandparents. "I have to go ..."

Skyler hurriedly ran upstairs, and frenetically began packing her bags. When she zipped up her carry bag, she was caught entirely off-guard when she found Gabriel standing in the doorway. "I'm so sorry, Skye. I don't know why I said that? I couldn't help myself, and before I knew it, I blurted it all out. I was just so angry with you. I know that doesn't excuse my behavior, so, I am so sorry. It's none of my business and it wasn't my place." Skyler could barely listen to him, and interrupted him before he could go any further. "Angry? Really? You were angry? Who gives you the right to be angry? What about me? Us? Your family? We had to carry on without you after you left! You left us here to pick up the pieces without you and because of you! You caused all of this! You drove a wedge in between your family and I. I begged you not to go, remember? I pleaded and begged with you to stay! You left me here alone! Don't you dare tell me that you were angry! You have no right! You lost that right the moment you chose Doctors Without Borders over us! You have no idea what I have been through since then! You know nothing of my life since you left!" Gabriel lowered his head when Skyler paused to gulp back on her tears, "You stand there and judge me like I am such a terrible person! You have no idea what you've done, and you sat there, thinking you knew everything. You're probably standing there right now, thinking you have all the answers!" She took in another deep breath when she realized she had begun to shudder frenziedly, "You know nothing, Gabriel! You have no idea about anything! Hope didn't deserve to come into this family when everything was so crooked after you left! All I wanted, all I ever wanted was to protect her from this family! I didn't want to expose her to all the heartache and pain that you left behind. The aftermath of your leaving destroyed us all! We were all just trying to breathe from one moment to the next! I did not want my child, my daughter, the love of my life to grow up with the scars of your destruction, Gabriel! I love her. I love her more than anything else in this world! I would do almost anything to protect her heart and shield her from all you left us in!" Skyler yelled out at the top of her voice before she picked up her bags, and gently brushed against him when she walked out past him.

Gabriel instinctively grabbed her by the arm, when he noticed the tears flowing discontentedly from her eyes, "Fuck, Skye, I didn't know. I never meant for any of this. I didn't realize any of this. You're right, I don't know what it was like for you. I don't know what you've been through and I'm sorry. It's so easy for me to forget what you all went through. One moment, I want you to be happy and carry on with your life with your little family, but the next moment, I am angry, and I so badly want you back. I hate this. I hate that you've found someone else. I hate that you're going home to him. I want to let you go, I just don't know how to? I don't know how to begin again, Skye, because, for so long ... it's always just been you." He whispered hoarsely before she looked him sternly in the eye. "I didn't choose any of this! But, I can't walk away from my life and try to pick up where you and I left off. We've changed, I've changed. I'm not the girl you left behind, Gabe. I'm nothing like her anymore. It's been five discouraging years. Five years, Gabe! Do you know how long that is when you're grieving? When you can't sleep at night because your heart won't let you forget? Do you have any idea how it feels to watch your child sleep, knowing how severely you are betraying her? No Gabriel, you couldn't know because you left me! You were not here!" Skyler hurriedly made her way downstairs, anxious to get as far away from him as possible, and return to Hope.

Donna had only minutes before arrived for lunch when Skyler began loading her bags into her car. "Skye?" Donna hurriedly made her way to Skyler, excruciatingly aware of a distressed and indignant expression on her sister's face. Skyler turned and glared at her, leaving Donna anxious when she recognized the plaguing expression on her sister's face. "You told dad! I told you about Hope in confidence because I trusted you! You swore to me, Donna!" Skyler was enraged and deeply hurt by her sister's betrayal. "Skye, I'm sorry..." "Whatever, just please drive me to the airport so I can get out of here! I never should have come!" Skyler responded with a trembling voice while overcome with fury. "Your flight doesn't leave for another ..." Donna began protesting before she decided that she should rather remain wholly silent. "I don't care, Donna! I want to get out of here. You can drop me off at the airport, and come straight back. I'd rather sit there for a couple of hours than be here." She paused for just a moment, "If you won't take me, I'll call a cab." "Of course, I'll take you, Skye, we can leave now if you want?"

While driving away from Logan's Bay, Donna was desperate to restore her credibility with Skyler, and nervously approached her sister, "What happened, Skye? Mom and dad barely said goodbye to you?" Skyler swabbed at a lost tear that had carelessly rolled down her cheek, "Gabriel, he told everyone about Hope at breakfast. I've never seen him like that before, so condemnatory and infuriated. Mom is so angry with me, she can barely look at me." The tears had begun to mercilessly shimmer in her eyes once again. "Does he know about Hope?" Donna became tense at once before Skyler glared anxiously at her, "No, I told him, I said that Gavin is her father." She lowered her head in her hands as she sobbed uncontrollably. "Oh God, Donna, I have just gone and made it so much worse!" Donna placed her hand on her sister's back in an effort to comfort her. "But, dad told mom that Gabriel is her father, and they both are insisting I tell him the truth. He made me promise, otherwise they will tell him the truth about her." Skyler was overcome with fear when she felt every inch of her body erupt into uncontrollable shudders. "I just, I just must tell Hope first, you know? I can't just spring this on her and hope she understands?" Donna nodded her head in agreement and felt immense pity for Skyler as she continued to drive to Kennedy.

When they reached the airport, Donna despondently turned to embrace Skyler, "It will be okay, Skye, you have to believe that. This mess will sort itself out, you'll see ..." She held Skyler firmly against her and stroked her long, blonde hair. After checking herself in, Skyler hugged her sister protectively for what felt like forever, "What if I just disappear again, Donna, where nobody could find me, could find us? What if I just run again? What if we just go away and never come back?" Skyler had become panic-stricken and Donna could sense the unmistakable terror in her voice. "Come on Skye, don't do that. Please, don't do that to mom and dad again. Don't do that to Hope and Gabriel. I am begging you. Before you know it, things will have blown over and be back to normal, as all things should be. Besides, you know mom will tell Gabriel, and he'll live the rest of his life looking for Hope, and hating you for running." Donna became increasingly desperate as she pleaded with her sister. Even though Skyler was tempted by the simplicity of her disappearance, she knew that it would only be a matter of time before it all catches up to her again. "No, I won't do that to Hope, I promise. I'll come back in a couple of days." Skyler whispered before she turned away from Donna.

After she had checked in her bags, Skyler made her way to the aircraft that would take her back to Hope. She turned back to wave a final goodbye to Donna, and was stunned to find Gabriel standing in the background. Her heart began soaring when she saw him standing there, and for the first time in what felt like an eternity, she knew that the time had come to set things right with Gabriel. At that very moment, all she wanted to do was run into his arms and hold him against her, while telling him the truth about Hope. She wanted more than anything in the world, to tell him how she could barely go on without him, and that Hope, his daughter, had saved her. She wanted to beg him to return to Point's Reach with her, and she wanted to tell him how much she still loved him, and how sorely he was missed. While standing there gazing at him, she wondered if he could sense how desperately she needed him, even after all the years that had gone by. She wanted him to know that she was lost without him, but more than that, she wanted him to tell her that he loved her still.

Skyler wretchedly turned away from him, and reluctantly boarded her plane back home. Gabriel stood motionlessly as he watched her turn away from him, without as much as a wave. She was about to leave his life just as he had once walked out of hers. He was desperate for a moment alone with her, to remind her of what they once had. He was anxious to beg her, her forgiveness for walking out on her, and he wanted her to know that she was all he had ever dreamed of. He wanted Skyler to understand that nothing that happened to him in Kenya, could compare with the torture he was going through at that very moment. There was no hunger pain, no beating, no thirst that could ever equate to the brokenness he felt as he watched her leave his life.

As Gabriel stood watching her until he could no longer see her, he knew that it was his burden alone, and that he was obligated to let her go. He wanted her back in his arms, but more than anything, he wanted Skyler to find the happiness he once promised he would offer her. It was over for him, he missed his one great chance with Skyler.

Gabriel turned his back on her, just as she had turned her back on him only moments before. Gabriel Galicia was devastated to realize that Skyler would be his one great sadness in a life he did not choose.

CHAPTER SEVEN

Barely an hour after take-off, Skyler's plane touched down in Point's Reach. She was relieved to finally be home and ecstatic by the mere thought of being reunited with Hope again. All the comfort she needed at that very moment, was simply to sweep her daughter into her arms and hold onto her as though there would be no tomorrow. Skyler brushed off all feelings of anxiety and distress before she hurriedly descended her plane. When she caught a glimpse of Gavin and Hope waiting for her, she was aware of a trouncing in her heart, and she was thankful that all her emotions of devastation and exasperation were replaced by exhilaration and love. Her heart had miraculously come alive again the moment she had set her eyes on her daughter. She could barely linger for a second longer to pick her up and hold her securely in her arms. "Mommy!" Hope was overcome with excitement when she noticed Skyler in the crowd. She swiftly ran through the mob until she finally made her way to Skyler. "Hey! Oooh, I've missed you sooo much!" Skyler blurted out as she held Hope close to her. "Gavin, I've missed you. Thank you so much for picking me up, and bringing Hope with you!"

Skyler felt guilt entirely consume and overwhelm her when she placed a gentle kiss on his cheek. "Well, we're glad to have you back. Welcome home!" Skyler could sense that Gavin was plagued by questions for her, and she realized that he, more than anyone else, deserved truthful answers from her. After collecting her luggage, they awkwardly made their way out to the car park. "Would you like something to eat, are you hungry?" Gavin stopped and turned to face Skyler, "Oh, no. Thank you Gavin. I just really want to get back home. I am exhausted."

She was desperate for Gavin to refrain from any interrogations, but more than that, she was frantic for a little distraction from the past couple of days. They had barely pulled out of the airport when Hope fell peacefully asleep in her car seat. Skyler smiled when she thought of how effortlessly Hope could fall asleep during the shortest of car rides. She gazed adoringly at the little girl she loved more than life itself, and became tense about all she was about to expose her daughter to. "So, Skye, what was all that about? You left so suddenly, what happened?" Gavin grew impatient about all the secrecy, and was itching for an explanation from Skyler. She lowered her head and locked her hands into one another, "Oh Gavin, everything's such a mess. I made such a mess of things with Hope." "Yeah, I gathered things were a little messy, but what does Hope have to do with all of this? I mean, you said you didn't have contact with your family and, all of a sudden, you're on a plane to them?" He glared at Skyler in utter disorientation, "I know. I know it seems a little weird, and I know I owe you an explanation ..." She paused as sudden exhaustion began overwhelming her. She knew that Gavin deserved to hear the truth, but she was depleted by her erratic emotions. "Skye, you need to tell me what's going on?" Gavin instinctively sensed dread in Skyler's voice and with fear creeping up on him, he abruptly pulled off to the side of the road. Skyler climbed out of the car, and gasped for fresh air as though she was fighting to inhale every breath.

It felt to her as though someone had taken her lungs into their hands, and began squeezing them with all their valor. Her entire body had begun to quiver, and she was frantic to take in just enough air to keep her from collapsing. It was as if the reality of seeing Gabriel again had only just begun sinking in. The sensitivity to Gabriel's return had overwhelmed her, while her heart was shattering into a thousand pieces by the sheer thought of his unanticipated and startling reappearance in her life. Gavin hurriedly walked over to where she was standing, instantly wearied by the sudden fear that had gripped a hold of his entire being. He placed his arms around her shoulders, and could feel her gently shuddering against him. "Skye?" He was desperate to know what it was that had started engulfing her so overwhelmingly. Skyler retreated slowly, and gazed intrusively into his eyes, "Hope's father, he's back. Gabriel is back." Her tears had once again begun to flicker in her eyes. "But, I thought, I thought he died?" The utter confusion was evident in Gavin's sudden, husky voice. "Yeah, we all did. And legally, he is dead. Anyway, they found him somewhere in Europe and, he came home. I don't really know much of anything else. I don't know what happened to him, all I know is that he was found and brought home. He doesn't look hurt, and he doesn't seem to have any defects, or anything like that. He's just, Gabriel, as if he was never gone?"

She smiled sadly, but could in no way at all, ignore the desolation and despondency in Gavin's eyes. Gavin gazed at her for a moment longer, and was at once unnerved to discover the intense agony and sorrow that had overpowered Skyler. He had never seen her so entirely depleted, than at that very moment. With a startle, he realized that it was something he would never want to see again. "I mean, I knew it had to be something huge for you to just leave like that, but I would never have thought … and Hope? Does he know about her?" Gavin realized at that very moment, how close he was coming to losing both Skyler and Hope. "Yes, he knows of her, but I lied to him about her. I told him that you were her father, and that I had moved on with you. I don't know why I did that?" Skyler's grief only moments before made way for immense disgrace and mortification. "I can live with that Skye." Gavin was at once relieved that she had, at the very least, considered him in all that had happened. "No Gavin, you don't understand? My parents know the truth about Hope. Donna, my sister, told my dad and he then told my mom." She was struggling to find the words to tell Gavin that she was duty-bound to return to Logan's Bay with Hope. "My parents gave me an ultimatum, if I don't tell Gabriel about Hope, they will. It was never my plan to keep Hope from him, but he was dead, you know?" Gavin gently stroke her cheek before her tears were once again, flowing unapologetically from her eyes. "I came back to speak to you and Hope first. Gavin, I don't know what else to do? She's so little, I don't even know if she'll understand any of this?" Gavin pressed Skyler firmly against him and held her protectively in his arms. When he let her go, he walked her back to the car, and they drove home in obstinate silence.

After Skyler held Hope in her arms for what seemed like an eternity, she placed her in her bed, and called for Maria to keep a vigil over her daughter. She was desperate to be alone with her thoughts as she tried to make sense of all that had happened in the last few days. As she leisurely made her way down to the beach, Skyler was once again aware of all the untaught and overwhelming emotions that had crept back into her heart. She could not get Gabriel's eyes out of her mind, and she could not help but wonder how he would react to the news that Hope was without a doubt, his daughter. Skyler loved Gabriel before he left her, and seeing him again after all the years that had cruelly passed them by, she was reminded once again of how her soul would not let go of his. She treasured the vision of having her little family include him, but she was terrified that the authenticity of her concept would be in direct opposition of her dreams. "Skye?" She was startled to hear Gavin's unanticipated voice behind her. "Hey?" She whispered hoarsely when she hurriedly wiped away the endless supply of tears that had once again rolled down her cheeks. "I know you want to be alone, but what I need to ask, can't wait. I have to ask you, and I know my timing sucks, but I just have to know ..." He paused to take in a deep breath as he caressed his fingers through his hair, "How did you feel? I mean, what did you feel when, when you saw Gabriel again?" He hesitated and stammered all at the same time. Skyler could barely face him, and gazed out over the ocean when she suddenly realized that the wind had started blowing fiercely. "I don't know? I'm so confused by all of this, Gavin ..." She turned to face him and tried her utmost to honestly identify her rollercoaster of emotions. "I mean, I remembered the way I felt about him once, and I'm sure that deep down I still love with him but, so much has changed. Too much is different now, you know? Everything has been changed. Everything is different now, and Hope, she is and must remain my priority. He left me, Gavin. I can't forget that and I'm not sure I can forgive him for walking out like that. I am furious at him for leaving us."

She looked up just enough so that their eyes could meet. "But more than that, I am terrified, Gavin. I don't know how he'll react to Hope being his daughter. I have no clue what he'll say or do. I don't know what happened to him over there? I don't know what state his mind is in, you know?" Skyler paused to wipe her hair from her face, "I mean, he was so enraged by the fact that I had kept Hope hidden from my family, if he discovers that he's Hope's father, can you imagine how disgusted he'll be in me?" Skyler was desperate to identify her feelings for Gavin. She was desperate to feel for him what she once, and still, felt for Gabriel. "I don't know, Gavin? It was just so sore seeing him again. But you, you're here. You're always just here and I feel safe with you. Hope loves you so much ..." Skyler realized that what she felt for Gavin could never equate to the powerful emotions she felt for Gabriel, and it left her heartbroken and devastated. She loved Gavin. She cared deeply for him, but at that very moment, she knew that it would always only be Gabriel that could claim her heart. Yet, Gavin was present for her and for Hope, and she knew that it would splinter Hope's heart into a million fractions if Gavin ever had to walk out of their lives. Hope did not know Gabriel. Gavin was the only father she had ever known and for Skyler, that was enough. "I've made such a mess of things, but Gavin, please believe me when I say this, I can't go back to him. I don't want to. It hurts, and I am miserable there. My life is here now, with you and with Hope. I'll go back with Hope and tell him the truth. We can work something out, but I want you to wait for me. This is where I want to be, if you want me?" She took his face in her hands, and smiled desolately at him. "I'll go back with you, Skye, if you want me to? I'd love to meet your parents, and I really want to be there for you?" He was desperate to insert his presence into her life, and into Hope's. Gavin loved Skyler and adored Hope, and he would do anything she needed him to do. "You will? You would do that for me?" Skyler was stunned by his sudden and unexpected gesture, "I mean, you would have to face the music just as I would have to, are you okay with that? I mean, you don't know how the Maxwell's and Galicia's can get?" Gavin took her hands into his, and smiled lovingly at her. "I would do anything for you and Hope, Skye. How can you not know this?" He chuckled softly before he kissed her gently. When she turned back to the ocean, Skyler realized that it might not be such a bad idea to have Gavin accompany them home. She could tell Gabriel about Hope, but at the same time, he would be forced to accept the fact that she had found a new life and love with Gavin. Skyler turned back to Gavin and smiled broadly, "Thank you, Gavin, this means so much to me. I would love to bring you home with me." She flung her arms around his neck, and held him dotingly against her. "Do you know that you are my safe place? Do you know how you cradle my heart? I wish Hope was yours, and I wish you knew that you are the crusader of my heart." She kissed him gently before she buried her head into the safety of his chest.

After saying goodnight to Gavin, Skyler hurriedly made her way back home. She quickly thanked Maria for staying with Hope and wished her a good night. When she turned back to Hope, she considered her challenge on how she would approach her daughter, and tell her that the father she thought had died, was alive and well. She had no inkling of where to begin, but she was positive that her daughter would be ecstatic by the promise of having another daddy. Hope would in no way at all, understand her mother's cruel betrayal towards her father and her grandparents. She was too young to understand how her grandparents on her father's side, had betrayed her mother too. There was no way at all for Hope to fully comprehend how discarded and rejected Skyler felt when Gabriel left for Kenya. She could not hope that her daughter would appreciate how devastated Gabriel's leaving had left her.

Skyler lifted Hope out of her bed, and laid her down beside her. While fast asleep, Hope looked like an angel, and was the spitting image of Gabriel, the little boy Hope evoked. Skyler's heart ached when she realized that all that was normal to them, was about to change forever. She reflected once more on what Gavin had said earlier. Skyler was convinced that it would almost certainly be for the best, especially for Hope, if he had accompanied them back to Logan's Bay. Unable to sleep, Skyler restlessly laid awake long into the night as sleep invaded her, and as she ceaselessly thought about Gabriel. She knew from the innermost core of her, that he would forever more be the only man that could ever make her experience anger, hurt, love and pain all at the same time. He could effortlessly enforce feelings of antagonism and wretchedness, yet, he could just as easily impose feelings of love and abhorrence all at once. She so desperately sought the shelter of her old life, the life she knew before Gabriel left, but she was sure that there was too much, that was wounded between them. They had become entirely dissimilar from one another. They were no longer the carefree and blithe teenagers they were before Gabriel had left for Kenya. She became a mother, and Hope was her first and only consideration. Her heart ached for Gabriel and for the family they could once have been. She wanted to share Hope equally with him. She wanted to raise Hope under his watchful eye, but her careless and irrational decisions of the past were coming back with a vengeance, to haunt and terrify her. There was nothing she could do to validate all she had done to both their families, to Gabriel, to Hope and to herself. Skyler prayed that Gabriel would intuitively know how desperately she loved him, and she secretly hoped that he would trust her love for their daughter.

As though she had fallen asleep only moments ago, Skyler woke up inexplicably exhausted and utterly defeated the following morning. When she sluggishly made her way over to her bathroom mirror, she disparagingly noticed that her eyes were bloodshot and swollen. Her mind instantly wandered back to Gabriel, and she was once again reminded of an intense ache for him that came from the very core of her. Staring back at her reflection in the mirror, Skyler realized that she must have cried herself to sleep the night before. Careful not to wake Hope just yet, she quietly made her way to the kitchen, and hurriedly poured them both a cup of coffee. Skyler stood mumbling in an effort to convince herself that it would not be the beginning of a day that would turn out to be one of the toughest days of her life, it would simply be the beginning of many more challenging days ahead of her. She unrequitedly gazed out over the ocean, and even though it was the dawn of one of the most picturesque days in Point's Reach, her heart refused to see the beauty or promise in anything that once mattered to Skyler.

"Baby Hope? Wake up, sleepy head ..." Skyler gently stroked her slumbering daughter's forehead while gazing lovingly at her sleeping child. She found peace and serenity watching Hope awake from her sleep. Skyler more than anything, adored the recognition in her daughter's eyes when she would lay eyes on her mother, first thing in the mornings. As Hope groggily awoke from her sleep, Skyler could once again see Gabriel in their daughter's eyes, almost as though she was seeing the uncanny resemblance for the very first time. "Hello, mommy." Hope whispered before taking her mother's face into her hands. "I've made you a cup of coffee ..." She smiled lovingly at the picture-perfect little girl she and Gabriel had unwittingly created many years ago. Hope sat up straight, and took the coffee mug from Skyler with both her sleepy hands. Skyler's heart began racing uncontrollably when she was once again reminded that the time had come to tell Hope about Gabriel, even though she was desperate for a moment more to consider her words cautiously and flawlessly. Gazing at Hope, Skyler knew that she was left with no more time, it had run out for her. For whatever the consequences of her deceptions may be from that moment forward, Skyler was duty-bound to waste not a moment more.

She had just opened her mouth to approach Hope with the news, when her phone rang suddenly, and instantly alarmed Skyler. "Hello?" She answered with a hint of exasperation in her voice. "Skye?" Her heart galloped incessantly when she heard the familiar voice on the other side of the phone, "Gabriel?" She was stunned to hear the voice she had so often ached to hear. "Hi, yes it's me. I am so sorry to call so early ..." He paused apprehensively while Skyler in turn, was aware of a faint shudder in his voice, "I just wanted to say again how sorry I am. I'm so sorry for my behavior the other morning. I am so sorry that I carelessly embarrassed you, and put you on the spot like that in front of our families, I don't, despite what you think, I don't want to hurt you, and I don't want to spoil things for you. Please forgive me, Skye?" Skyler hesitated when she detected the sheer sadness in his voice, "That's alright, Gabe. You were right and actually did me a favor. There is nothing to forgive ..." She was suddenly and unexpectedly overcome with compassion and empathy for him, and for the first time since seeing him again, Skyler realized that Gabriel had been going through a tremendously challenging adjustment himself.

She had no intention of adding to his problems or his guilt. She was certainly not motivated at all to make him feel shoddier than he already had, and she definitely could not condemn him when she carried around her own devastating secrets that would most certainly, crush Gabriel in the not too distant future. "That's all I wanted to say. Skye, take care of yourself ..." "Gabe, wait ..." Her voice trailed off, not wanting the call to end just yet. "Can we talk? I mean, I'm, I'm taking Hope to meet my parents, and I'd, I'd really like to talk, a chance to talk to you alone?" She was desperate to prepare him for the hardest thing she would ever have to tell him. "Sure, I look forward to your visit ..." He replied swiftly before he brusquely hung up on the call.

Skyler's eyes straggled back to Hope. She was once again astounded by the fact that her daughter never failed to boast an energetic smile on her face. Hope presented Skyler with an enormous amount of comfort, yet, Skyler felt as though she had bitterly betrayed her daughter through all her shameful lies and equally devastating deceptions. "Listen, baby ..." Skyler slid in beside her daughter who was slowly sipping her coffee, "There's something really important that mommy needs to talk to you about, so I need you to really listen, okay?" Hope frowned and nodded, and Skyler had no inclination of how to successfully, yet gently or effectively, approach her daughter with the news of her father. "You know how mommy told you about your daddy, your real daddy, and that he ..." Skyler paused when Hope interrupted her, "Daddy's with the angels in Heaven, mommy! He watches me and looks after me with Jesus!" Hope pointed to the ceiling when she gawked upwards. "Yes, that's what we all thought." Skyler hesitated and realized that it was so much trickier than she could ever imagine, "Your daddy came back, back from the war. He was never with the angels in Heaven like we all thought he was." Hope glowered as she gaped at Skyler with utter confusion in her eyes, "He wasn't?" "No, he wasn't. Do you remember when I went away the other day?" "Yes?" Hope nodded inquisitively, "I went to grandma and grandpa to see daddy again." She paused and smiled sadly at Hope who was attempting to process all that Skyler was telling her, "You see, Hopie, daddy wanted to become a doctor, and he wanted to help little children like you. But the war was going on there where he went, and everyone was fighting. He had to go and help the little children in the war, do you understand?" Skyler was desperate for Hope to understand what she was trying to tell her, "He was hurt in the war, but nobody knew that he was still alive, and when they found him, they brought him back to grandma and grandpa."

Skyler had no suspicion of whether her daughter could make sense of anything she was saying, or even if she was old enough to understand what she was trying to tell her. Hope beamed from ear to ear while clapping her hands excitedly, and jumped up and down on Skyler's bed. "I can see my daddy now! My real daddy!" Hope shouted out enthusiastically at the top of her voice. Skyler knew that her daughter did not quite grasp what she had just told her, but she was happy and relieved to have finally told Hope the truth about Gabriel. "What about Daddy-Gav?" Hope sat down on the bed and was unexpectedly, yet entirely confused as she stared inquisitorially at Skyler, her tears lay shallow in her eyes. "Oh, baby, Daddy-Gav will always be here with us. He loves you, he will always love you ..."

Skyler was frantic to console her daughter when she gathered that not only was Hope disordered and afraid, but that Skyler could hardly make sense of much herself. Skyler knew that it was a promise she had no right to make, she could barely persuade herself that she would be able to keep it. "Would you like to meet your real daddy and see your grandparents?" Skyler knew instinctively what Hope's answer would be. "Yes!" Hope shouted out in pure delight.

Alice VL

CHAPTER EIGHT

Skyler called her father and reluctantly, and nervously informed him of her plans to fly out with Hope the following day. She made it clear to her father that Gavin would be accompanying the two of them, and she requested that he appropriately prepare Tabitha for their visit as a family. "Do you think it's wise to bring the new man in your life home for such an intimate visit?" Skyler was staggered to discover the hesitation in her father's voice, "I'm with Gavin now, dad, and Hope sees him as her father. She is going to be surrounded by strangers. The best thing for her is to have Gavin there with her. He's been here for us, and he has been so good to us. He is a part of our lives, and if you and mom can't accept that, then I'd rather not come. Please talk to mom before we get there, okay daddy? If Gavin isn't welcome, Hope and I won't be either. I have nothing left to lose, daddy. Gavin comes, or we stay." Skyler was entirely conquered when it came to her mother. She knew that a confrontation between the two of them would put an end to any possibility of Hope meeting Gabriel and their families. "I'll make it happen, baby. I look forward to meeting him, and I can absolutely not wait to meet our little girl. What time will your plane be landing tomorrow?" "Jjust after ten, but Gavin has arranged for a rental at the airport, so, you don't have to pick us up." "Alright then, honey, I am looking forward to seeing you and meeting my granddaughter and of course, Gavin. Have a safe flight and see you all tomorrow!"

When Dave hung up the phone, he was unsure of how to groom Tabitha for Skyler's guest. He worriedly made his way into the kitchen, where he discovered her unloading the dishwasher. Walking up behind her, heplaced his arms firmly around her waist, "Hello, beautiful …" He whispered before he gently kissed her on the cheek. Tabitha giggled and turned to face him, "Hello, handsome …" Placing her arms around his neck, she gazed dreamily into his eyes, "Can I make you a cup of coffee?" He smiled before he turned and took an empty seat at the kitchen table, "I want you to come and sit with me, so we can talk for a minute …" Tabitha frowned and hurriedly dried her hands on a dishcloth before she swiftly made her way to an empty chair next to Dave. "What's going on?" She was at once worried when she noticed the frustration in her husband's eyes. "I just spoke to Skye. All the arrangements have been made. She'll be home tomorrow." Tabitha smiled and squeezed Dave's hands, "That's wonderful!" As she was about to get to her feet, Dave gripped her by the arm and indicated to Tabitha to remain seated, "She'll be bringing Hope and her new fellow with her." Sarah glowered and was about to respond when Dave stopped her, "This is what we're going to do; we are going to welcome him into our home, just as we've welcomed Gabriel and Christopher into our home. We will treat him with the respect he clearly deserves, and we will not forget that he's been taking care of our daughter and our granddaughter for a long time. There will be no uncomfortable silences, Tabitha, do you understand? We are going to be the perfect hosts for Skyler, her daughter and the new man in her life. You will be the perfect host to Gavin, alright?" Tabitha lowered her head, unable to look Dave in the eye. "If you don't promise me this, I will call Skyler back, and she will cancel her trip, it's as simple as that. If that's who she wants, and if that's who she chooses, we will support her, no matter what. I am not prepared to lose Skyler again, and I have no problem in setting this ultimatum for you." Dave took Tabitha's hands into hers, "She's our daughter, Tabby, we must support her. Look what happened the last time we failed her. I won't let that happen again, and you shouldn't want to either."

Tabitha smiled sadly before she firmly squeezed his hands, "I promise to try, honey. I have a four-year-old granddaughter that I never even knew existed. I am so mad at her!" "I know, but rather now than never, right?" "I guess so ..." Tabitha whispered before she got up and made her way back to the dishwasher, "You should've told me about Hope, Dave."

"I know, darling, there's a lot of things I should have done. We can't turn back the time, but we don't have to lose any more of it." "She is going to break Gabriel's heart. I worry about him..." Tabitha mumbled while unloading the dishes. "But, Skyler is our daughter, and her heart was broken a long time ago. We're not going to take sides here, Tabby. We are going to support our daughter in whatever decision she makes, and we are going to embrace and dote on our granddaughter. It could not have been easy for Skyler to go through all this on her own. I can't imagine how tortured she must have been by all the secrets. We are going to welcome her home, and we are going to love her. We are not going to give her a reason to run from us again. Okay?" Tabitha nodded reluctantly before Dave made his way over to her, and held her lovingly in his arms.

After her phone call to Dave, Skyler tossed the phone onto her bed and carried on packing her bags, watching Hope from the corner of her eye excitedly pack her toys. "Don't take too many, I'm sure Aunt Donna will have plenty for you to play with. You have two little cousins waiting to play with you." Skyler smiled lovingly at her daughter, "Mommy, what if daddy gets sad?" Hope turned to face her mother. "Why would daddy get sad, Hope?" "He doesn't know me, and what if he thinks that I love Daddy-Gav more?" Skyler was devastated by the sheer thought that her daughter would so intensely carry the burden of another's happiness. At that moment, she was immensely proud of Hope, but she feared the emotional toll it was taking on her little girl, "Oh Hope, you are far too young to worry about things like that. Daddy knows you love him and he is okay with you loving Daddy-Gav too. You can love as many people as you want, okay?" She took Hope in her arms, and held her protectively against her, "Okay, mommy."

When she placed Hope down, she turned around to find Gavin standing in the doorway. "Hey, you two …" He handed both Skyler and Hope a red rose. He slowly veered away from Skyler and towards Hope, before he seized her into his arms, "You know, Hope, I also had two daddies once and I loved them both, equally." Skyler was mortified that he had eaves-dropped on their conversation earlier. "Really?" She frowned while staring into Gavin's eyes, "You had a daddy?" "Yes, really, and I loved them both, and they both loved me back." He placed a quick and gentle kiss on her cheek before he put her down, "Listen …" Gavin turned back to Skyler, "Are you okay with all of this? If you need some time, I get it?" Skyler turned away from him and sat down at the foot of her bed, before she lowered her head, "I don't want to go without you, nor does Hope. I can't face them all on my own Gavin, but if it's too overwhelming for you, I get that too. I never want to put you in a position you're not comfortable in." Kneeling in front of her, Gavin took her hands, "I want to go for you, for Hope, but most of all, for me. I want to meet your parents and see where you come from. I want to meet the man that owned such an enormous fragment of your life, the one that brought Hope to us. I love you, Skye and I'll stick with you for as long as you want me to." He leaned forward and kissed her gently. Skyler cherished the safety she felt when Gavin was around her. She adored his gentle nature, and she admired his strength and courage. When he kissed her, she felt an immense sense of comfort, and she realized that Gavin had found her at exactly the right time.

When they landed at the Kennedy International Airport the following morning, Gavin sensed that Skyler had grown extraordinarily anxious. He took her hand and gently squeezed it, silently reassuring her that he would let no harm come to her. Skyler took Hope into her arms, and gently wiped her unruly hair from her eyes, "This is where you were born ..." She smiled sadly at her daughter. "Is my real daddy here?" Hope frantically looked around her. "No baby, daddy is with grandma and grandpa. We'll be there in a little while."

Less than an hour later, Gavin had collected the rental, loaded their luggage into the car before they finally drove to Logan's Bay. The closer they came to the village she grew up in, the more anxious Skyler grew. Only moments before they drove into the quaint little village she had adored so much, Skyler glanced back at Hope who was fast asleep in her car seat. She prayed that she was doing the right thing by bringing Hope to meet her parents and to meet Gabriel's parents, but most of all, to meet her father. She still could not bring herself to tell Gabriel about Hope, and she prayed that she could find the words that had continuously failed her as she attempted rehearsing them in the days leading up to their trip.

When they pulled up into the driveway of the Maxwell home, Dave and Tabitha were anxiously awaiting them from the front porch. Skyler's stomach turned when she saw them there, but Gavin ignored the glances from the porch, and instantly turned to face Skyler, before courageously smiling at her. Skyler cautiously and apprehensively opened her door to discover her parents had already made their way over to welcome them. "Hello, Dave Maxwell, pleased to meet you." Dave had wasted no time into introducing himself to Gavin, "This is my wife, Tabitha, and that little bombshell over there is Tallulah, Skye's youngest sister." He hurriedly introduced Tabitha and Tallulah to Gavin. "Hello everyone, Gavin Storm. I am so pleased to meet you all. Skyler has told me so much about you." He smiled awkwardly, but was instantly comfortable around Dave. Tabitha smiled and politely greeted him, but it was undeniably apparent that she could not wait a moment longer to meet Hope.

Skyler had just barely lifted a sleeping Hope from the car seat, when Gavin began unloading their luggage. "Oh, Skye, she is a little beauty. She has your eyes but other than that, she looks just like her father, she looks just like him! I mean, it feels like I'm looking right through them and into Gabriel's." Tabitha became slightly uncomfortable, but when she realized that Hope had woken up, she eagerly turned her attention back to her granddaughter. "Hello, Hopie ..." Tabitha took Hope's frightened hand, and smiled adoringly at her. When Hope burst into tears,

Skyler realized that her daughter had suddenly become enormously anxious of all the strange faces that were suffocating her. Dave approached Skyler, and gently placed his arms around her, "Hello princess, and this must be Hope?" He smiled pompously at the little girl with the dark hair and the greenest of eyes he had ever seen, "Hello Hope, I'm Grandpa Dave and this is Grandma Tabby. That young lady over there is your Aunt Tallulah." He smiled tenderly before he took her little hand into his, "We are so happy to meet you." Skyler was sure that she detected hidden tears in her father's eyes, and was sad to realize that she was responsible for stealing time with Hope from them.

Skyler glanced over at her mother, and noticed her swab violently at a lost tear that had rolled down her cheek. She was unexpectedly infuriated at herself for treating them so harshly, for reasons that no longer seemed as important to her. When Hope noticed Gavin come around from the trunk of the car, she frantically held her arms out to him. Skyler realized that her daughter was in no way at all, ready for all the new faces around her. She was terrified and confined by all that had begun to surround her. Gavin took Hope from Skyler, before he turned back to Dave, "She's just woken up and it was a long flight. Everything is just a little strange to her right now. Lovely place you have here, Mr. Maxwell ..." Gavin glanced curiously around him while Hope rested her head on his shoulder. "Thank you, Gavin, but please, call me Dave." He smiled and turned to lead the way back into the house. "Skyler …" Skyler could at once detect the accusation in her mother's voice, "Oh mother! I came, didn't I? I said I'd tell Gabriel, and I will! Just give me a second to breathe! We only just got here, for Pete's sake!" Skyler replied callously before she made her way into the house, to where Gavin and Hope were.

"Hello Skyler, I didn't expect to see you again so soon?" Gabriel seemed to have come out of nowhere, and joined them where they all met up in the dining room. Skyler's heart hammered recklessly when she saw Gabriel standing there. She was sure that her breaths were getting shorter when she caught a glimpse of him, and knew that she was running out of time. At that very moment, Skyler realized that the time they were to spend in Logan's Bay, would quite possibly turn out to be of the hardest days of her life yet. "Gabriel? Hi, I didn't expect to see you right now, at this moment. I, I was going to find you later, but, you're here …" She was stammering excessively, and what Gavin saw, made his heart ache into the innermost hub of him. It was the first time since he had known Skyler that he saw something untaught in her eyes. Something he had never seen before, but something that told him there was still something hiding inside of her; a kind of a light she had reserved only for Gabriel. "Gabriel, this is Gavin, the man I told you about," She turned back to Gavin who was still carrying Hope in his arms, "and this is Hope, my daughter." Gabriel shook Gavin's extended hand, and was surprised to discover that he no longer felt any anger or resentment towards the two of them. He smiled, and for the first time since he had returned home, Gabriel knew that his heart would ultimately survive losing Skyler. "Hello Hope ..."

Gabriel smiled in wonder when he turned his attention to Hope and for a moment, he thought he saw something proverbial in her eyes. "Are you my real daddy?" Hope excitedly blurted out and gazed beseechingly at him, her eyes growing brighter by the minute. Skyler let out a vibrant, despondent sigh before she defeatedly lowered her head, excruciatingly aware that her entire body had begun to jolt in the knowing that she could never retract what Hope had blurted out only seconds ago. "This cannot be happening ..." Skyler mumbled as she shook her head in utter despair, sensing at once that the entire universe was conspiring against her. Gavin stood motionlessly and stunned. He glanced tensely around him while Tabitha and Dave simply stared at one another in silence.

Gabriel frowned when he heard the little girl ask him if he was her father. He could in no way at all, shake the nudging feeling that Hope considered him, and not Gavin, her father. "Your real daddy?" "Mommy says my daddy didn't go live with the angels. I'm going to see my daddy …" "Gavin's not your daddy?" "He is my daddy, but I have a real daddy, mommy said so …" "Did she? Should I ask her about it?" He whispered while gazing explicitly and questioningly at Hope. She nodded, and pointed directly to Skyler.When he stared at her for only a moment longer, he abruptly turned to Skyler, who at once identified the uncertainty in his eyes, and by the look in her eyes, Gabriel knew in his heart that she had lied to him about Hope. "Skyler?" Skyler felt fear grip a hold of her heart when the restricting lump in her throat had managed once again to compromise her ability to explain Hope to Gabriel. His heart was pounding fiercely as he studied the little girl staring optimistically back at him, waiting to hear him say that he was her father. She seemed fearful of him, yet it seemed to Gabriel as though he was looking back at himself. He was shattered by the very thought that Skyler had lied to him about the child she had kept a secret, not only from her family, but from him too. He was utterly confused by the conflicting emotions that had begun to consume him. He was angry. He was sad, but at the same time, he was meeting his daughter for the very first time.

He walked up to Skyler, and overcome with rage,

grabbed her by her arm, "Skyler? Do you think now is a good time to tell me what's going on here?" Skyler knew that he had seen in Hope, all she had seen so many times before. She turned apprehensively to Gavin, who noticed the sudden wretchedness in her eyes. The time had come for Skyler to tell Gabriel the truth about their daughter, and for an instant, Gavin was again overwhelmed by a nudging feeling that he was about to lose them both. "Go on, I'll stay with Hope." He smiled assuredly before he gently rubbed her arm. Gabriel took Hope's hands into his, desperately fighting off the tears that were threatening to roll down his cheeks, "Hope, mommy and I are just going to talk. We'll be back soon, will you stay with your other daddy?" "Okay …" Gabriel smiled gloomily before he grabbed Skyler by the arm once again. Still clutching at her arm, Gabriel led her down to the beach while Dave, Tabitha, Gavin and Hope made themselves eerily comfortable on the back porch. Dave and Tabitha both agreed that they liked Gavin enormously, and were at once relaxed in his company. Although they knew that Skyler had lost her heart to Gabriel a long time ago, they were delighted that she had met a man who adored her as much as Gabriel loved her.

"What Hope said earlier?" Gabriel began trembling as he searched for clues in Skyler's eyes, when they finally reached the shore. "Why would she ask me that? She's, she doesn't look anything like Gavin, she doesn't look like him at all, Skye? What the fuck is she on about, her real daddy? Her daddy didn't go live with the angels?" Skyler sensed the utter anguish and desolation in his voice. Gabriel's heart was racing as he incessantly searched her eyes for answers. In all the years he was held captive by the enemy, he had never felt terror as he felt it at that very moment. "God, Skye, what are you not telling me? Why would she ask me if I was her father? Why on earth would she think that the man in there isn't her father?" Gabriel felt as though his entire world had begun to crumble, and he immensely feared what she was about to say next. Skyler bowed her head in shame, unable to look him in the eye. She felt an enormous sense of culpability for having kept the truth about Hope from him, from the very beginning. "I felt, I mean, when I first saw her, it felt as though … Skye? Help me out here, what am I seeing? Am I going crazy?" Gabriel was growing increasingly restless by Skyler's silence. "She isn't Gavin's daughter, is she? Is she, Skye?" He raised his trembling voice, desperate to hear Skyler tell him that Hope was his little girl. He wanted Skyler to know that he could sense it, "I can feel it. My heart can feel it, Skyler. I am so confused. Why aren't you saying anything? What the fuck is the matter with you?" Skyler felt the tears sting in her eyes, but the crushing lump that had formed in her throat had once again constrained her ability to say anything. She knew from deep within the innermost core of her that Gabriel knew the truth about Hope, yet she could not manage to utter a word to him. "That little girl over there, that beautiful, confused little girl ..." He pointed furiously at the house, "That's my little girl, isn't it? Isn't it, Skye? That is our daughter, yours and mine? You lied to me! You lied to us all! How could you, Skyler? Just a few days ago, you told me that Gavin was her father?"

Skyler remained silent while swallowing aggressively over the constricting lump in her throat, but it was of no use when her tears began to roll unreservedly down her cheeks. Gabriel was enraged by her failure to deny it, and when she started sobbing, she finally validated the truth about Hope. He turned his back on her and hopelessly, ran his hands through his hair. Skyler lowered her head into her hands and wept violently, unable to maintain her composure. There was nothing she could say to justify all she had done to him. There was no way at all she could alter what he had discovered with his very own eyes. She anxiously wiped the warm, unforgiving tears from her cheeks, and hurriedly made her way over to Gabriel. "All these years, Skye, you lied. You lied to my parents, you lied to your parents, you lied to Hope, and then you so effortlessly lied to me. You looked me in the eye and told me you had a daughter, another man's child. You didn't even bat an eyelid? How did you even get

Gavin to go along with it?" "I didn't lie to Hope, Gabe, I told her you were gone and that you, you were her real daddy. Gavin was just trying to protect Hope and I. I didn't have the courage to tell you …" Skyler was desperate for Gabriel to understand that she had never lied to Hope about him. He lifted her chin just enough to meet her eyes, frantic for answers. "Why would you lie to me about her, Skye? I don't understand? Help me understand? Just tell me!"

He grabbed her by her arm once again. Skyler felt as though her heart had shattered into a thousand pieces. She swallowed back ferociously in an effort to respond to him, and give him the answers he so desperately needed. She wanted to tell him how truly sorry she was. She wanted him to know that it was never a deliberate attempt to hurt him, or their parents. She wanted him to understand that she felt entirely alone and abandoned after he left her. She wanted him to know that she couldn't accept that he was gone, and how angry she was that their parents had so easily discarded him, but when she opened her mouth, she could barely find the words to begin. "We had it all Skye, you and me. We had a life. We had a future. I loved you so much, and you threw it away as though it meant nothing?" He yelled out at her, immensely frustrated by her silence. The longer Skyler looked at him, the harder his eyes became. Gabriel became quiet suddenly, and turned to gaze out over the ocean. Skyler could almost see his heart shattering, and she knew that she had to say something. "Gabriel, please. I want to explain. Just give me a chance to gather my thoughts and find the words to tell you ..." She grabbed his hand before he abruptly freed it from her grasp. "I loved you, Skyler. I couldn't live without you, but right now, right now I can't stand the sight of you! I don't want to hear it, Skyler. I don't want to hear it, and I don't want to see you, understand?" "Gabe, don't do this. Please, don't do this ..." He abruptly turned his back on her in anger and crippling frustration, before he hurriedly made his way back to the Maxwell house. Gabriel had turned his back on her, and as much as she tried to hate him for it, she was candidly reminded of the fact that she had only herself to blame. She watched him walk away from her, and was overcome with an ache she had never known before. Skyler knew that he would never pardon her for betraying him in such a cruel and unforeseen way. She made a feeble attempt to wipe the tears from her eyes, but they were relentless and continued to flow as though she had an endless supply just waiting to seep from her eyes.

From where Gavin was seated on the porch, he witnessed the bitter warfare that Skyler and Gabriel had engaged in, and when he looked down at Hope, he knew that she was right in the center of it all. He watched Gabriel make his way back to them, and by the expression on his face, Gavin knew that he had taken the news enormously grueling. Gavin felt pity for him, and knew that he would hardly have acted any differently, if he was placed in Gabriel's position. Skyler had betrayed Gabriel and her family, and he questioned whether they would ever be able to recover from her dishonesty. Gabriel impulsively approached Gavin, who was aware of the tears burning in his eyes, "You look like a nice guy, Gavin, and you've clearly been good to her, and you obviously love Hope. This isn't on you, but, you can have her. I don't want her anymore. She's just not worth any of this shit!" The anger had overwhelmed Gabriel. His voice was broken and yet, Gavin knew that it was the hankering of a broken heart that had entirely conquered him. Gabriel made a distinctive effort to avoid Hope when he refused to glance into her direction, and left as quickly as he arrived.

Skyler apprehensively made her way back to the house, and when she reached Gavin, she quickly took Hope from him. He was saddened to notice her sorrow when she looked at him with sore and puffy eyes. "We shouldn't have come here …" She held Hope firmly against her, before glancing back at Gavin. At that very moment, he had an overwhelming urge to hold them both in his arms, before taking them back home with him, leaving this almost once-forgotten life of hers behind. He smiled sadly when he gazed over at Hope, and hurriedly kissed her on her cheek. "I'm going to take her upstairs and lay her down, will you be alright?" Gavin nodded before Skyler turned to leave. Watching Skyler take Hope upstairs, Gavin was once again aware of a nagging feeling that he was about to lose them both to Gabriel. From the moment he saw Skyler's eyes on Gabriel, he knew in his heart that there were too many things unsaid and unspoken between them. Gavin knew what love looked like, and he saw it when Skyler looked at Gabriel. He tried to think of only one time that Skyler looked at him like that, through the eyes of a woman who loved a man so unconditionally as he knew Skyler loved Gabriel, but not one moment came to mind.

There was a soft knock on the bedroom door, but Skyler ignored the intended intrusion, and turned to gaze at Hope who had fallen asleep beside her. "Mom?" Skyler whispered when she noticed her mother standing at the door. "Poor baby, she must be exhausted?" Tabitha made her way over to the bed, and sat down beside Hope before she gently stroked her hair. "It was a long flight and then the drive, and all the excitement that followed. She doesn't know what's going on, and I still haven't been able to tell her that Gabriel is her father. She couldn't wait to get here, mommy. She couldn't wait to meet her daddy and now, all she knows is conflict. My daughter has never known conflict before today, and I hate it. I hate that she is exposed to so much antagonism." "I've invited the Galicia family for dinner tonight, and Donna will be joining us. I think we must get this all out in the open for once and for all, and find closure so that we all can move on from this. We must make peace with one another for Hope's sake, and Hope must be formally introduced to her daddy." Tabitha smiled at Skyler who was gazing disconsolately at Hope. She turned to face her mother, and knew without an ounce of doubt what the evening would have in store for her. "Dad and Gavin have gone into town, why don't you take a nap with Hope and I'll see you later?" Tabitha gently stroked Skyler's cheek before getting up to leave. She had no sooner left when Tallulah walked in. "Hey Skye, is she asleep?" Tallulah was desperate to steal a peek at Hope. "Yes …" Skyler smiled fondly at her youngest sister. "What's up?" Tallulah sat down beside Skyler, and took her hands into hers, "I saw Gabriel earlier on the back porch next door …" Tallulah nervously glanced around, desperate to ensure that they were alone, "He was crying, Skye. I felt so bad for him." Skyler got up from the bed, and made her way over to the window, "I don't want to hear it, Tallulah, please just leave it alone. I don't know how to say sorry, and I do not want to hear how I destroyed everybody, including my daughter's life. I should never have come home." Skyler yelled out through her tears before Tallulah made her way over to her sister, and placed her arms around her, "I'm not mad at you, Skye ..." She hugged her sister tighter before she left Skyler to take a nap with Hope.

She must have been asleep for what felt like hours when Skyler heard Gavin calling out to her, "Skye, wake up ..." He placed a cup of coffee on the pedestal beside her. She looked over at where Hope was sleeping only a short while ago, and was horrified to discover that she was no longer there, "Hope?" She was anxious suddenly, and sat up straight on the bed. "Don't worry, she woke up earlier and your dad took her." He sat down beside her on the bed, "She's next door with Gabriel's parents. I think they've had that talk with Hope?" Skyler fell back onto the pillow, and covered her face with her hands, "Oh no, that's all I need right now." She rubbed her forehead at the mere thought of Gabriel's parents' reaction concerning Hope. "Come on, Skye, you can't keep her away from them. Let them have this. They suddenly find out they have a four-year-old granddaughter, and technically, their first grandchild." "I know, I know. I just wish we never came. Life was so much easier back in Point's Reach."

When Tabitha summoned her family to dinner, Gavin was the first to make his way downstairs. Skyler quickly brushed her hair, and stared accusingly at her swollen eyes and bloated face. She prayed that her heart would not betray her during dinner, but the vulnerability she was feeling inside reminded her of how fragile she felt around Gabriel. Skyler knew that if she could just get through the next couple of days without losing her heart or mind to Gabriel again, her chances were excellent of leaving Logan's Bay with Gavin, and successfully starting a whole new life with him, while placing the past distantly behind her.

When Skyler hesitantly made her way downstairs, she could clearly hear voices and laughter coming from the dining room. She heard Sarah and Gabriel play with Hope, and was pleased to hear Hope's laughter echo throughout the house. When she entered the dining room, she could barely hide her delight when she saw the three of them. "Mommy!" Hope waved excitedly when she saw Skyler enter the dining room. "Look mommy! Daddy!" She pointed excitedly to Gabriel who had lowered his head, not wanting to face Skyler just yet. When Sarah saw her standing in the doorway, she stood up and made her way over to Skyler, "Thank you for bringing her home, Skye. This fighting must end. I'm not mad at you." She smiled at Skyler before she turned away from her. Finding an empty seat next to Gavin, she realized that he was caught up in conversation with Dave and Carlos. She hurriedly glanced around her, and noticed that Donna had not arrived as yet. As she was about to ask her mother about Donna and Christopher, they all walked in, almost as though Skyler had supernaturally summoned her. She smiled when she noticed her sister carrying both her boys who were doing their very best to break free from their mother. "Skye!" Donna yelled out and excitedly embraced her sister, "Where is Hope?" She glanced around her, and when she saw Hope, she rushed over to the niece she was meeting for the first time. Gabriel smiled when he saw Donna, and lovingly placed his arms around her, "Hey sis, you're looking more beautiful than ever?" He winked at her before Donna smiled bashfully at him. She leaned closer to him, so that only he could hear what she was about to say, "That's because I'm pregnant again …" Gabriel smiled broadly and turned to Skyler who was watching them with a despondent smile on her face. She quickly turned away when she realized that Gabriel was staring at her, and for just a moment, Gavin recognized that look in Skyler's eyes again. "Skye!" Skyler turned around to find Christopher make his way over to her, "Wow! Look at you! I am so glad you came! I can't wait to meet our little princess." He lovingly embraced her before he enthusiastically made his way over to Hope. Skyler walked up to her rugged nephews and lovingly embraced them, sad that she had missed out on so much time with them.

They had all gathered around the dining room table

when Sarah and Tabitha brought in the food. Dave got up from his seat and lifted his glass, "Tonight, two families are joined together in more ways than one. Christopher and Donna, and their brood ..." He winked at his eldest daughter, "and Skye, Hope and Gabriel." He turned to Gavin who had suddenly felt completely out of place, "And, I would like to welcome a new member of this family, if he will have us, Gavin ..." They all raised their glasses while Skyler smiled bashfully at Gavin. "Gavin, thank you for bringing my girls home. Thank you for bringing Hope to us. Thank you for being there for them both, it takes one hell of a man to take those two on. True to her name, she has given us all a little bit of hope today." Every single person nodded in agreement and giggled at Hope, who had started clapping her hands. Skyler smiled at her father before Hope suddenly appeared behind her, "Mommy?" She held her arms out for Skyler to pick her up. "Oh, come to grandma ..." Tabitha knew that Skyler was desperate to spend much needed time with her sisters. "Here's your plate, come sit next to me." Tabitha whispered before Hope happily made her way over to Tabitha and Dave. Skyler glanced over at Christopher who had stood up and raised another glass, "I, we have an announcement to make ..." Donna smiled timidly when she noticed the awkwardness on Christopher's face, "We are, we're going to have another baby!" They all broke out in applause and almost simultaneously, congratulated Christopher and Donna. Skyler smiled and winked in approval and pride for her sister. She was tremendously delighted by Donna, and for a moment, Skyler wished she was a little more like her.

After they all had dished up their dinner, Gabriel turned to Donna, "Tell me, Donna, you being a mother almost three times over," He paused and turned to Skyler, "Would you hide your child from Christopher or your parents?" Skyler's heart began hammering once again before she turned to Gavin who took her hand and gently squeezed it. "I …" Donna was struggling to find the words but realized at once what Gabriel was trying to do, "I don't think, I just think, it depends, but …" She was desperate not to create an unpleasant atmosphere and began stumbling over her words before Gabriel interrupted her, "But what, Donna? Why would any mother want to keep her child away from a father who would sacrifice his life for her?" Donna grew anxious suddenly. "Gabriel, come on, leave it alone. We're all trying to have nice dinner. We are all together for the first time in a very long time. Don't scare Hope, bro …" Christopher stepped in before Donna could respond. "No, Chris, I don't want to scare my daughter, I just, I really want to know? Do you know that Skyler hasn't given me one explanation for any of this? She hasn't yet said one word to me about any of this? She hasn't even said it out loud, that Hope is my daughter." By the look in his eyes, Skyler was convinced that he was piercing invisible daggers her way. Gavin held her hand tighter, before Dave realized that the conversation had become awkward and unpleasant. Skyler felt that familiar lump in her throat make its presence known once again She knew that there was no way on earth that she would leave Logan's Bay with her heart intact. "Hope ..." Skyler turned to her daughter. "Did you have fun with your other daddy today?" Hope nodded in delight before Skyler turned away from her. She had barely lifted her knife and fork when she heard Hope's voice echo, "Why are you sad, mommy?" Skyler was once again reminded of her daughter's excessive compassion for her, "Oh, I'm not sad, baby." She smiled at Hope before she lowered her head.

"So, Gabriel, it must've been tough for you out there?" Gavin was desperate to break the somber mood that was beginning to overwhelm them around the dinner table. "To be honest, when enough time had passed, none of us ever thought we'd come home. We became numb to our surroundings and eventually, we lost track of how long it was, or what day we were in. We never thought we'd leave there alive ..." Skyler was devastated when she heard how defeated he sounded. Her heart was trouncing by the mere suggestion of all Gabriel was made to endure. "I'm sure. I don't know how you did it?" Gavin shook his head at the sheer thought of Gabriel being held a prisoner for such an extended period of time. "But, do you know what kept me going, Gavin?" He turned to Skyler, "And I don't mind saying this to you, and in front of everyone else. You should know what you're getting into. I knew, I thought, I was so sure there was someone waiting for me. I had a duty to come home to the girl I had met and fallen in love with when I was only a boy. I knew she was waiting for me, and I was sure, I was so sure that she'd wait forever …" Gavin could hear the extreme agony and discontentment in his voice. "And you know what I came home to? My home was gone, and she was gone. I came home to a daughter that was passed off as another man's child. I came home to hear that she had broken off all contact with her family for the past five years or so. But at the same time, I came home to two nephews who knew me. They knew who I was. My brother told them all there was to know about me, but she couldn't afford me the same respect." Everybody turned back to their food when the silence became deafening. Skyler tried to wipe the tears that had begun flowing down her cheeks. She prayed fiercely that no-one would notice how shattered she was. "I mean, it was all I could think of. She begged me not to go, you know? And all I could think of was how she begged me to stay, but I left, I left her. I thought I was doing the right thing for us and for our future. Now, now thankfully, she is your fucking problem." Gabriel smiled miserably at Gavin who had bowed his head, unable to look him in the eye.

Gabriel got up and hurriedly made his way out to the back porch before Gavin turned to Skyler, "Go, go talk to him. You owe him an explanation, Skye." Skyler tensely hesitated but quickly excused herself, and made her way out to the porch to where he was standing. "Gabriel?" She nervously placed her hand on his shoulder, "Gabriel, I don't know how to fix this, or how to make things right with you? You make it sound so cold, so deliberate?" She paused in a desperate attempt to swallow back on her tears, "If I could go back and do things differently, I would. I made so many mistakes, I know that. I was hurt and angry. I was alone, and I felt so lost without you, Gabe. And, after a while, I mean, when you didn't come back, I thought, just like everybody else did, I thought that you died ..." Skyler felt the tears escape through her eyes while distraughtly trying to shut them off. "Skye, tell me one thing? That's all I want to know ..." He turned around to face her, "Gavin, do you love him? He seems like a good man, and Hope is without a doubt, very fond of him, but, do *you* love him?" He once again found himself searching for the answers in her eyes. "He was there for me, Gabriel, and he loves Hopie ..." She was frantic for Gabriel to understand that she owed

Gavin more than she was giving him. "Do you *love* him, Skye?" Skyler turned away from him. She knew from the innermost part of her, that Gabriel already knew who her heart belonged to. "It's a different kind of love, Gabe. It doesn't hurt as much as loving you did. It's just easier to love him. He makes me feel safe. I can't do this with you, Gabe, I don't want to discuss Gavin with you, it's not fair to him." She whispered hoarsely before she turned, and made her way back to the dining room.

Gabriel stood gazing out over the porch, and was devastated that Skyler had confessed her devotion to Gavin. It was finally over for them, yet his anger for Skyler had profoundly increased. He felt immensely betrayed by her supposed love for him; deceived by all the broken promises she once made him. He was angry that he had lost out on being the first man Hope would ever love and look up to. Gabriel was devastated by the fact that time had stolen all that had ever mattered to him. He lowered his head when he could no longer bear to feel the excruciating pain that had engulfed his entire heart. When Skyler returned to the dining room, she scanned the area looking for Hope, "Where's Hope?" She was anxious at once. "Mom has put her to bed, she's loving every minute of this." Dave smiled at Skyler. Skyler found it challenging to finish her meal, and made a desperate attempt to act as though nothing had happened. Shortly after Skyler had taken her seat, Gabriel joined the rest of them. Gavin noticed that things were becoming increasingly strained between them.

After Skyler and her sisters helped Tabitha wash up the dishes later that evening, Gavin called Skyler out to the pool. "Skye, listen …" He took her hands into his own, "I know things are a little rough for you right now, and I realize how complicated everything is. I don't want to be the reason things are tougher for you …" Skyler was instantly bothered by what he was going to say next. "I shouldn't be here now. I shouldn't have come here with you. I am going back to Point's Reach tonight. I really want to give you time to sort things out with Hope and Gabriel. I don't want to be in the middle, and I definitely don't want to distract you." He turned away from her before Skyler anxiously grabbed his hands, "Oh Gavin, please don't go. I want you here. I don't know if I can get through this without you? I don't want you to leave …" She was desperately pleading with Gavin to stay. Skyler knew that Gavin was all that was keeping her firmly grounded and sane amidst all that was going on around her. She was dreadfully afraid that if he left, she might give in to her emotions and, lose her heart to Gabriel all over again. "I want to give you the time, Skye …" He paused to take in a deep breath, "I can see the way you look at him. You don't look at me like that? And that's okay, but, I need you to work through whatever feelings are left between you and Gabriel. I want you to choose me, but I want you to be honest about how you feel. You need this time, Skye, you know you do." He was incapacitated by the pain that had suddenly made its way through his entire being when the mere thought of losing her to Gabriel became a sudden and unexpected reality to him. Skyler turned away from him, afraid to admit how much sense Gavin was making to her, "Gavin, I know I still have feelings for Gabriel, I know that. I thought he was dead, and now he isn't. But, I don't want to lose you." "If you want me, you can have me. I'm not going anywhere, Skye. You know where to find me, but, I can't and don't want to stand in your way either. I don't want to be that guy, and I know my presence is placing much more strain on you than you need. There are so many things you and Gabriel need to work out. There are so many things unfinished between the two of you. Do it now, before it is too late and when, if you come back to me, I'll know that you chose me, alright?" He took Skyler in his arms, and held her protectively against him. Skyler held onto him and was reminded once again of how safe he made her feel, "How did I get to be so lucky, so lucky to have such a wonderful man like you, Gavin?" "I'll be waiting for whatever you decide, Skye, but Gabriel deserves to have his answers too. He deserves more than this."

Gavin made his way upstairs and kissed Hope goodbye before greeting Dave and Tabitha. Dave was sad to see him go. In a tremendously short period of time, he grew immensely fond of Gavin, and thoroughly enjoyed his company. Skyler walked him out to the car, painfully aware of an intense sadness and horrifying fear that made its way into her heart. "Skye, Gabriel deserves more, he didn't ask for any of this." Gavin held her in his arms before he reluctantly drove off into the night. Skyler wiped the tears from her eyes before she headed back inside where Dave was waiting for her in the living room, "Hey dad. I want to go for a walk on the beach, will you keep an eye on Hope?" "Sure, do you want me to come with you? I can ask mom to look after Hope?" He was saddened to detect the sorrow in his daughter's eyes. "No, that's okay. I just want to be alone for a while ..." She bent down and gently kissed him on his forehead.

Skyler sat down on the beach when she reached the shore and gazed out over the ocean. She thought of what Gavin had said to her, and she wondered why it sounded so simple when he told her what she already knew. She was greatly indebted to him for the emotional relief and safety he had offered her since moving to Point's Reach, but she realized that she could never love him the way she unwillingly, still loved Gabriel. She felt a cool breeze surround her, and she wondered whether Gabriel would ever forgive her. She tried to consider all that had been altered between them. Gabriel had matured tremendously over the last couple of years, as did she. Skyler was horrified to admit that she loved him more at that very moment, than she did the day she said goodbye to him. "I saw Gavin leave earlier, is everything alright?" Skyler was at once alarmed when she heard Gabriel's voice break the silence which had surrounded her only moments before. "Gabriel? I didn't hear you …" She rose to her feet when she saw him standing behind her, "Sorry, I didn't mean to frighten you." Gabriel was once again horrified to witness the extreme wretchedness in her eyes. "He, he had to get back …" "I'm sorry to see him leave. Hope, she's something, isn't she?" He made his way next to her before Skyler turned to face him. She smiled forlornly at him as he stood beside her, "Yeah. She is everything good in my life." "Skye, I know things weren't easy for you when I left, and I know that I'm not making anything easier for you now. Like I've said before, I didn't really expect to find you waiting for me, you know? And, you had every right to carry on with your life. That's what I would have wanted for you, you know?" Gabriel was determined to let Skyler know that he no longer bore any resentment towards her, "I overreacted, and I am so sorry about that. I just couldn't understand why you kept Hope from our families, but Donna told me how you refused to accept that I was gone, and that you were so angry that my parents had given up on me. I get it, I really do. I don't agree with it, but I get it. I think I probably would have reacted in the exact same way, although, I wouldn't have waited so many years. You were wrong there, Skye." She smiled when he spoke. She was sure that she could detect traces of the old Gabriel coming back to her.

While gazing at Skyler, his heart nudged him to look closer at her. He could almost sense that Skyler's heart continued to hunt his. She unexpectedly burst into tears, and began pounding at Gabriel's chest with all her might, while her tears flowed unreservedly down her cheeks. "I waited for you, Gabe! I wanted to die when everybody tried to convince me that you were dead. I wanted to die with you! I didn't want to live without you, and then, then Hope came along! You left me, you left me with a baby all on my own! Your mother was adamant I sell the house, my home! She she said I was drowning and that I had to get up, you know? And then, all I wanted to do was get back at her, punish her for hurting me and destroying all our memories! Hope was the perfect way to punish her, and then, when I realized how wrong I was, it was too late, Gabe, I couldn't take it back ..." She continued to pound relentlessly when she felt her entire world come crashing down on her. She was finally ready to release all the pent-up anger and hurt she had been carrying around her since Gabriel left for Kenya.

Leaving her was something he never chose to do, and Gabriel realized how immensely she fought to carry on without him. "I hated your parents for what they did! They made me give up on you. I had to sell our home, Gabe! I am still so angry with your mother, and now you walk back into our lives? It's as though you have come back from the dead. What do you want me to do, Gabriel, what?" She shouted through the tears when she finally let go of him. Gabriel moved closer to her, and took her face in his hands, "I don't want you to forget, Skye. I don't want you to forget us and that, that I love you. I know you love me still, I know it, Skye! I want you to say it!" Skyler realized for the first time that she was by no means at all, the only one to suffer, but that Gabriel had suffered tremendously too. "I don't want to throw away the one chance we have now, Skye. I don't want to let go of us, of the family we are. I want you to come back to me, Skyler! I can't stand the thought of another man taking care of you and Hope. I am her dad. I don't want to lose any more time with her!" He gazed intently into her eyes, trying to find something there to tell him that it was not too late. He wanted her to surrender herself into his arms, and tell him that she loved him still, but all Gabriel could see was the ruins of destruction that was left behind in her overpowering wretchedness.

Skyler fell to her knees when she realized again that they were no longer the two people they once were. It seemed a lifetime ago that she could place her arms around him, and tell him how intensely she adored him. Skyler knew that she could never step back into the past and pretend that he never left. They were simply two broken people, damaged by circumstances they did not choose. She couldn't erase the last five years, and she knew into her soul that they would never be the same again. She turned away from him when she thought of Gavin. He had unwaveringly stood by her over the past few years. He had grown to love and accept Hope as his own daughter. He had presented her and Hope with the solidity that had escaped her since Gabriel left. She was in no way equipped or prepared to sacrifice her daughter's heart simply to save her own. "Gabriel, I would do just about anything to get back what we've lost. I wish I could erase the last few years, and I wish it was as simple as giving it all up, but I am different now. I have changed, and I'm committed to Gavin. He has given my life meaning and a sense of normality has come back to me. I can't just take him away from Hope, it would shatter her. I can't ignore what he's meant to me or Hope these last couple of years?" She paused when she became excruciatingly aware that her heart was besieged by a pain so severe, she could scarcely breathe, "I don't want to hurt him. I love him, I do …" "I don't, I don't believe you, Skye. Look me in the eye and tell me that it's Gavin you love, that you choose him. Tell me that he is what's best for Hope." He grabbed her arm, silently pleading with her to come back to him. Skyler was devotedly aware of the fact that Gabriel knew her better than the performance she was putting on, but her loyalty to Gavin compelled her to place him behind her, and move forward without him.

She turned to face Gabriel squarely in the eye, but when she saw the devastating grief in his eyes, she felt her legs grow weak underneath her. Instinctively, she held onto him, but at the same time, she was anxious to remain steady and walk away from him, and the unconquered love she had for him. She gently placed her hand on his cheek as he gazed intrusively at her. She knew into the very core of her, that no matter how much of her she would devote to Gavin, and how long she would be apart from Gabriel, she could only ever faithfully and honestly love the man standing in front of her; the man who was begging her to come back to him. Skyler gently kissed him before he wrapped his arms around her. He frantically searched her eyes as she clung desperately onto him. When he closed his eyes, he recognized her lips on his, while he inflexibly held her against him. Her hands found their way to his face when she stubbornly clutched it into her hands, unable to release her lips from his. She felt her body come alive again when she lowered her hand just enough to feel his beating heart from the tips of her fingers. It was a reminder that he was alive, that he had come home to her. When her body began aching for him, she squeezed his chest. She hunted him as enthusiastically as she once did. Gabriel pressed her closer to him, at once sensitive to an immense hunger for her. "Let's go away?" Gabriel's desire for her was entirely consuming him. "Let's go too far …" She responded by digging her fingers into his back. She wanted him more than she had ever wanted him before. Once again, she was swept away into a world that only Gabriel could hold her hostage in.

Skyler was only moments away from surrendering her body entirely to him, when she breathlessly stepped back, and glared at him. She had begun shuddering from head to toe, feeling once again as though her heart had started to bloom again. As she stood staring at him, she knew that she could never place her heart in the treacherous hands of Gabriel Galicia again. "Gabriel, I've loved you for my entire life. You were my first love, my everything. There was a time when I thought, no, I was so sure that I couldn't carry on without you. I wanted to die when I thought you weren't coming back, but then Hope came into my life, and it was as though she was a replacement for losing you, the next best thing to having you." Skyler began telling Gabriel all that her mind was instinctively instructing her to tell him. She lowered her head, and prayed that Gabriel would not suspect how in conflict her heart was with her mind. "She saved me. She brought me back, and she gave me a new normal. There is so much of you in her, and that consoled me, you know? When I met Gavin, he just picked up all the broken pieces, and made me realize that my life didn't end with you, Gabe. A part of me died when you left, but Gavin, he brought something back to me. I know it's nothing like what you and I once had, but it's safe and I owe him so much. If I cross this line with you tonight, I'll be exactly who you thought me to be, and I can't. I can't do this to Gavin. I'm not that person, and I'm afraid, I am so afraid to walk away from you and never feel this way again. But Gabe, Hope, you know? Hope will be destroyed if Gavin leaves. It will crush her, and I can't, I just can't ..."

Gabriel turned away from her when he realized that his heart had begun to strictly command him to let go of Skyler. The time had come for Gabriel to move on with his own life, and let the girl he had been dreaming of for his entire life, it was time to let her go. He turned back to her and placed his arms around her. He held onto her, afraid that he might never again feel the way she made him feel at that very moment. "Then go back to him, Skye. If that's what you want and if Gavin is who you need, go back to him. But please, I am begging you, don't keep Hope away from me, don't let Gavin be all that Hope knows?" He whispered as he held her tighter against him. Skyler's heart was crushed once again when she heard him say that it was alright for her to go on without him. She ran her fingers through his hair, and she wondered for a moment, why he was not fighting harder for her. From deep within her, a fragment of her wanted him to engage into warfare for her, but she knew that it would be of no good, nothing could change the way she felt at that very moment. "I could never keep her away from you, Gabe, I swear. Besides, that little girl will never allow it ..."

Skyler realized that there was nothing else left to say to one another. They were finally closing off the chapter they had begun many years before. She cautiously, yet unwillingly walked away from him. It felt to her as though he had died again, it was finally over for them. She walked away from him, overawed by the battle between her heart and her mind. She did not want it to be the end. Her heart reminded her that what they had once had, could never be all there could ever be for them. She gasped for air when she absorbed the cruel reality that she had given up on the only man her heart could never let go of.

Gabriel stood watching her until he could no longer see her. He was unreservedly splintered by the fact that she had fallen in love with another man. He was devastated by the reality that Hope's first love, was for a man she had recognized as a father. He cursed all that had happened to them, and he damned the day he left Skyler behind. He had obsessively devoted himself to his country, and in return, he had lost all that had ever really mattered to him.

When Skyler made her way upstairs to her bedroom, she found Hope fast asleep in her bed. She leaned down to kiss her daughter on her forehead when her mind turned back to Gavin. She promptly picked up her mobile phone, and tautly dialed his number, but there was no reply. When she glanced at her wrist watch, Skyler realized that he was more than likely still in the air. "Gavin …" She whispered before she realized that her call had been redirected to his voicemail. "Hi, I just called … I wanted to say, I choose you, Gav, if you'll have Hope and I? I feel safe with you, and I choose you. Gavin, I love you, I do. You made us a family, and Hope, she just loves you so much. Please tell me I'm not too late?" She abruptly hung up and prayed that she still stood a chance with Gavin. When she turned around, she was at once startled to find Tabitha standing in the doorway. "Mom, you scared me …" Tabitha placed her index finger to her lips in a motion for Skyler to remain silent before she signaled for her to follow her. They both made their way down the stairs and into the kitchen. "I heard you on the phone ..." Tabitha hastily poured each a cup of coffee. "Mom, please, I'm too tired to hear you lecture me." Skyler turned away, exhausted by her meeting with Gabriel, and desperate to return to Hope. "Skye, wait!" She instinctively grabbed Skyler's arm, "I didn't bring you here to lecture you. I know things have been hard on you, and I realize that I haven't been very supportive of you. I'd like, I would really like another chance with you, and if Gavin is the man you want, then I won't stand in your way. None of us will. You deserve to have some good in your life, and if it turns out to be Gavin, then I want you to have that. We are all just trying to make sense of everything and cope with all of this the best we can." She smiled tenderly and spoke in a soft and nurturing tone, "Your father and I know that you are quite capable of making your own decisions. You've been doing it for so long, but all I'm asking from you is please, please, please don't keep Hope from us." Tabitha had resigned herself to the fact that Skyler and Gabriel were lost to each other, yet she feared her daughter's heartache and anguish would keep her away from Logan's Bay. Tabitha Maxwell was no fool and knew precisely how sincerely Skyler still adored Gabriel.

"What is it with all of you? Why do you guys think I'll take Hope away from you all? I love you guys, and I want nothing more than for us to all be together. I'll never keep Hope away from you, or from Gabriel. It's just that my life is over there now, and I don't want to displace Hope if I don't have to. She is extremely confused by all that has happened this last week. Besides, mom, what keeps you from visiting us?" Skyler placed her arms around her mother, and gently hugged her, "We'll see each other all the time, mommy, I promise. It won't be like it was before. I won't do that to Gabriel." Tabitha was at once aware of a pained expression on Skyler's face, "I love him, mom. I love Gabriel so much, it hurts, but Gavin, you know? I love Gavin too. I am so confused, mommy, and Hope, I don't want to hurt her. I can't take Gavin away from her." Tabitha placed her arms around Skyler and hugged her firmly, "Just do what feels right for you."

Skyler was almost fanatical about returning to Point's Reach the following weekend. Even though she was secretly thrilled to be close to Gabriel again, she knew that if she had stayed in Logan's Bay even a moment longer, she might give in to the nudgings of her heart, and in a moment of one of her many weaknesses, she might confess to Gabriel that she continued to find it exhausting and crushingly challenging to resume her life without him. Skyler grudgingly accepted the truth that she would never quite recover from losing him, but she was relieved that the worst of her days were finally over. She spent the next few days engaging in a concerted and determined effort to avoid him or even, run into him, but she gracefully allowed him the time that was left to spend with Hope, time with her he so desperately sought. While Skyler cautiously scrutinized Gabriel and Hope from a distance when she thought that no-one was looking, she beamed with pride and valued the individual moments he would spend with her. It was distinctly clear to Skyler and both the Maxwell and Galicia families that father and daughter had grown extraordinarily close to one another in an incredibly short interlude of time.

Hope was thrilled and grew increasingly animated while spending almost every waking moment with Gabriel, while he in turn, cherished all he was discovering about his daughter, for the very first time. From a distance, Skyler would keep a watchful eye on them, and more the ever, she found the resemblances between the two of them impressively remarkable. While watching her daughter form an indestructible attachment with the man of her dreams, Skyler could in no way at all, help but feel a little redundant. Just as an outsider, looking in on someone else's life, she coveted with all her heart to be invited into their fairytale, and become a small fraction of the world they had escaped to. At times, she was convinced that there was no room for her in the little world they had created, and sometimes, she was secretly enraged at Gabriel for abandoning her, and leaving her to bring Hope into this world without him. Ever since their confrontation on the beach, Skyler noticed a transformation in Gabriel's disposition and mindset. She could barely reject the idea that he had so effortlessly accepted the sincerity that their life together was over, yet to Skyler, it seemed as though he no longer presented any traces of dread or misery in his eyes. Although Skyler was cautiously relieved, it by no means lessened her sorrow when she realized that he seemed to encourage a life without one another so apparently painlessly.

Gabriel was unenthusiastically determined to create a safe volume of distance between Skyler and himself in a resolved effort to spend the time he had left with Hope. He was desperate to fill up each day creating adventures with her, and absorb all there was to know about the daughter who had been gone from him for years. He was anxious to form a connection with Hope, and he knew that once they were to leave Logan's Bay, his moments with her would be few and far between. He furtively prayed that Skyler would rediscover the love she once had for him, and in a moment of unimaginable insanity, she might confess her undying love and devotion to him, and stay. He detested the notion that they were about to leave to return home to Gavin, but he knew that there was nothing he could do to force her to stay. He was cautiously sensitive to the hopelessness in Skyler's eyes, and the dispirited tone in her voice became enormously unsettling for him. He persistently speculated as to how he would succeed in bringing a new kind of normal into his life, with Skyler was no longer a feature in his future. For the time being, he was pleasantly distracted by Hope, and he refused to allow the uncertainty of his future with his daughter overshadow what little time they had left with one another. He absorbed all there was to soak up about Hope. How she laughed and squinted at the same time, how she would enthusiastically clap her hands when she laid eyes on him, and how she would run into his arms and frantically hold onto him. He was terrified that he might forget all that he was learning about his daughter for the very first time.

Christopher and Donna had stopped by often, and although Donna was courageously strained to discuss Gabriel with Skyler, Skyler avoided any conversation that would lead back to Gabriel, as though mentioning his name would bring about a devastating plague. Sarah and Skyler had halfheartedly placed their discrepancies aside, and had succeeded in becoming friendly with one another again.

Gavin had called Skyler on the morning after he received her message, and although he was pleased by Skyler's decision, he however, could barely shake the feeling that Gabriel would be the only man who would undoubtedly own her heart. He had a prodding suspicion that even though Skyler had every intention of keeping her promise to him, she had failed miserably in convincing herself of her veritable emotions, and refused to admit that Gabriel would remain the one great love of her life.

The evening before Skyler and Hope were to return to Point's Reach, Donna called at the last minute to change the agreed upon plan of driving her and Hope to the airport, "Skye, I'm sorry, I didn't plan on getting sick, but I've arranged with Gabriel to drive you and Hope to the airport." Skyler was at once disoriented and could barely imagine the drive to the airport alone with Gabriel. "Come on, Donna! You seemed fine this morning? Why did you have to go and make plans with Gabriel for me? I could've just asked mom and dad?" "I know, I was feeling fine this morning, but it just hit me out of nowhere. I'm really sorry. I didn't even think about mom and dad. But, it would be rude to change it now?" Skyler hung up almost immediately and angrily cursed her sister. She knew Donna well enough to know that she was deliberately orchestrating a set-up between her and Gabriel. While packing their bags, Skyler was entirely overwhelmed and wholly unnerved by the awareness of being alone with Gabriel once again. She had only moments before packed the last of Hope's toys when she was at once caught off-guard hearing Gabriel's unanticipated voice Gabriel behind her. "So, this is it, then?" He moved closer to her, unsure of what to say next. "I guess it is. I'm so sorry to put you out like this, the airport and everything. I could just ask my parents to drive us?" "I'd love to drive you to the airport. It would give me an hour or so extra with Hope, I don't mind …" Skyler glanced around her as though she was saying goodbye for the very last time.

The thought of never returning to Logan's Bay was almost too severe to bear, yet, there was really nothing left for her to return to anymore. "I'm leaving for Kennedy next week. I've decided to start my own practice there, and look for another place. I thought you'd like to know that our old place is in the market again." He carefully scrutinized her, intrigued to discover how she would react to his surprise. Skyler glowered in surprising, yet downright misery, and turned away from Gabriel. Her heart began battering when she reflected on all the perfect and captivating moments they had spent in their home, the very first home that had brought Hope to her. Gabriel came up from behind her, and placed his hands on her shoulders, "I want to know if it's okay, if you're okay with me buying it back? What I'm trying to say is, I'd like to have Hope visit me holidays, and I'd really like it if it was in that house?" Skyler turned to face him, and for the first time since she had come home, she could once again detect animation in Gabriel's eyes.

She discovered a slight sparkle that she had once known so well return to him, and she recognized the charmingly handsome man that she had fallen in love with so many years ago. "That was basically her very first home, you know? She'll love that. She'll love the idea of being there once before. She is such a sensitive soul, it would mean so much to her." Skyler turned away from him, unexpectedly overawed with emotion. She was entirely unprepared for how she would feel. She was wholly devastated by the idea that Gabriel wanted to return to the home she was forced to give up and move out of, without her. She hurriedly scribbled down her landline number on a tiny piece of paper while anxiously reminding herself of all that she too, had lost, "I'm really bad with mobile phones. Here's my home number. Call me when you're ready. You can call this number to speak to Hope." He smiled sadly when she handed him her number, which to Skyler, was one more intrusive fragment of her life. Skyler grew increasingly anxious by the mere thought of allowing Hope to visit him in Kennedy. She had barely spent a regrettable two nights away from her daughter, yet, Skyler knew that she could hardly keep Gabriel or Hope away from one another.

"Thanks Skye, I just really wanted your approval, it means

everything to me. Good luck with Gavin, he's a great guy, I mean it. I want you to be happy, and if it has to be another man, I am glad it's Gavin." He placed his arms around her, and held her protectively against him for what seemed like longer than was necessary. Skyler glanced up at him when she recognized the familiarity she felt when his arms were around her. When she gazed into his eyes, she could swear that she saw a promise from him, a slight glimmer of hope for them. She placed her arms around his neck and gently kissed him on his lips. She closed her eyes, frantic to absorb all she might forget about him not too far from that very moment. He kissed her back, and held firmly onto her. She felt safe. She felt sheltered. He felt as though he once again, belonged in her world. She retreated slowly from him, afraid that she might surrender her heart back to him and announce to him how desperately she wanted him to take her back with him, to their home in Kennedy. She felt a devastating shudder make its way into her entire being, and she was sure that her tears were never really far off. "Thank you, Gabe ..." She whispered croakily, unable to look him in the eye. "I'm glad you're alive. I know I haven't said it to you, but I am. I'm glad that Hope will get to know the wonderful man I once knew, and still know. I am so, so grateful that you didn't flatly discard her because of me, thank you for that." Skyler hurriedly swabbed at the tears that were threatening to spill from her eyes, "None of this was ever her fault, and she shouldn't have to pay for our mistakes." Gabriel moved closer and wiped a lost tear from her cheek, "I love her, Skye, nothing else in this world matters more to me than Hope does. That little girl has given me a new lease on life. I don't even care about all the things that happened in Kenya, or the torture, the pain or the suffering. Nothing matters more than being the best man and dad for that little girl. I can't imagine my life without her, and even though I just met her a few days ago, I cannot even remember anymore what my life was like before her."

Skyler squeezed his hands, and turned away from him. Gabriel once again walked up to her and from behind her, he placed his hands on her shoulders. "I'm proud of the woman you've become, Skye. I am so enormously proud of the mother you are to Hope. I know it must have been hard for you, but you did such an amazing job with her. I'm sorry I wasn't here. I'm sorry I let you down, and more than anything in this world, I am so, so sorry I left. My dedication to my job has cost me much, you and Hope too. For that, I am so desperately sorry. All I can do now is to try and be present for Hope, and for you, if you ever need me." He held her vehemently in his arms and when he realized that he could barely control the tears that were about to show up in his eyes, he walked out of her bedroom.

When Skyler put Hope to bed later that evening, she laid quietly staring at the ceiling. Sleep had mercilessly escaped her mind, while she continuously wandered back to Gabriel as she considered a reality where it would be far easier for him to move on with his life, than it was for her to pick up all the broken pieces of the life they had once shared. She felt sudden fear tugging at her heart when she considered a possibility that Gabriel could meet and fall in love with someone else, just as she did. Falling in love with a man like Gabriel would be the simplest thing in the world for just about any woman. Her eyes trailed back to Hope as she was reminded by the choices she had made. It was time for Skyler to accept all that was lost to her, and that she was compelled to move forward, not only for Hope's sake, but for hers too. As she lay almost frozen and unable to sleep, she climbed out of bed and glanced over at the house next door. When she saw Gabriel's light burning, she threw her robe over her, and tiptoed downstairs. She unlocked the front door, and slipped out of her childhood home unnoticed, as she did so many nights before. She bare-footedly ran around the back, and squinted up at Gabriel's bedroom window. She quickly glanced around her, and picked up the only pebble that was lying at her feet. She aimed, and with the very first throw, she struck his window. While waiting for a response from him, she smiled casually when she saw Gabriel's shadow appear at the window.

She waved excitedly, before Gabriel hurriedly made his way down to her. "I couldn't sleep ..." "Skye, shit, you scared me! I thought something was the matter?"

She grabbed his hand, and smiled at him. "Come with me!" She pulled at him until he surrendered and followed her down the path they knew so well, and onto the beach. When they reached the shore, Skyler stood inertly and closed her eyes. Taking a deep breath before she opened her eyes, she looked up at Gabriel. "Let's pretend just for one night, Gabe. Let's pretend we are the two teenagers we once were. Let's forget you left, let's forget I left. Let's go back to before. Let's go back there, let's go too far..." She flung her arms around him, and fiercely kissed him without considering the consequences of one last night with Gabriel. "I don't want to talk about it. I don't want to think about it, I just want to be with you, just once more. There is no Hope and there is no Gavin, just you and me. Like we used to be. Let's not live in this world now, let's go back to before. I know I'm asking for much too much, but, just once more. Let's go too far one more time, just one last time." She whispered hungrily to him before she held feverishly onto him. Gabriel laid her down on the shore and gazed ravenously into her eyes. He kissed her again when he rested his warm body on top of hers. She placed her arms around him, and pressed him against her, desperately aching for his warm skin on hers. She grabbed at his t-shirt, and pulled it over his head before he freed her from her robe, and lifted her nighty to expose her bare skin. His lips trailed her entire body as she began responding passionately to his. She pulled his face back to hers, and pressed his lips against hers once more. "Let's go too far …" She was desperate to feel him against her, and she was frantic to forget all the pain and anguish of the past few years. She wanted Gabriel to sweep her away into a world she once understood, one they knew so well and one, they were home in.

Gabriel felt her entire body shudder as he gently moved inside of her. He looked into her eyes while she dug her fingers into his back, moaning softly. She closed her eyes and drifted back into a world she was once pleasantly and intensely acquainted with. She lingered for as long as she could, and when she could no longer control her body, she cried out in exhilaration. Gabriel collapsed beside her, and turned to face her. He smiled when he noticed the beam on her face. She turned to face him, and gently stroked his cheek, "I'm glad you're back, Gabe …" "I love you, Skye …" Skyler sat up straight and quickly pulled her nightgown back on. She frowned when her eyes hauntingly trailed back to his. "I know, Skye, just for one nigh, I know." "I'm not sorry, Gabe, I will never be sorry. I knew what I wanted, but that's all I could have and ever will have, because now, now it has to be about Hope again." When Gabriel put on his t-shirt, he rose to his feet and held his hand out to her. She took his hand when he helped her to her feet, unwilling to let go of him just yet. They strolled back up the path they had snuck out on so many nights before, and when they reached Skyler's house, Gabriel hurriedly kissed her on the cheek, "See you tomorrow ..."

"Goodnight, Gabe ..." She radiated happiness and smiled, before she turned to head back indoors. Gabriel stood gazing at her until he could no longer see her. He smiled contentedly as he made his way back to his bedroom. When Skyler climbed back into her bed, she could still smell Gabriel on her. She closed her eyes without feeling as though the entire world had rested on her heart, and drifted off to sleep with Gabriel still fresh on her mind.

Gabriel drove Skyler and Hope to the airport the following morning, both aware of obstinate silences between them. Gabriel and Hope were engaging in childlike chatter while Skyler remained silent and withdrawn for most of the trip. She would smile often when Hope let out faint giggles, and she would smirk each time Gabriel nudged Hope into fits of laughter. Skyler was unpredictably emotional and awfully close to tears when she said goodbye to her parents and the Galicia family. She realized for the first time how dreadfully she had missed them, and how much she longed to be around them. She glanced over at Gabriel often. She was fraught to take in all there was that she loved about him one more time, afraid that she might forget all she had cherished and valued about him, in the not too distant future. She was afraid that not too far from that moment, she might wholly forget all the little things she had once adored about him. His dark hair was neatly combed, and the look in his eyes told her that for the first time since he had left, Gabriel Galicia had found happiness and peace once again. From the destruction they had faced not too long ago, he had finally found joy and contentment in this world again. Her heart would thump each time he turned back to check on Hope where she had finally fallen asleep in her car seat. Skyler was desperately afraid that she might never feel again, the way she felt at that very moment. Their moment had passed them by. She was convinced that she was destined to miss him for the remainder of her life. Skyler was abruptly and frantically fearful of the certainty that Gabriel Galicia would turn out to be her one great sadness.

Skyler's unusual silence overwhelmingly unnerved Gabriel as they drove in stillness to the airport in Kennedy. He checked on Hope often, but was stunned by the fact that he would be obliged to say goodbye to the only two women he was frantic to keep close to him. Gabriel worried about Skyler, and he was concerned about Hope. He was desperate to keep them sheltered and shielded, but he knew that he had no authority or influence over Skyler any longer. Gabriel was enormously reassured by the fact that Gavin would be waiting for Skyler, and greatly relieved that he would care for them and keep them safe. He would secretly catch glimpses of Skyler as often as he could in a feverish attempt to memorize everything about her, one more time. Gabriel's heart was frantically nudging him to beseech Skyler to stay and give him one last chance to prove himself worthy of her. He was desperate for one last opportunity to love her. Gabriel's mind had engaged in a warfare against his heart, until he ultimately realized that to love Skyler perfectly, he would be compelled to let her go.

When they reached the airport, Gabriel spent as much time as he could in a heartbreaking effort to saying goodbye to Hope. He was wholly thrown off-guard and utterly surprised to witness the tears that had begun glistening in his daughter's eyes. His heart could barely endure separating from Skyler, but to witness the shattering in his daughter's eyes, was almost too devastating to bear. "Daddy, I don't want to leave you …" Hope clutched Gabriel's hand firmly, and held distraughtly onto him as she buried her head in his chest. "Hopie, please don't cry my angel. I'll come and see you all the time, and you'll come and visit me often. Daddy's going to get you and me a beautiful house, and you'll have your own bedroom, okay? Please don't be sad. Daddy loves you, don't you ever forget that, okay?" He embarked upon a gallant effort to comfort and reassure his daughter, but Gabriel was convinced that he had failed miserably as he desperately attempted to mask his own pain.

"Hope? What's the matter?" Skyler cautiously approached Gabriel and Hope. "I don't want daddy to die again!" Hope was inconsolable as she clung dreadfully to her father. Gabriel turned to Skyler, unsure of what to say to Hope, but overwhelmed and devastated by his daughter's utter hopelessness. His heart felt as though it was being cruelly shattered into a million pieces, and he fought vigorously to find the words to adequately console his little girl. Gabriel was devastated and outraged by the fact that the universe had chosen those he had loved the most to exercise its cruel tricks on. His eyes pleaded with Skyler's when she felt her own heart begin to splinter. "Daddy's not going to die, Hopie, he's just going to live here, and we are going to live in Point's Reach. He's going to come visit you, and he'll call you all the time. Daddy's going to come and fetch you to visit him here, and grandma and grandpa too. Please don't be sad, Hopie ..." Skyler was enormously distressed while trying in vain to reassure her daughter of her father's significant presence in her life. "But, I love him, mommy. Why can't he come with us? Why can't daddy come live with us? I'm scared daddy will forget me?" Hopie began wailing inconsolably once again, before she tightened her grip on Gabriel. Gabriel was stunned and remained silent, desperately trying to regain his composure, "Hopie, I love you so much. How can I ever, ever forget you?"

Gabriel could barely control the tears that were brimming in his eyes, and silently prayed for the courage to let his daughter go. Skyler could virtually see Gabriel's heart shattering inside of him when he discovered Hope's disappointment and inability to grasp all that was happening around them. She could barely suppress the prodding feeling that her daughter and Gabriel's pain was entirely her own doing, and that it all could have been entirely different for them. Not only was Skyler solely accountable for the agony and anguish of her own heart, but she alone was answerable for the extreme and undeniable distress that Gabriel and Hope were suffering. She gently freed Hope from Gabriel, and smiled wretchedly at the devastated man unwilling to release his daughter, "I'm so sorry, Gabe, for all of this. I know this is me. I just, I don't know how to fix things with you or with Hope. Please call Hope as often as you can, please, Gabe, don't punish her because of my failings. Don't let her down, Gabe." She whispered hoarsely over the accustomed, narrowing lump in her throat. "I'm not going to let her down, Skye, I won't hurt her ..."

She brusquely turned away from him just as Hope began weeping hysterically again. Skyler felt as though she could not at all, endure the anguish and ordeal of hearing her daughter cry out for her father. When they finally reached the plane, she turned back to Gabriel who had remained unresponsively where they had left him only moments earlier. She waived miserably when she realized that she was totally dislodged for a moment, especially when she could see him wipe the tears from his eyes.

"Goodbye my girls. I love you." Gabriel whispered when he could no longer see them. Climbing back into his car, he noticed a teddy bear that Hope had left on the back seat. He picked up the bear and pressed it firmly against him while he permitted his tears to flow freely from his eyes. When he bowed his head in defeat, he sobbed violently, and silently cursed the day he had boarded his flight to Kenya. Gabriel realized that nothing that he had endured on his trip with Doctors Without Borders, could prepare him for the torment and aching he was suffering at that very moment. He felt disoriented and entirely deserted as he sat weeping for his daughter. Gabriel was desperately afraid that he may never feel the way for another woman, as he felt for Skyler. He swiftly took his mobile phone from his pocket, and hurriedly dialed Skyler's number. When he reached her voicemail, he was sure that their plane had since taken off. He remained silent for what felt like forever, before he turned his thoughts back to the call, "Skye, I can't do this. God knows, I can't. I love, love you and Hope, how I love that little girl so much. Please Skye, I need her and I need you. Please, I'm begging you for just one more, one last chance. You can deny your feelings all you like, but I know, I know you love me. I can feel it. If, if there is anything left of what we once had, you owe it to Hope. Skyler, you owe it to us." He burst out sobbing once again as soon as he curtly disconnected the call. As he gazed through the windscreen of his car, he noticed her plane take off and sat watching until he could no longer see them. His heart was shattered. In a matter of moments, he had returned to the broken man who had come back to them.

When Skyler's plane landed, she quickly switched on her mobile phone. Before she could dial her parents, she noticed a voice message that had come through. She swiftly held the phone to her ear, and was shattered to hear Gabriel's fragmented voice. Through his pleading and begging for her to give them one more try, Skyler's heart felt as though it could not survive resisting Gabriel Galicia, over and over again.

Alice VL

Pearls in Ashes

She tossed the phone into her bag, before she picked Hope up and quickly made her way out of the plane.

Alice VL

CHAPTER NINE

When Skyler descended the flight of stairs from the plane, Hope was fast asleep in her arms. She had cried herself to sleep shortly after they took off even though Skyler had tried her best to pacify her. She repeatedly wiped away her daughter's warms tears that were rolling relentlessly onto her cheeks as she lay sleeping. Skyler at once recognized Gavin in the crowd waiting to meet them, and was instantly pleased and tremendously gratified to see his welcoming face. She smiled at him, but she was once again aware of the certainty that he could in no way at all, have an equal effect on her heart, as Gabriel did. "Hello, beautiful!" He was ecstatic to see Skyler again, and gently kissed her on her cheek. "Ooooh, I missed the two of you!" "Hey, it's so good to be back." Skyler was sincerely pleased to see Gavin. He snippily kissed Hope on her forehead before he placed his arms around Skyler. When Hope opened her eyes, Gavin was immensely troubled to realize that she had been crying. "Daddy ..." She whispered dejectedly when she held her arms out to him. Gavin glared incredulously at Skyler, and was devastated to discover that she was not calling out to him, but to the man that had thoughtlessly stolen their hearts away from him.

While driving home from the airport, Skyler told Gavin all about her trip to Logan's and how pleased she was that she had finally taken the plunge and returned home to her parents with Hope. She reluctantly told Gavin how dreadfully she had initially wavered in introducing Hope to the Galicia family, but that she was ultimately indebted to Gabriel and his family, for embracing and welcoming Hope into their family. She skipped all the parts that included Gabriel to Gavin, who in turn, did not dare mention him. Gavin suspected that Gabriel would forever be her first and one true love, but he was sure that he was emotionally equipped to accept whatever it was that Skyler felt she could offer him. He hoped that in time, Skyler would eventually recover from her broken heart, and look to Gavin for her very own happy-ever-after.

Gabriel called Skyler often and spoke to Hope for hours

on end as he excitedly informed her of his new home and the bedroom he had painstakingly and lovingly decorated for her. He enthusiastically told her how thrilled he was to see her again, and that he was looking immensely forward to her visits with him. Although it enforced feelings of discomposure for Gavin, he realized that there was nothing at all he could do to change the fact that Gabriel was Hope's father, and that he had stepped back into her life, as though he was never gone. Gavin too, felt betrayed by the universe. He had embraced Hope long before Gabriel had made his unexpected appearance.

Skyler bravely endeavored and committed to working on a new novel, but the fact that there were no more clues left in her life that she thought she could leave for Gabriel, she surrendered to and was depressingly captured in the remorseless clutches of writer's block. There was no longer anything to dream of when it came to Gabriel. She could no longer pen down on paper her unspoken emotions, and fantasize of a life with him, out of dread that she might irresponsibly reveal her true desire for an existence with him. There were no longer any characters living in her head, and there was no magical world left to create for them, and ultimately, escape to. All she could think of was how life had let her down, and how brutally it had scorched her.

Life had continued on characteristically for Skyler and

Gavin, almost as though Gabriel had never returned, but late at night when Gavin laid awake long after Skyler had fallen asleep, he recognized a jolting sensation which forced him to admit that their story had forever changed. He suspiciously listened while Hope spoke to Gabriel each day, and he scrutinized Skyler as he watched her progressively pine for him. Gavin was overawed by her despondency, and he wondered how much longer she could carry on heedlessly deceiving herself, and those closest to her. He would often walk in on her contemplating dismally as she gazed purposelessly out over the ocean, in the darkest of the night after Hope was asleep and when she thought no-one was looking. Gavin unquestionably caught glimpses of the sorrow in her eyes, and often noticed how she irritably swabbed at the frustrating tears that were flowing irrepressibly onto her cheeks. He began sensing a gradual change in Skyler with each call Gabriel made to Hope, and resentfully realized that Skyler's mood would become enthusiastically animated each time she heard his voice. At times, he was positive that he could almost visualize her heart battering just for him. He was distraught by the fact that he had never seen her react in a way vaguely as hungrily for him.

Skyler aligned herself into a fierce campaign with her emotions from the moment she returned to Point's Reach. She convinced herself that as the days went by, she would steadily recover from her brief confrontation with Gabriel, and carry on as normal with her life in Point's Reach and with Gavin. She was disparagingly plagued by her emotions each time Gabriel would call, and she would berate herself for the startling emotions that would intimidate her. It would entirely demoralize her when she heard his voice, leaving her discouraged and shuddering for the remainder of the day. She desperately tried to conceal her unanticipated and disturbing reactions from Gavin as she valiantly struggled to focus on her bond with him. Skyler realized that Gavin's patience for her would eventually expire. She had grown increasingly desperate to numb her unsolicited feelings for Gabriel. Yet, the stronger she became, the sadder she would be. She cautiously heeded the plans Gabriel made with Hope, and she could barely ignore how intimidating and daunting her future seemed without him. She felt like an intruder, desperate to find her place in someone else's life, a life she could belong in and be loved in. As solemnly as she tried, Skyler could by no means at all, banish Gabriel from her mind or from her heart.

Gabriel had succeeded in buying back the house he had once shared with Skyler. He was secretly thrilled to reclaim a significant fragment of the life they were once united in. When Gabriel first moved in, it strained him to come home at night to an unfilled, eerily quiet house whose deafening silences haunted him into the early hours of most mornings. The memories of Skyler and the love they had once shared were enormously challenging and weighed profoundly on him. As the days went by, Gabriel effectively demonstrated his mark on the house he adored, and was exhaustively delighted by how his home had once again turned out. He was equally thrilled by the sheer prospect of bringing Hope to visit him, and he could effortlessly visualize her running and squealing through their home. On more occasions than Gabriel would care to confess to, he could swear that he saw a silhouette of Skyler in their home. It would appear to him as a shadow, leaving him instantly unnerved as he impatiently searched for her throughout the entire house, only to discover that it was in fact, his inventiveness and unstinting hunger for her that were playing cruel tricks on his mind. As effectively as he had pieced his life back together, Gabriel could in no sensible way, shake the feeling that his life had remained unfinished. He was thriving at his medical practice, his profession introduced him to a bunch of people in his community who had successfully managed to distract him from all that had once entirely beleaguered him. He had begun dating a string of women in a frantic bid to establish steadier friendships, but could never quite connect with any of them, as he once did with Skyler. The climax of his day remained his one phone call to Hope. Each time he dialed Skyler's number, he implored the universe that she would take the call, anxious to hear her familiar voice again.

When Skyler answered his calls, his heart would race at the speed of a freight train while he bravely endeavored to remain untethered. With nothing much to say to one another, Skyler would cut short their call and hurriedly hand the phone to Hope.

When Gabriel met Michelle, he had reached a point in his life where the solitude and stillness had begun to expose a life of intense loneliness for him. He alarmingly discovered just how discouraging and tiresome it had become to meet someone he would consider spending much of his life with. Michelle was a beautiful brunette, of slender build and highly sought after in the dating world. She was a highly-qualified surgeon and colleague of Gabriel in The Tygerberg Children's Hospital where he would often run into her while doing his rounds. Gabriel was unexpectedly thrilled when she invited him to dinner after a shift late one evening. He was tremendously spellbound by Michelle's persuasive energy and her head-strong individuality. He was bowled over and intensely attracted to the tall, self-supportive surgeon who shared his love for adventure, science and children. For the first time since Gabriel had returned from Kenya, he was sensitive to an incontestable attraction to someone else other than Skyler.

They had much in common and would spend hours consulting on patients with one another, and seemed to engage fluently with each other. They fully understood the other's work schedules and they accepted that their free time together, was restricted. Gabriel was unexpectedly, yet pleasantly infatuated with Michelle, who in turn, fell intensely in love with Gabriel. After a frenzied number of dates and social gatherings, Gabriel was wholly relieved to confess to the prospect of a future with Michelle. Without intending to, and without deliberately seeking one another out, they fell head over heels in lust with each other. Gabriel and Michelle became inseparable, and keen to spend all that was left of their uninterrupted time with each other. He was anxious to introduce Michelle to Hope, and he desperately implored a higher power that she would fall in love with Hope, just as he had. Yet, Gabriel was intimidated by the gentle, yet muted nudges that were continuously reprimanding him as his feelings for Michelle intensified. He was wholly discouraged by the fact that he had never felt lonelier, than when Michelle was around. He had never felt as isolated as he felt when he was amongst close friends, and it terrified him to admit that he might be carrying the scars from his ordeal in Kenya, along with losing Skyler. Each time he would spot a stranger that would vaguely resemble Skyler, he would subconsciously drift back into a world where he would desperately yearn for her. He grew extraordinarily frustrated when he was unintentionally consumed by thoughts of her. His heart would cruelly criticize him for seeking to abandon her, even though he wanted nothing more than to draw her closer. Gabriel deliberately sought to suppress all the unsought emotions that would creep up on him. He would bravely sneer and carry on as though she had never before, consumed his entire body and mind.

With each devoted gaze into Michelle's eyes, he would be inadvertently reminded of how Skyler would often peek at him. Gabriel resentfully accepted that no other woman would ever look at him, in the way that Skyler once did. He realized once more that Skyler was all his heart would undeniably recognize and intentionally pursue. As he bravely confronted his emotions, he was determined to rebel against his heart, and for once, embark on the journey his mind was leading him on. He had been left feeling defeated and spent by the interminable conflict that had engaged in a bitter combat within him, and he was desperate to rebel against it. Skyler was lost to him, she had made it clear that she had elected Gavin to spend the rest of her life with. There was nothing more Gabriel could do, to try and win Skyler back. All that was left of their plans and promises for the future they had once made to each other, was Hope. The little girl who sought no-one's permission or approval to enter the world. The child who showed up at exactly the right time, the daughter that saved Gabriel and Skyler from themselves.

Gabriel noticeably beamed each time his heart would placate him and remind him of the little girl that was waiting for him. She was enough, and if that was all Gabriel was left with, he swore that it would be all he would ever need.

Alice VL

By the time Christmas arrived, Gavin could no longer disregard the discernable fact that Skyler had grown increasingly disillusioned as the days had dispiritingly passed them by. He was irrefutably sensitive to the certainty that her soul was fading and dying a protracted and frightening death. Gavin often tried to draw her out into an argument in a desperate attempt to coerce her into admitting to her feelings for Gabriel, but Skyler would simply walk away from him with nothing to say. He was sure that she had finally given up on her heart, and that she was merely wandering around aimlessly for Hope's sake. There was no longer anything he did that made her happy, and the more frantic Gavin was to include her in his life, the less available she was to him. He waited patiently for Skyler to deal with the inner battle that she was fighting so bravely against, but as his frustration towards her increased, he finally understood that she had been suffering the side effects of a crushed heart. Gavin no longer knew how to approach Skyler, and he had no inkling of how to reinstate the woman she once was.

Gabriel had called early in the week leading up to Christmas, to coordinate his much-anticipated holiday with Hope. Skyler unenthusiastically consented and agreed that Hope spent Christmas with Gabriel and their families in Logan's Bay. Skyler was trampled by the realization that Gabriel's life was progressing flawlessly according to his new plans, and that he had painlessly carried on without her. He sounded exultant and contented, yet, she in no way at all, expected to feel such an enormous amount of agony inside of her. She was not equipped to deal with the anguish their disconnection had caused her, or how her love for Gabriel would come back to haunt her.

It was just before noon on the day that Gabriel had arranged to pick Hope up when Skyler heard a car pull up into her driveway. She promptly called out to Hope, while at once apprehensive about Hope's absence from her. "Hope!" Skyler hollered down the passage before Hope came running out breathlessly, fanatically aware of the fact that her father had come to pick her up. "I think daddy's here!" Skyler seized Hope into her arms when she noted the exhilaration on her daughter's face. Hope was overcome with animation, and excitedly clapped her hands in anticipation of seeing Gabriel again. Skyler hesitantly made her way to her front door. She was entirely unrehearsed for the vision that greeted her when she opened her front door. Gabriel was complemented by another woman. When Hope ran into Gabriel's waiting arms, Skyler's heart stung dreadfully when she caught a glimpse of the picture-perfect brunette that had accompanied him. "Skyler, hi!" Gabriel smiled uncomfortably when he noticed her standing unresponsively at the front door. "Hi ..." She was at once distressed and livid at herself for allowing Gabriel to create havoc upon her heart once again. When he placed Hope down, Skyler instinctively moved closer to them in a desperate attempt to remain unruffled and composed. "Skye, this is Michelle. Michelle, this is Skyler, Hopie's mom ..." He tensely, yet nonchalantly introduced the two women before he awkwardly clutched Michelle's hand and held it firmly in his. He gently squeezed her hand before he picked Hope up again, and glanced over at Michelle, "... and this is Hope." He playfully tickled his daughter before he gently kissed her on her forehead. "Hello ..." Hope timidly responded before she clasped her father's face in her hands, and smiled adoringly at him.

After exchanging gracious, yet awkward smiles, Skyler was positive that her world was disintegrating around her, and had suddenly stood ghostly still. She was desperately afraid that Gabriel might discover the demolishing of her heart when she could barely move as her body began to carelessly shudder. She was in no way at all prepared for seeing him with another woman. She felt her entire body become numb with devastation, and she was aware of a nauseating sensation in the pit of her stomach the moment she realized that Gabriel had finally picked up the broken pieces he had returned to.

While she stood staring at Gabriel and Michelle, she was

convinced that she was morbidly presented with a depiction of two people undeniably passionately and vehemently smitten with one another. Skyler knew instinctively that for Gabriel to bring Michelle along, could only mean that he had embarked upon an earnest and heart-felt association with her. Skyler hurriedly veered away from them, and hastily made her way back into her home. She picked up Hope's luggage, and was at once strained by all the conflicting emotions that had found its way into her heart. She had always understood the likelihood that Gabriel might find someone else to replace her and share his life with. She had often tried to prepare herself for that very possibility, but when Gabriel and Michelle stood in unison in front of her, she was overcome by the most excruciating and debilitating pain she had ever felt, an incapacitating ache that was absorbed into the innermost core of her.

With the ever-invasive mass in her throat, Skyler cautiously made her way back to Gabriel, and handed him Hope's bags. She made a strenuous effort to seem unflustered and calm in front of them, and smiled broadly at Hope, "Bye, mommy ..." Hope waved cheerfully before she lovingly glanced back at Gabriel. "I love you, Hopie." Skyler barely managed to utter the words before her tears cruelly found their way into her eyes, "Enjoy the holidays, and be a good girl for daddy, okay?" She smiled miserably and was at once mortified by the apparent huskiness in her voice. She rapidly steered back into the direction of her home, knowing that if she had stood there for only a moment longer, she might reveal how totally devastated her heart was.

Gabriel was utterly bewildered by Skyler's unforeseen emotions and apprehensively glanced back at Michelle, "Would you mind taking Hope and waiting in the car for me?" He could barely disregard what he had seen only moments ago in Skyle, and; he could not leave her so enormously and so apparently defeated. Gabriel was conquered by an inexplicable need to check up on her before they were to leave. "Sure." Michelle took Hope from Gabriel, and hurriedly made her way to the car. "Let's go wait in the car for daddy." Gabriel was yet again unnerved by Skyler's wounded appearance. He could in no way at all, overlook the tears that were about to burst through her eyes. He was convinced that she was simply experiencing great difficulty in separating from Hope, and Gabriel was aware of a critical need to assure Skyler that he would take superb care of their daughter. When Gabriel entered through her front door, he was at once aware of her sorrow as she stood gazing out over the ocean, "I'll look after her, Skye, I swear. I'll take such good care of her. I know this is all very new for you, and I know it's your first Christmas without Hope, but I'm sure you and Gavin could use some time alone. I mean, maybe being without Hope isn't such a disaster? I promise you, Skye, she'll call you every day. I swear it, okay?"

Skyler was disconcerted to find him standing behind her and hurriedly dabbed at the tears that had begun rolling enthusiastically down her cheeks. "I know, Gabe. I just never expected to feel like this, about any of this." She knew that Gabriel would take extraordinary good care of their daughter, but she struggled to find the words to disclose how distressed she was to see him with another woman. When she studied him closely, Skyler realized once again that Gabriel possessed the uncanny ability to disrupt her life, and repeatedly break her heart. "I just didn't expect this to hurt so much, you know? It's hard, Gabe, it's just so hard ..." She paused while wiping the warm tears from her cheeks, "It feels like, it's just that, I can't help but feel like we are living day to day with Hope, you know? She needs more than this, Gabe. She needs stability and family. She needs to grow up with the security of, of us." Gabriel moved closer to her and took her hands, "Skye, I can't do this either. You're right, Hope needs the security from both of us ..." He hesitated before he squeezed her hands and took in a deep breath, "What do you mean?" She whispered hoarsely, when it felt to her as though someone had clutched at her heart and began ruthlessly tugging at it. "You're sad all the time. I become angry with you all the time …" Skyler stood staring at him, afraid of what he was going to say next. "I've made a decision with my life and I, I wanted to be the one to tell you before you hear it from anyone else. I just didn't want to tell you here like this …" His words began to desperately fail him as he considered the repercussions of what he was about to say. "Tell me what, Gabriel?" Skyler cautiously advanced closer to him, distraughtly frightened by the unexpected and sudden indignant expression on his face. "I,I've been thinking so much about everything lately, and since I've come back, I've, I've just realized how short life is, you know? Everything can change in the blink of an eye, you and I know that only too well, don't we?" He began stammering on the words he had perfected in his mind, only moments before, "I need more, Skye. I need my own kind of shelter, like you have with Gavin. I like Michelle, I'm comfortable with her and we just sort of fit. We have the same interests and we have almost the same ideals when it comes to our careers. She is good for me, and she brings out so much good in me. I'm a different man around her, a better man, so, I'm, I'm going to ask Michelle to marry me. I want to give Hope the security of a home with us, and that of a family. I want her to have brothers and sisters. I still want these things, Skye, I mean, don't you?"

Skyler was crushed to hear Gabriel tell her how Michelle invoked such intimate feelings for him. She was devastated that he envisioned a future family with her, and a family he had once dreamed of with her. "No, I don't, Gabe. I have that now." "Yeah, it's just, I don't, not really." Besieged by guilt, he suddenly turned away from her. Skyler glared at Gabriel, unable to fully comprehend what he was saying to her. Her heart could not shatter any more than it had at that very moment. She could barely breathe. She was sure that she could no longer bear the physical pain that had so vindictively crept up on her. She walked away from him, and began collecting the toys that Hope had left scattered on the floor in a desperate attempt to hide the unrestrained tears that were cramming so unrelentingly in her eyes. "Skyler, don't do that. Don't turn away from me. You always walk away from me. Just for once, look at me!" Gabriel raised his voice as he irately grabbed her arm. She turned to face him, and gently rubbed her forehead with the palm of her hand. "Say something! I don't know any more what you think or how you feel? I can no longer read you, and I honestly, honestly feel like I don't know you anymore. Just say something?" "What do you want me to say, Gabriel?" Gabriel was horrified to detect the sudden, unpredicted defeat in her eyes. He scrutinized every inch of her face, convinced that she had grown old and exhausted in a matter of moments. "Tell me how you feel! Tell me what you feel? Just anything, Skyler! Look at you! You're a wreck! You are broken and sad! You're a shadow of who you once were. I don't know, I don't know what's going on with you? Tell me?" "I have no idea what you're talking about? I'm not broken, Gabriel, I am going to miss my child! The child I was raising on my own, remember? I'm happy for you, Gabe, really. I mean, I don't know this Michelle, but I know you, and if she's good for you, if she's who you want ..." Skyler knew she had to conquer her silence and at the very least, acknowledge his unfortunate decision to entirely destroy her world. "I know that you came back to chaos and nothing was as it once was. Gabe, you deserved so much more than you came home to. I want you to have life and I wish you everything that is good, and if you've found that with her, then I am truly, truly happy for you." She could in no way at all, express to him how she truly felt. Her voice was quivering, her heart had slowly continued to shatter bit by bit, as though it was harshly punishing her for abandoning and betraying Gabriel when he needed her the most. "We are worlds apart, Gabe, we've always been, even at school. I was foolish to think that you and I stood a real chance. You were popular, loud and outgoing when all I wanted to do, was retreat into my own little world. But, there was a time when I so stupidly thought that we'd become wonderful someday, together, and now, now there is nothing left for us, but Hope. So, Gabe, I get it. I can't fit in where I don't belong. I never belonged with you. Michelle can, she's more like you. She is basically you, just a woman you."

Gabriel shook his head in frustration, and even though he had hoped that she would say something to change his mind, he knew that Skyler Maxwell had surrendered and given up on him a long time ago. "Yeah, she's great. And as usual, you have all the answers, you know everything? I left you that voicemail, Skye, do you remember? I begged you for just one more chance, even after you lied to me. I was willing to put everything bad behind us, and build on the good, on Hope, and the fact that she is our daughter, Skye, ours and not yours alone. Not Gavin's, not Michelle's, ours. But still, you won't admit to anything, you have all the answers and you just know it all, don't you?" She lowered her head in anguish, knowing that she could barely escape his anger that had come back to haunt her. "Your silence, Skye, is worse than anything I've ever had to go through. Your silence says more than you ever could." He whispered sadly before he turned to leave.

When she could no longer hear his car, Skyler crushingly fell to her knees and devastatingly sobbed just as a vulnerable and wrecked child would. For the first time in all the years since Hope was born, she was truly alone again. She was outraged by the circumstances she found herself in, and she questioned how it was possible for the universe to play such remorseless and malicious hoaxes on her. She felt wholly alone when she realized that the man she had been dreaming of for her entire life, had driven off with her baby girl to spend Christmas with his new love. They were to become a family that Gabriel was assembling without her. Envy and resentment entirely consumed her, yet, when she considered the fragments of her broken heart for a moment longer, she realized that she had brought all the agony and despair upon herself.

She failed to spot Gavin standing in her doorway, who had been watching her in silence from a distance. It aggrieved him to witness her fall to her knees when Gabriel walked away from her. Gavin was once again aware of a niggling feeling that he could never compete with the man she had lost her heart to decades ago. He was powerless to win her over, and bring her back from her immense heartache. Her soul hunted him, and hankered for Gabriel in a way that it would never seek his. Gavin stared at her, overcome by his own sadness, and reluctantly conceded that it was time to set her free, and let her go. He had fallen hopelessly in love with her and the little girl who had brightened up his life in a way he never thought possible, but Skyler Maxwell could never love him the way she loved Gabriel, no matter how vigorously she tried. Gavin knew that she was doing all she could to wholly commit to him and to their relationship, but as much as she tried to convince herself that her life with Gabriel was over, Gavin knew without a doubt, that she was simply conning herself. "Skye ..." She soared to her feet when she spotted Gavin grudgingly approach her. Skyler hurriedly dabbed at the tears that had become an almost enduring fixture on her face. "Are you alright?" He dried the warm tears from her sore and distended eyes, unsure of how much more destruction he could bear to witness on her distressed face. Skyler was at once relieved and comforted to see him. She fell dismally into his arms, as a fresh batch of tears began rolling down her cheeks. She shook violently as she sadistically wept into his chest. He could feel each shudder with every tear that fell from her eyes as his own heart thumped with each defeated whimper from her. He held her close to him, and left her to snivel in his arms. He knew that the moment he let go of her, would become the moment from which he would never be able to hold her in his arms again.

He was frantic to alleviate her pain and wipe away all her tears, but for the first time since he had met Skyler, Gavin understood that his love for her would never, ever mend her crushed heart or ease her sorrow, even just a little. When she finally looked up at him, he ultimately grasped how profoundly she still loved Gabriel. "Come, come sit with me ..." He took her hand and led her to an empty couch in her living room. She slowly sat down beside him, at once degraded by her irrepressible hysteria only moments earlier. "Skye, when I first met you, I knew that, I knew that you were carrying around an enormous amount of hurt inside of you ..." When Skyler searchingly glowered at him, he realized that she was about to interrupt him. He gently placed his index finger on her mouth, in a desperate attempt to keep her silenced. Skyler knew that what Gavin was about to say, was weighing worryingly on him, but at the same time, she was sure that he was about to tell her that he could no longer live as they had been living for months already. "I thought that, in time, maybe things could work out for us, and that perhaps, you would eventually fall in love with me, even just a fraction of how I fell in love with you and Hope ..." He gently wiped the unsolicited tears that were carelessly flowing from her eyes, "But Skye, what you feel for Gabriel is something that doesn't come along often, and for some people, it never comes. They never find it, and I know, I know that you don't want to hurt me. I know that you said you wanted to be with me. I know all about what you intended for us, and I believe that you really wanted all of that, but I can also hear the things you aren't saying. What I'm trying to say is, I know you'll never feel that way about me, and I can't stand by and watch you do this to yourself." He smiled admiringly at her, desperate for her to understand that he was in no way, wrathful towards her, "I've seen the way you look at him. I see the way Gabriel constantly succeeds in hurting you even though he doesn't intend to, and I know, I know that I'm holding you back, Skye. I know you are trying. I know that you chose me." Skyler was desperate to interrupt him, but Gavin carried on speaking before she could say anything, "I can't see you like this anymore. I feel that you are vanishing slowly and you are fading away bit by bit each day. I cannot be responsible for that. It's not your fault, Skye, and I don't blame you. I don't hate you for it, either. I wish you could understand that I am so okay with all of this." He slowly rose to his feet, "I'm not Hope's father. I know, I know with all my heart that you don't want to hurt me, but the best thing I can do for you, Skye, is to let you go." He paused as he sorrowfully gazed at her, "I don't want your loyalty for me to keep you with me. I don't want to wake up to all your regrets and what-ifs someday, because it will happen, Skyler. I want you to be truly happy, and I don't want you to surrender to me and settle for the next best thing. I can't help you, Skyler. I can't fix things for you. You must stop this. Stop telling yourself things you don't even believe. Stop fooling yourself." When Skyler looked at him, she noticed that Gavin's tears were unapologetically glistening in his eyes. Skyler got up from the couch and moved closer to him while she instinctively, placed her arms around his neck, "Gavin, I am so sorry. I tried so hard. I wanted it to work. You are such a good man, and I am such an idiot. I so dreadfully want to shut off what I feel for Gabriel, because, it just hurts. You don't hurt me, Gavin. You've never hurt me. Perhaps Gav, perhaps I just miss what we were once, and maybe I'm just finding it harder to move on than I thought it would be, you know? But, I do love you, Gavin, and I so badly, so badly, wanted to make it work with you ..." She whispered almost inaudibly in his ear.

"I know you did, Skye. I know your intentions were pure and honorable, but we're honestly just duping ourselves, and I don't want to drag this out for longer than I have to." He gently kissed her before he sadly scrutinized at her, "I am going to leave now. Merry Christmas, Skyler, and I pray that you and Gabriel can work things out somehow. Please tell Hope that I love her, and that, that I'll never, ever forget her." He hurriedly walked out and shut her front door firmly behind him. For a moment, Skyler instinctively wanted to run after him, and beg him to stay. She wanted to plead with him for one more chance to prove that she could love him better. She wanted to remind him of how absolutely Hope adored him, but when she stepped back for a moment, Skyler was ready and unexpectedly equipped to acknowledge that she could no longer live the lie she had created for herself. She could no longer willfully deceive her heart. She turned away from the front door, and gazed out over the ocean, aware of a surprising release that had come over her. She smiled sadly when she conceded to the fact that it was perhaps, too late for her and Gabriel to pick up the broken pieces of their hearts, but at the very least, she was comforted by the fact that she was unobstructed to love him in her mind and through Hope. There was no longer anything that could stand in her way of secretly loving Gabriel, even from a distance, and even, from another world. She was at once enthusiastic to return to the world she had secretly created in her mind, when Gabriel had first left. Once more, she could find him there when the world became quiet and was asleep. She was free to open her notebook, and batter down words that could once again, create a life where only she and Gabriel would exist in. Skyler was free to live in that world, dream of Gabriel, and how he once loved her. Once more, she could leave clues for him and pray that someday soon, he would find them and make sense of them.

Alice VL

CHAPTER TEN

Skyler spent the next few days in an all-embracing haze. She realized for the very first time how utterly deafeningly quiet and hauntingly hollow the house seemed without Hope. She walked around in circles for most of her days, and she would lay at night in total darkness on Hope's bed, desperately longing for her daughter, and frantically searching for Gabriel. Each time her phone would ring, her heart would miss a beat. She would jump to her feet and almost in one foul sweep, she would hold the phone in her hand. Skyler was extremely gratified to Gabriel that he allowed Hope to call Skyler almost daily. Hope's voice would at once calm her fears, and enormously improve her disposition.

Gabriel and Michelle had taken time off from work to spend with Hope in Logan's Bay. Gabriel was eager to introduce Michelle to both the Galicia and Maxwell families. He was relieved that they all welcomed Michelle with open arms, even though he could barely escape feelings of betrayal towards Skyler each time they would take a walk on the beach, or take their places around the dinner table. Gabriel would be persistently reminded of the sanctity of their walks on the beach, as though moments like those belonged only between him and Skyler. He was desperate to eliminate and discard all reminders of her during their holiday in Logan's Bay, but it seemed to Gabriel that the harder he tried, the less able he was to successfully discard the memories of the life they had once been united in. At times, he felt as though he was losing a grip on his emotions when he engaged in a bitter conflict with his passionate state.

On one particular warm night after Hope had fallen asleep, Michelle implored Gabriel to take a walk on the beach with her. "Come on, Gabe? Itt's still early!" Gabriel hesitated before he reluctantly agreed to accompany her on a late-night stroll on the romantic shores of Logan's Bay. They had barely reached the shore before Michelle seductively turned to face him, "I love you, Gabriel, and I love it here. I love that the stars that shimmer on the water. I love that I can see our future in your eyes." She took his face into her hands, and ardently kissed him. Gabriel spontaneously placed his arms around her waist, and pressed her firmly against him. Michelle began unbuttoning his shirt, as Gabriel spontaneously laid her down on the beach. He closed his eyes and hungrily kissed her, intensely aware of an irresistible need for her. His body had begun to pulsate for her, as hers was quivering with his every touch. She breathlessly reached for him, and when Gabriel opened his eyes, he was at once, enormously disturbed to see Skyler's embittered and shattered eyes glaring back at him, overwhelmingly conquered by an excruciating sadness. He promptly retreated and glowered incredulously at Michelle. "Don't stop …" Michelle moaned hoarsely when she pulled him back to her. Gabriel frantically resisted her, and sat down beside her before he bowed his head in crushing wretchedness. "Gabe?" Michelle immediately sat up and stared at him in total disbelief. "Gabe?" He glanced over at her, and was instantly relieved to discover that it was simply his mind playing tricks on him. "I'm sorry, Michelle, I don't know what just happened there?" He lied before he bowed his head again. "I can't do this, not here." It was yet another innocent reminder of his life with Skyler. It felt to Gabriel as though every corner and each turn held an unsolicited and unsought souvenir of Skyler, or a recollection of what they had once shared. The beach, making love on the shore was sacred to Gabriel, and he was in no way at all, ready to create a brand-new kind of devoutness with Michelle. "Let's go back …" He whispered when he buttoned up his shirt and held his hands out to her.

After he took a quick shower that night, he climbed in beside Michelle and speedily kissed her, unable to banish Skyler's haunting eyes from his mind. "Goodnight …" He hurriedly turned off the bedlamp, and turned his back on her. Michelle laid silently behind him, and placed her arms around him, "Goodnight, handsome ..." She whispered sleepily before she promptly drifted off to sleep. Gabriel laid awake thinking of Skyler. He was entirely unnerved by the vision of her as he was about to make love to Michelle. He was overwhelmed by a hollow pit in his stomach which made him feel physically revolting. For one brief moment, Gabriel was afraid that she would unceasingly come back to haunt him for the remainder of his life.

Skyler could detect thrill in Hope's voice to be back with her grandparents in Logan's Bay. She was jubilant when she energetically told Skyler about all that she and Gabriel had done for the day. When Skyler once asked her where she slept at night, Hope eagerly told her that granny Sarah and granny Tabitha were making turns in having her sleep over. She elatedly told Skyler about her bedroom at Gabriel's home in Kennedy, and how beautifully Gabriel had prepared it for her. Skyler was keen to discover if Michelle was in Logan's Bay with them, and was at once saddened when Hope giggled and bashfully informed her that they were inseparable, "They kiss a lot, mommy ..." Hope would whisper almost inaudibly. Skyler was reminded of the fact that Michelle had recklessly and greedily taken her place in Gabriel's heart as she sat on the outside looking in, desperate to merely feel his familiar arms around her once more. She had become hostile towards Michelle for stepping into the life Skyler had initially belonged in, and she was angry that Michelle was instantly rewarded with Gabriel and Hope's love, simply for imitating her life so callously.

On Christmas morning, Skyler hurriedly called her parents to wish them a Merry Christmas. She spoke to each of them for what felt like hours, before they eventually handed the phone back to Tabitha. Tabitha knew it would be tormenting to break the news to Skyler, but she was duty-bound to inform her of Gabriel and Michelle's engagement on Christmas Eve. "I'm happy for them mom, and if she treats Hope with kindness, then there is nothing I can do about it. I want Gabriel to be as happy as I am." She lied and made a valiant effort to remain brave in front of her mother.

Tabitha could detect the shudder and sadness in Skyler's voice that she was so desperately trying to hide, but remained helpless in offering her daughter the comfort she so dreadfully needed from her mother. "Why don't you come home for Christmas? Your father, we all would love to see Gavin again." Skyler hesitated for a moment before she decided to tell her mother the painful truth about Gavin, "I can't come home now, mom. I have a New Year's deadline. Besides, there's no way I could get a flight out on Christmas morning. I rather just want to stay home. Gavin and I, he left me, mommy ..." Skyler stammered wretchedly, leaving Tabitha deeply saddened by the fact that Skyler was spending Christmas on her own. "Oh honey, would you like me to fly out? I might be lucky and be able to get a cancellation seat?" "No mom, please, don't do that. Enjoy your Christmas. I just, I just really want to be alone. Please don't say anything to Gabriel ...." "Skye ..." "Merry Christmas, mama. Please tell dad and the girls that I love them. Give Hope a big hug and kiss from me, and tell her I miss her." Skyler silently wiped a tear from her eye, conscious once again of the never-ending, confining lump in her throat. "Speak to dad quickly, he's been anxiously waiting to speak to you again." When Tabitha handed the phone to Dave, he could at once detect the utter dejection in Skyler's voice. "Honey, is there something I can do?" "No daddy, I'm fine. I just miss Hopie." She whispered hoarsely and unexpectedly, and longed to feel her father's protective arms around her.

Dave Maxwell knew his daughter well, and he knew that no matter how hard she tried to convince them otherwise, her heart was shattered as she secretly pined for Gabriel. "She's fine, my girl. She is being spoilt rotten. Gabriel is so good with her, and she barely leaves his side." Skyler smiled when Dave gave her a quick run-down of Hope's comings and goings. When she eventually spoke to Hope, Skyler was intensely aware of the fact that Hope was in a hurry to end the call, and return to Gabriel. "There were so many presents, mommy! Santa Claus brought a truck with a lot of presents for us! Daddy gave Aunt Michelle a shiny ring because he's going to marry her! I can also wear a pretty dress like Aunt Michelle. But, mommy?" She almost whispered, "Yes Hopie?" "Can I go now? Daddy's waiting for me?" "Of course, you can, my girl. Merry Christmas. I love you." Skyler was devastated that she was not spending Christmas with her daughter, even more so when Hopie was anxious to end their call. "Okay, bye, mommy!" As she was about to replace the receiver, she heard Gabriel's voice echo through the phone, "Skye?" Her heart hammered intensely when she hesitated before she finally held the phone against her ear once again, "Gabriel?" "So, sorry that Hope was so quick to get off the phone with you. We're, we're taking her for a ride on her pony, and she's just so excited." Skyler smiled despondently when she discovered how unruffled Gabriel sounded, "Oh, my hat, a pony?" She giggled through her sniffles. "I know, but, my parents, you know?" She sniggered again when she detected the embarrassment in Gabriel's voice. "So, anyways, I'm glad I caught you. I wanted to wish you and Gavin a Merry Christmas. I hope Skyler, I pray that all your dreams come true and I wish you all that is good for the New Year. I, I, man, I'm bad at this. Merry

Christmas, Skye …" He chuckled when he began stammering, "Merry Christmas, Gabe, and thanks, we sure could use a new year right about now. Congratulations on your engagement. I hope that you and Michelle will be happy, I mean it …" She had only barely managed to whisper the words when her heart began splintering all over again.

She abruptly ended the call, and swiftly wiped away the tears that were once again, threatening to roll from her eyes. Gabriel handed the mobile phone back to Tabitha, and smiled sadly at her. Dave placed his hand on Gabriel's shoulders and gently squeezed it, "She sounds so sad? Is everything alright with Skyler?" Gabriel gazed questioningly at Tabitha. "It's Christmas, you know how emotional Skyler gets at Christmas, and all that was before she had Hope. Tis' definitely not the season to be jolly for Skye." Dave chuckled and turned away, unable to look him in the eye, afraid that he might blurt out that Gavin had left, and that Skyler was alone for Christmas.

After she had ended the call, Skyler resolved to take a long walk on the beach. She instinctively looked back at Gavin's house, and realized sadly that he had probably left for the holidays. His doors were shut, the windows were closed, and all the curtains were drawn. Skyler could not help but feel that she alone was responsible for the confusion and chaos she had found herself in. She berated herself for letting Gabriel go, and then she hated herself for letting Gavin go. She sat down on the beach, and allowed the wind to blow through her hair as she reminisced and relived the moments she had once spent with Gabriel. She was overcome with grief when she considered all that had happened in the past few weeks, but Skyler was determined to do her best not to dwell on all that she had lost any longer. She realized that she had in no way at all, felt as alone in her life than at that very moment, but she contentedly blamed her solitude on the fact that it was Christmas. It had truly turned out to be the loneliest time of the year for her.

She glanced at her mobile phone, and was at once tempted to text Gabriel, "Tell Hope I love her." She pressed the send button moments before she considered the consequences of her impulsiveness. She stood staring at the screen, and was disappointed that there was no response. She had just given up on receiving a reply, when the red light began flickering on her phone. Excitedly and almost as though her heart was about to hammer right out of her chest, Skyler opened her text messages and was at once, thrilled to see Gabriel's name appear on the screen. "About to climb on pony. Can't talk. Will tell her." Skyler smiled when she pictured her little girl on a pony, with Gabriel close by and frantic to keep her from falling off.

When Skyler climbed out of the shower later that evening, her heart began thumping excessively when she noticed that red little light flickering once again. She grabbed her phone, and excitedly began reading Gabriel's text to her, "So much fun! What a girl! What a pro! xxx" It was hurriedly written, but Skyler was ecstatic that it was followed by a picture of Hope on her pony. She stared at the little girl staring back at her with Gabriel beside her, but all she really saw, were the three little kisses below her message. She climbed into bed, and smiled at the screen in front of her, "What a dad!" She typed nervously, before she speedily sent the message, afraid that her audacity would fail her. "Handsome fella' that!" Was his immediate response, followed by a smiling face. "No secret that! xxx" She accidentally included her three kisses. "Shit!" She unknowingly typed and sent in succession of her previous message. After what seemed like hours for Skyler, she placed the phone on her nightstand without receiving another text from Gabriel. She laid staring at her phone in anticipation of that red flickering night, but it never came. As she drifted off to sleep, Skyler returned to the world she hadn't been back to since Gabriel had returned.

Skyler struggled to get out of bed in the mornings, and almost as though she had given up entirely, she allowed herself to sleep as often as her body requested it from her. She found it a welcomed escape from all the hurt and anger she was carrying around with her, and she was relieved to be able to cut off from the world at the drop of a hat. She feebly attempted to work on her newest novel, but all she could think of was Gabriel and Hope. The silence was becoming increasingly deafening and overwhelming. She longed for a little cluttered noise when her thoughts became too loud for her. She watched the clock in her living room that seemed to have stood still. She learnt to despise Michelle when her mind tricked her into thinking how Michelle had replaced her not only in Gabriel's life, but in Hope's too.

Gabriel was once again sensitive to Skyler's presence after their quick phone call on Christmas morning and subsequent text messages. He was immensely protective of her, and suspected that all was not well with Skyler. He would listen closely when Dave or Tabitha spoke, but he could in no way at all, shake the feeling that Skyler needed him. During the day, he would surround himself with activities for Hope, and he would spend hours playing with her, or walking on the beach with her and Michelle. At night, when darkness surrounded him, he would drift back to her eyes, and he would clearly hear her voice. It would overpoweringly frighten him, he would fall asleep unable to exile her from his mind.

By the time New Year's Day had arrived, Skyler realized

that she had spent the majority of her days in bed. She felt displaced and scarily removed from her normal day to day routine. She hardly ate anything, and she refused to do much to distract her from Gabriel. Skyler punished herself enormously, and convinced herself that she deserved to feel the pain and resentment Gabriel had felt not too long ago. She deserved to be penalized. Less than two hours after she had woken up on New Year's morning, Skyler's landline unexpectedly rang, "Hope?" She was sure that it would be Hope, and was excited to hear her daughter's voice again. "It's me, Gabriel ..." She was stunned to hear Gabriel's stammering voice on the other end of the call. "Gabriel? What's wrong?" Skyler instinctively knew that something had gone horribly wrong. "It's Hope, she's hurt ..." Gabriel bravely tried to remain composed even though Skyler could hear a deathly and frightening shudder in his voice. "Gabriel?" Skyler was panic-stricken and feverishly yelled at him from the top of her voice. "We've taken her to The Tygerberg Children's Hospital in Kennedy, we're here now ..." Gabriel spoke calmly and hesitated when he detected the grave anxiety in her voice. "What? Tell me what happened!" She grabbed her bag and car keys, and frantically made her way out to her car, before she hurriedly ran back into her home again. Skyler was entirely disoriented and had no intimation of what to do first. "Hope was with Donna in the car when another car drove in in front of them.

They're all okay, but Hope, she's not doing well …" Gabriel did his best to explain the events of all that had happened to her daughter, before he burst out sobbing into the phone. "They don't know, Skye? They're busy running tests and checking. They're waiting for the results of her brain function tests. Michelle is on standby in the theatre, if it comes to that. The best surgeons are with her …" He wholly broke down, unable to inform Skyler that Hope might not survive the wreck.

Skyler tossed her phone onto her couch, frantic to reach her daughter without delay. When she realized that she was still in her pajamas, she ran back into her bedroom, and hurriedly slipped on a pair of jeans and a sweater while she unconsciously put on her sneakers in her car. She impatiently made her way to the airport while desperately pleading with God for an available flight out to Kennedy at once. Gabriel frenetically redialed her number, and was anxious when Skyler failed to take the call. He placed his phone in his pocket, and urgently made his way back to the ward where his daughter was lying unconscious, fighting for her life. He sat down beside her, and lowered his head as he begged God to save his daughter's life. He pleaded for mercy and he swore to do better for both Hope and Skyler. He was desperate for God to keep Hope with them, and all he could think of was how broken Skyler would be if she had lost the child she loved more than life itself. He was deathly afraid that he might lose the child he himself, found a reason to live for. Michelle dismally watched him from a distance as she anxiously awaited the verdict of Hope's EEG scan. She was ready to fight for Hope's life, and realized for the first time, why it was that she was destined to become a pediatric surgeon. As she stood gazing at Gabriel, painfully aware of her own thumping heart, she knew that there was nothing she could do to reassure him of Hope's well-being and recovery.

Skyler had become panic-stricken by the time she had reached the airport, and realized that she could barely remember leaving her home and driving to the airport. She was profoundly appreciative, and at once relieved that there was a seat available for her on the very next flight to Kennedy. She hurriedly called Gabriel from her mobile, but was promptly redirected to his voicemail. She quickly turned off her phone, and tossed it in her bag. After boarding the plane, Skyler sobbed silently as she desperately prayed that Hope would be alright. The flight seemed to take forever, but when she realized that they had landed, she hurriedly leaped from her seat. She quickly made her way through the airport, and she said a silent prayer of gratitude that Gabriel was with Hope. Gabriel Galicia was a brilliant doctor, as was Michelle. Skyler knew that Hope was in extremely capable hands.

When she reached the well-known Tygerberg Children's Hospital in Kennedy, she frantically made her way towards admissions, "Hope, Hope Maxwell?" She had barely uttered Hope's name before she hysterically broke down in tears. "Just a moment …" The desk nurse quickly turned to the computer, "Ward 101, to your right." All Skyler could hear was the ward number before she sprinted down the passage until she spotted Michelle in the hallway. "Where is she?" Skyler yelled out anxiously. When Michelle pointed through a glass window, she saw Gabriel sitting beside her daughter, holding her hand. She opened the door, and was devastated by what she saw. Hope was laying unresponsively, as though she was in an entrenched slumber. Skyler failed to detect any marks or bruises on her body, yet, by the disconcerting sounds the machines around her were making, she knew that her daughter's condition was ominous. "Skye?" Gabriel shot to his feet when he spotted her standing there, shaking hysterically as her tears were uninhibitedly scuttling from her eyes. "Gabe?" When her legs grew weak underneath her, Skyler collapsed in his arms, and sobbed violently into his chest. Michelle turned away from them, and precipitously felt as though she had no right to be there. "She'll be okay, Skye. We have to believe that. Do you hear me? She will pull through." Gabriel was desperate to believe all that he was warranting Skyler of Hope's recovery. "What's wrong with her? Gabriel, you're the doctor? This is what you do! This is what you left us for!" Skyler was at once overcome with fear. "She took a severe knock to the head, and although they can't pick up anything wrong on any of the scans, she just won't wake up? Her scans are all normal, Michelle doesn't have to operate. She's just asleep, Skye. She is just asleep and won't wake up."

Skyler noticed his inflamed and distended eyes for the first time, and realized that she was hardly the only one to agonize over the fear of their daughter's state. When Skyler pulled herself together, she made her way over to Hope, and gently placed her hand on her head. "Mommy's here, Hopie. You have to be okay baby, please, you have to ..." Skyler whispered delicately to her daughter, and prayed that she could hear her. "I'm so sorry, Hopie." She whispered hoarsely, swallowing through the restricting lump in her throat. She sat down on an empty seat next to Hope, and firmly held her hand as she continuously prayed for Hope's recovery.

Gabriel turned to leave when he realized that he could no longer bear to see Skyler so unnervingly fragile. It crushed him to imagine her in so much pain, and it devastated him to realize that there was nothing he could do to reassure her that Hope would be alright. He made his way to the door before he glanced back one more time. He was conquered by an overpowering urge to hold her protectively in his arms, while he swore to her that Hope would fully recover. As he stood staring at her from the doorway, he knew that it was one promise he could not make her. He was relieved to find Michelle standing on the other side of the door, and took her into his arms. Michelle held him close to her while gently stroking his hair, leaving Gabriel to sob bitterly in her arms. "She must be okay, she has to be okay …" Gabriel pleaded as he held onto Michelle.

Skyler realized that she must have fallen asleep when she felt a warm hand on her shoulder. "Skye, here. Have a cup of coffee …" Gabriel cautiously handed her a warm cup of coffee. "Hope …" Skyler whispered while totally disoriented before she turned back to her daughter.

Alice VL

Pearls in Ashes

CHAPTER ELEVEN

Skyler and Gabriel had unfalteringly remained at their daughter's bedside for the next couple of weeks. The Maxwell and Galicia families came out to see Hope often, but Skyler noticed Michelle's growing absence, and realized that it had been a while since she had noticed Michelle stop by. On their second night at their daughter's side, Gabriel came up from behind Skyler, and placed his hands on her shoulder. "I am so sorry, Skye ..." He was desperate to make her understand how deeply saddened and distressed he was by Hope's accident. "Not now, Gabe ..." She was filled with abhorrence and rage towards him. She was angry that he had left her, and she was once again, incensed by the fact that he had left her to raise Hope on her own. "When Skye? When? Are we never going to speak to each other again?" Gabriel was devastated by how effortlessly she had managed to shrug him off, time and time again. Skyler got up from her seat next to Hope, and tugged at his arm. "Not in front of Hope!" They had just walked out of the hospital ward when she turned to face him, intensely reminded of the hostility that had entirely overwhelmed and blinded her, "I hate you for this! I hate that you let this happen! I hate that you left to treat and cure other children, strange children, but you can't do anything for your own! What was the point then?" The words came spilling out of her mouth as she released all the pent-up anger and hurt that was festering inside of her. Gabriel lowered his head and took her hands. Skyler abruptly freed them from him, dangerously close to falling apart, "You left me! When you walked out of that door that day, you left us both! When you walked away from us, you chose your work, and you left me to have and care for Hope on my own! I lost our home, I lost you. I lost everything! And guess what? I keep losing! That is my little girl laying there. She is all, all I have, and all I will ever have. She will love me always, even when you don't. She loved me long after you stopped! That is my baby!" Gabriel determinedly took her hand and squeezed it, "I didn't know, Skye. If I knew about Hope, I would never have left you. I went for us, for a better future for us. I didn't know that it would turn out like this?"

He was desperate for Skyler to understand that he did not choose to leave her for all those years. She leaned against the wall and slid hopelessly to her knees. She entirely surrendered to her broken heart, and could no longer deal with the intense sorrow that had wholly beleaguered her. "I couldn't breathe. I wanted to die, Gabe. I didn't know what to do? I didn't know where to go? You left me with Hope and I thought, I thought you were never coming back. Everyone told me you weren't coming back. I loved you so much, but you just left me." Gabriel knelt beside her, desperately afraid that Skyler was finally surrendering to her pain. "I love that little girl, Skye. She's our daughter. I just thought that I could make the world a better place for us, and for our children someday. I know that doesn't make any sense to you, and I know it means nothing to you now. I choose you, Skye, and I choose Hope. I wish I could go back to that very day, I would never have left. Never, Skye, never." He was frantic to tell Skyler how desperate he was to become a better man for her.

"I get it, Gabe, I know. I know you and I know you never meant for any of this to happen. I just, I just need someone to blame. Who else can I blame for all of this? I'm sorry, Gabe, you did the right thing. You are a good man. I think that I just don't want to admit to what happened to you over there? It's just easier being angry at you, you know?" She quickly dried the tears from her cheeks when Gabriel helped her back onto her feet. He placed his arms possessively around her, and held her confidently against him. When she let go of Gabriel, he held onto her arm, acutely mindful of Gavin's absence, "Will Gavin be coming out to see Hope?" He studied her eyes in a fraught attempt to empathize with her sadness, but when her eyes frantically avoided his, he was at once baffled by her increasing desolation. "He doesn't know, I, I haven't told him ..." "You haven't told him about Hope's accident? Why would you not tell him, Skyler? That man loves Hopie. I don't understand?" "It's complicated, Gabe ..." He turned her around to face him once more, "You left without telling him?" Gabriel was completely puzzled by Skyler's unanticipated secrecy. "Do you want me to call him for you?" When Skyler recognized the confusion in his voice, she could barely find the courage to admit that Gavin too, had mercilessly discarded her. "No, we're just, he just, he left and I don't, I haven't even told Hope yet, she doesn't know ..." "He left? What do you mean, he left? When?" She bowed her head when he tightened his grip on her arm, "The day you came to get Hope. It wasn't his fault, Gabe, he just, he thought that I couldn't get past you, you know?" Skyler whispered hoarsely, desperate to make Gabriel understand that Gavin was in no way at all, liable for the end of their relationship. "Wow. You've been alone since then? And Christmas?" "It's no big deal, Gabe ..." "I'm sorry, Skye, it is a big deal. Huge. I didn't know? I would never have taken Hope if I thought you'd be alone on Christmas."

She smiled gratefully through the threatening tears that were lying shallow in her eyes, before she anxiously returned to Hope. "She deserved this, Gabe. She was so happy. I could hear it in her voice. I'm glad she came." Skyler and Gabriel began talking to one another again while they kept a close vigil at their daughter's bedside. Skyler was once again, astounded by how fluently she could engage with him. While they were waiting for Hope to wake up, they spoke about the past, and they gushed over the little girl who had become the center of their lives. Gabriel told Skyler how he cherished his daughter, and how saddened he was to lose such an enormous fragment of her and Hope's life.

Skyler tried to teach him all there was about her, and what she was like before he met her. How readily she took her first steps for the very first time, and how besotted she was with her feet that seemed to her, had a life of its own. She grudgingly told him about her first big fall, and how she cried herself to sleep afterwards. Skyler whispered stories of her first meeting with the tooth fairy, and how she feared Santa Claus when she first laid eyes on him. Although she did her very best to include all the specifics of Hope's first years, she knew that they were moments Gabriel would never reclaim. "So, listen, Skye, would you mind if I left you for a while? There is something I have been putting off that I need to take care of. I won't be too long, I just really want to take a quick shower while I'm home?" It was just before sunset when Gabriel gently drew Skyler away from Hope's doctor, who was about to examine her. "Sure, Gabe. There's nothing you can do here anyway." Skyler was convinced that he was eager to spend an evening alone with Michelle. "I'll bring us something decent to eat. I don't think I can stand another cafeteria meal. Crab sticks?" He smiled when he recalled how Skyler fancied crab sticks and lobster. "Yummy! That sounds great! But really, Gabe, why don't you take the night off? You've been sitting here for weeks. You deserve a night out with Michelle. I don't have much of an appetite anyway ..." She smiled sadly before Gabriel placed his hands on her shoulders, "I am a father, Skyler. I don't get nights off, especially when my daughter is in hospital. I want to be here with Hope, and with you. Michelle understands, she knows that this is my place now." He gently pulled her closer and tightly hugged her, before he finally made his way to the elevator. He turned around and smiled when he saw her watching him leave. He hesitated, but waved before he finally disappeared before her eyes.

Gabriel slowly made his way to the front door of the home he had shared with Michelle for the past few months, the home he had shared a lifetime ago with Skyler. When he reached the front door, he hesitated for a moment. All he could think of was Skyler, who was waiting at their daughter's bedside for him to return. Michelle was beautiful, spirited and successful. She was independent and tremendously supportive of Gabriel and his work. She understood and wholeheartedly accepted his devotion to Hope, and she not once questioned his intentions as he sat beside her sick-bed. She was honest, and she adored Hope, but he could not think of one instance where she took his breath away. Michelle had fallen unstintingly in love with him, but Gabriel was badgered by a pestering feeling that he could never unleash himself from his love for Skyler. When he opened the front door, he noticed Michelle in the kitchen, about to pour herself a cup of coffee. "Hey! This is a nice surprise?" She was ecstatic to find him standing in the door way. "You're just in time. Coffee?" She smiled enthusiastically when Gabriel shut the door behind him. "Smells good, thank you." He was unexpectedly overcome with exhaustion, and made his way over to where she was standing. "I thought I'd grab a quick shower and change into fresh clothes before heading back to Hope." He spoke softly when Michelle handed him a cup of coffee. "Ooooh, can I join you?" She straightened out his collar and undid his top button. Gabriel placed the cup of coffee on the kitchen counter top, desperate to avoid eye contact with her. "Gabriel?" She was staggered that Gabriel had turned away from her and at once, turned him around to face her, "What's going on?" He gawked at her, unable to find the words to tell her that he could no longer carry on simulating a life where he could effectively choose her, and live a life without Skyler or Hope. "Gabe, you're scaring me?" She grabbed his hands, and looked him sternly in the eye. "Michelle …" His voice was quivering, and he had no clue of how to walk away from her without breaking her heart, and perhaps his own a little. "Just say it, Gabe. This is about Skyler, isn't it?" Gabriel lowered his head when he let go of her hands, "I just need time, Michelle." "Time? For what?" Michelle was unnerved by the sudden disillusionment in his eyes. "She, she needs me. Our daughter needs me. I need to be there for them." Michelle was unnerved and at the same time, haunted by Gabriel's embitterment, "You are there for them, Gabe. You haven't left Hope's side for a single moment. What more can you do? What has Skyler asked of you?" Gabriel walked up to her, and placed a hand on her shoulder, "Skyler hasn't asked anything of me. I just, I don't want to lose Hope. I don't want to be a part-time dad, Michelle. I've lost out on so much with her. I don't know how to balance being her dad, and being with you? I must, I have to be her dad first, you know?" Gabriel tried his best to be as conceivably honest as possible with her. "You are a great dad, Gabe, but, what if Hope doesn't make it, Gabe? What if she doesn't pull through?" Gabriel was horrified to hear Michelle hint at the possibility that Hope might not survive. "Michelle! I can't think like that now, okay? Hope must pull through, she has to. She has to …" He felt his legs grow weak beneath him as his heart began to race irrepressibly. "But Gabe, what if she doesn't? You must consider the possibility, you must be prepared for it." "I can't lose her, Michelle. I am not going to lose her!"

Gabriel abruptly found his way into the living room, at once beleaguered by antagonism towards Michelle. It felt to him as though the entire world had crash landed on his shoulders, and there was nothing he could do to save Hope. "Hope or Skyler?" She hurriedly made her way towards him where he sat with his head in his hands, and knelt before him, "Who Gabe? Who are you afraid to lose, Hope or Skyler?" She yelled out in anguish before she clasped his face in her hands, "Gabe?" His tears were flooding his eyes when he noticed the distressing tears roll down her cheeks, "I have tried, Michelle, I've tried so hard to ignore my feelings for Skyler. I swear, and I thought, I just thought that I just needed time. I just, I love them, Michelle ..." She half-heartedly rose to her feet, and quickly wiped the tears from her eyes, "I could have told you that, Gabe. I just wanted to hear you say it and I needed you to hear yourself. And that, you did." She turned away from him and speedily made her way into their bedroom. Gabriel followed closely behind her when acute self-reproach began consuming his entire being. He did not intend to hurt or destroy Michelle, but he could no longer carry on defeating Skyler. He could barely remember when it was that he had fallen in love with Skyler, but he could no longer hand over his heart to Michelle. "Go take your shower. I'll be gone by the time you get out." She dejectedly began packing her bags before Gabriel regretfully made his way into the shower.

When Gabriel returned to the hospital, he was astounded to realize that it had been a little over three weeks since Hope's accident. He was flabbergasted by how rapidly the days had gone by. Skyler was pleased to see Gabriel walk in, carrying in their dinner for the evening, and smiled when she caught his eyes, "This smells divine!" She enthusiastically grabbed the bags from him, and hurriedly opened them up. Gabriel took a seat next to Hope and gently stroked his daughter's cheek. Skyler had no sooner opened the food when she noticed a strained expression on Gabriel's face. "Are you okay, Gabriel? Where is Michelle? I never see her here anymore?" Skyler realized at once that Gabriel barely spoke of her. "Yeah, I'm fine, just stressed out about Hope, but fine. I mean … it was unfair towards Michelle with Hope, you know?" Gabriel shook and lowered his head all at the same time, "After the accident, I promised God that if Hope pulled through that I would never leave her again. I swore to Him that I would be there for her, and watch her grow up. I can't put her first *and* put Michelle first. I don't want to do that to her, you know?" He seemed defeated and spoke almost indistinctly, "Michelle just didn't fit in with the picture I had in mind. Hope comes first and she'll always come first. There is nothing, nothing more valuable to me than this little girl. I just love her so much." Skyler hesitantly made her way over to Gabriel and knelt before him, before she took his hands into her own. For the first time since Hope's accident, she was overwhelmed by authentic sympathy for him, "I am so sorry, Gabe. I know you love Hope, and Hope loves you. I think you're underestimating Hope's spirit. She can handle it."

Skyler felt enormous culpability, and was hesitant to admit that a weight had been lifted from her heart. She realized at once that her daughter had given her something to hope for, yet again. She glanced over at Hope, and smiled sadly at her little girl who laid sleeping, almost like an angel in her hospital bed. When her eyes trailed back to Gabriel, she was aware of a critical need to break the uncomfortable silence between them, "I am truly sorry, Gabriel, but Hope, she's so resilient. Have faith in her. I know you could have worked it out with both of them." He gazed at her and smiled despondently, before he glanced back at Hope again. "I am going to fight you for her, Skye, I'll fight you into the highest court if I have to. I will use every penny I have in the process to get Hope. I want my daughter with me. I want to watch her grow up. I want to be a set fragment of her life. I never wanted to be a part-time dad. I never, ever asked for or agreed to this. I want to go to daddy-daughter dances with her. I want to tuck her in at night and read her bedtime stories. I want it all, Skye. I want to teach her to play the piano and ride a bike without training wheels. I want her to wake up knowing I am close by. I don't want another man to raise and love my daughter. I love her. Me." Skyler's heart missed a beat when she heard him so recklessly threaten her. It felt to her as though Gabriel was once again, devastating her entire world as it all began to crumble around her. "What? You can't do that, Gabe. You are being a jerk! You see her plenty! I will never keep her from you. You can't take her? Do you think that I'm a bad mother?" She shot to her feet, and glared prodigiously at him.

He stubbornly stood up, and when Skyler gazed questioningly into his eyes, she knew that Gabriel was utterly committed to his fight for Hope. "No Skye, I don't think you're a bad mother, you're a great mother. I just cannot have Hope live between us like this. I don't want her shuffled between your home and mine, between the strange men and women that come into our lives. I don't want to have to plan visits and holidays. I don't want her every other Christmas! I don't want to miss out on her birthdays and milestones. What about her first day at school? Where will I be? And her last day someday, where will I be?" He raised his voice, desperate to make Skyler understand that he could not live without his daughter. She grabbed his arms when fear entirely engulfed and enslaved her heart, "Gabe, don't do this to me. I am begging you! Don't take her away from me. She's all I have. She is all that keeps me going! When you left, if Hope didn't come along, I would surely have died. Gabe please! I'll move closer. I'll go back to Kennedy. I'll do whatever it takes, just please, I am begging you ... don't do this to us. She's my little girl, and as much as she needs you, she needs me too. There has to be another way!" She cried out in desperation as she relentlessly tugged at his arm. "There is one other way, but, you won't like it, and before you turn me down, think about what I'm saying, okay?"

He silently prayed that his accidental strategy would work in his favor, "You could come back to me? You and Hope? Let's go too far, Skye, let's go too far forever?" He paused for a moment to absorb the confusion in her eyes before he gently touched her cheek, "Do you really think that, after all that's happened, I would take Hope away from you? I couldn't do that, Skye, but I wanted you to feel how it would make you feel if you had to live without her. I want you to understand that that's how I feel. I just, I have never stopped loving you, Skye. I don't want to live without you anymore. I know you love me, I know it. I don't know what you're afraid of? I just don't know why you won't admit to it?"

He desperately prayed that Skyler would declare her unspoiled love for him. "I'm not afraid of anything, Gabe. I'm not afraid to admit to anything, not anymore, not when I have nothing to lose anymore, and not, not when it comes to you ..." Skyler smiled as she stood quivering, immensely relieved by Gabriel's confession. By the expression in his eyes, she was sure that she had rediscovered the man that had left her behind so many years ago. She moved closer to him and gently kissed him, "I just thought, I thought you'd never ask ..."

She whispered softly before he took her in his arms and gently kissed her, as though he was once again, feeling her lips against his for the very first time. "I'm not afraid to admit how I miss you, Gabe. I'm not afraid to tell you how afraid I am of losing you again. I'm not afraid to stand here, and tell you that I love you and that I don't want to do any of this without you. I'm not afraid to tell you that I felt no remorse whatsoever when you told me about Michelle, and Gabe, I could have stopped Gavin from leaving, but, I'm not afraid to admit that I didn't want to. I'm not afraid to stand here, and tell you that it has always, always only been you. Let's go too far ... forever ..." She held onto Gabriel, afraid that if she let him go, she would wake up to find that it had all been a dream. She was exactly where she was meant to be. Her heart reminded her that he was the only man she could ever love so powerfully.

"Hello mommy ... hello daddy ..." Skyler was startled, but ecstatic to hear Hope's faint voice behind her. Gabriel and Skyler abruptly glanced over at their daughter, and let out an exhalation of relief to see her open her eyes. Gabriel and Skyler smiled at one another, and hurriedly made their way over to Hope.

The little girl lying in the hospital bed was the exact same little girl that had saved her life so many times before. Skyler was overjoyed to have her little family back. She was thrilled that she was given the opportunity to piece them back together, with Gabriel by their side.

Skyler turned to Hope and gently kissed her, while Gabriel softly whispered, "Hope, who knew that you were all we ever needed to find our way back again?"

Gabriel, Skyler & Hope, with love.

THE END

Alice VL